Across the Wounded Galaxy

Rex Hurst

Interior art by Michael Osadciw, James Carlton

Cover art by Matt Olson

ISBN: 0-9993803-0-3

ISBN-13: 978-0-9993803-0-7

DEDICATION

To Peggy Cwiakala – who demanded I dedicate my first book
to her
&
To the boys at SSDC who let me play in their sandbox.

Table of Contents

Across the Wounded Galaxy- Visual Glossary vi

Chapter 1- Brethia Stargate Project 16

Chapter 2- Trishmag 25

Chapter 3- Hyperspace aboard The Arc of Blood 37

Chapter 4- Stilt 51

Chapter 5- Trishmag 67

Chapter 6- Hyperspace aboard The Arc of Blood 78

Chapter 7- Stilt 105

Chapter 8- Myntal 5 123

Chapter 9- Myntal 5 146

Chapter 10- Myntal 5 161

Chapter 11- Myntal 5 176

Chapter 12 – Stilt 202

Chapter 13 – Stilt 217

Chapter 14 – The Arc of Blood, orbiting the moon of Stilt 232

Chapter 15 – Stilt 248

Chapter 16 – Stilt 273

Chapter 17 – Stilt 284

Chapter 18 – Leaving Stilt aboard a Strange Vessel.......300

Chapter 19 – Passage..321

Chapter 20 – Passage 339

Chapter 21 – Trishmag...347

Across the Wounded Galaxy- Visual Glossary

Mutzachan

Orion

Zen Rigeln

Eridani

Fott

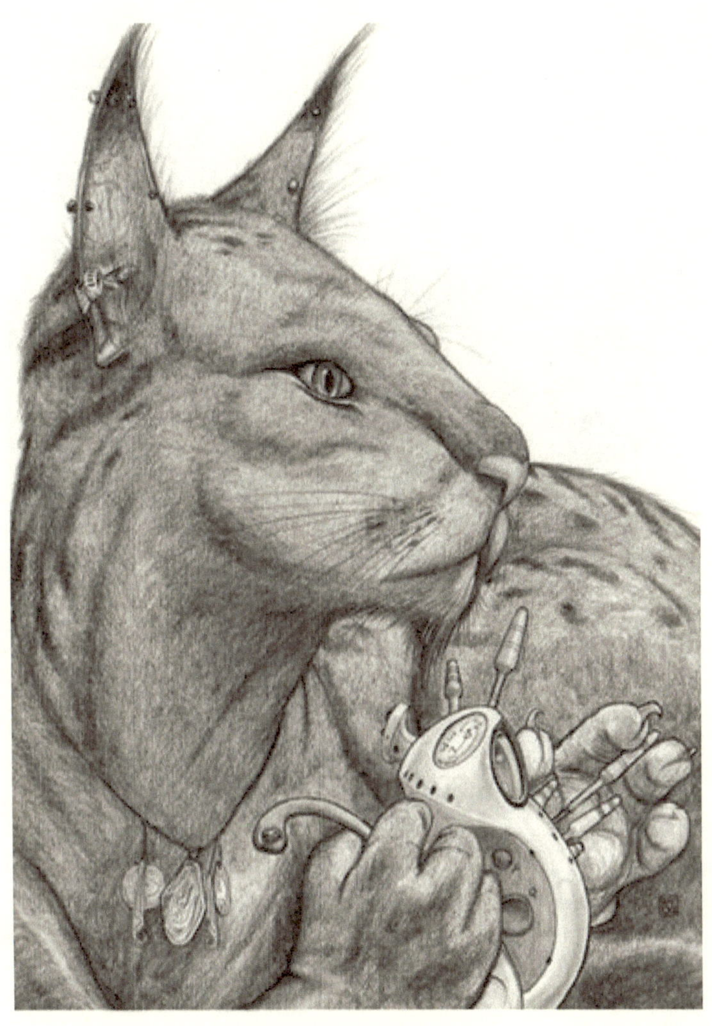

Cizerack

Ram Python

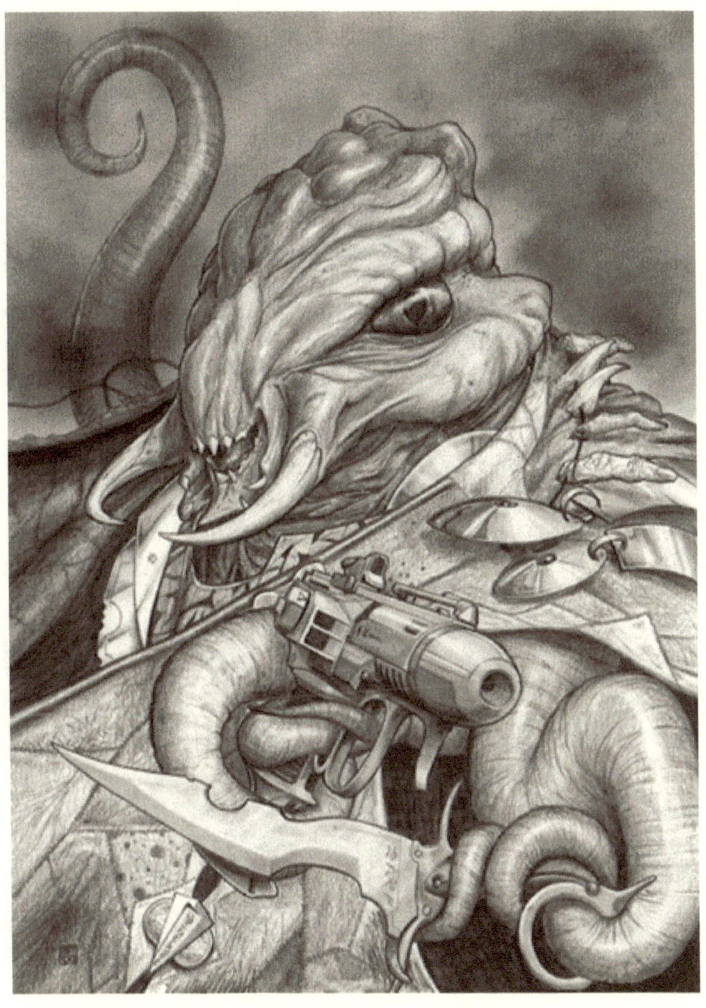

Phentari

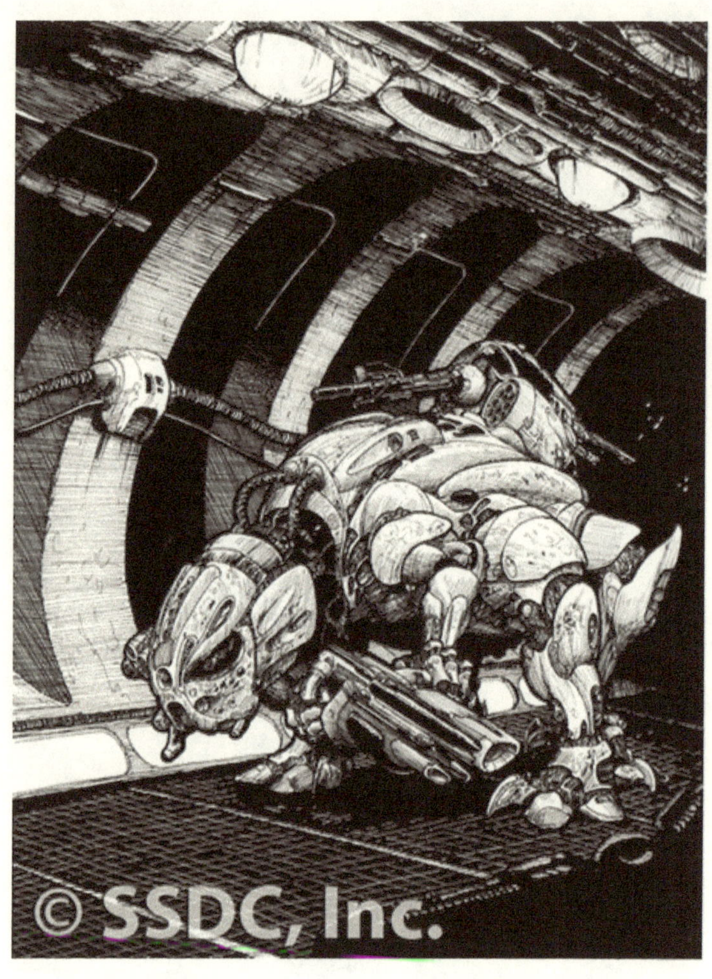

Tr'laa (Arachnid) Warrior

Mazian

Chapter 1- Brethia Stargate Project

Species: Gen-Human

Planet of Origin: None

Description: An artificially engineered species, designed to shore up the ranks of the genetically wounded Human race. They are force-grown in vats with an average gestation period of four months. Their occupations are predetermined according to commercial demand and a skill set is chemically implanted into their brains. They are mostly employed in bureaucratic and middle management careers or commissioned as lower echelon military officers. While their memory and physical skills are a step above the average Human, their emotional growth varies greatly from their parent race.

Freaky Fact: Due to a lack of childhood indoctrination and societal bigotries, Gen-Humans tend to be attracted to people who they feel are "interesting looking"; ie those who differ wildly from the high standard of beauty to which Gen-Humans themselves are sculpted. Those people usually believe that they've hit the jackpot.

***

There was a splash of gore and intestines. The masked Phentari whirled, a chainsword clutched in each of its four tentacles. The guard fell apart before him, sliced into four sections across the torso. Ah what skill, what nerve, it took to do that. An accomplishment requiring hours of practice. The Phentari swiped at a cowering nurse, carving off half her face. It was an act of pure sadism, doing nothing to advance the plot. The Phentari revved its swords and lurched into the maternity ward.

BEEP

There were two guards in the ward, both firing pistols with impunity. Rather risky thing to do in a hidden room filled with babies. After taking a few hits, the Phentari somersaulted over a crib and speared one guard in the abdomen while simultaneously decapitating the other. The obstacles dealt with, the Phentari raised its weapons. Remember, babies were worth 10 points and preemies 20.

BEEP

With the second warning Drake flipped off the game, *Lone Phentari 2: Mass Murder is My Hobby*, and sat up in his steel chair, pretending to be engaged in his work. He had uploaded a restricted program into his system that warned him whenever the supervisor or any of his cronies were logging in to monitor Drake's work, giving him time to spruce himself up.

Drake- DKE-k0018 (as was his full name) was employed in an administrative capacity on the Brethia Stargate Project. Stargates created a stable wormhole from one gate to another. They allowed a ship to move easily from star to star, galaxy to galaxy, without needing to employ warp drive or dip into hyperspace. Easily the quickest method of travel, the demand was so great that a ship could wait for weeks before getting clearance to enter. And with the energy required to maintain these holes, the cost for Stargate travel was appropriately astronomical.

The Brethia Stargate was an attempt by the Mutzachan Trade Council to create a structure to power hundreds of stargates. To achieve this, they were building a Dyson sphere around the system's star (with a surface area of ninety two billion Earths) to absorb every iota of solar energy emanating from the heavenly body and, after one hundred and four years of construction, it was only thirty five percent complete. It was, quite simply, the single greatest feat of astro-engineering ever attempted. And Drake was bored silly by it.

By its nature this amazing attempt created incredible amounts of administrative difficulties in all areas- from storage of construction supplies, to housing the ten million workers, to the acquisition of enough paper products so that everyone could clean themselves. This is where Drake came in, or rather Drake's batch. The entire DKE series, all fifty thousand of them, had been developed to address the organizational issues, specifically spoiled food indexing, hazardous material disposal, and septic management. Laugh if you want, but the amount of excrement generated each month could have created its own small moon orbiting the station.

Day after climate controlled day, it was the same grind. Type figures, check figures, adjust figures, order figures. Then walk back to his designated rest area, consume the daily food allotment, complete the regulation exercise regimen, engage in the compulsory social hour with his assigned friend group, watch the film being shown that night, and pass out in his sleep cylinder. One day meshed invisibly into another.

A waterfall of tiny numbers streamed over Drake's monitor. It took all of his effort not to sigh or yawn. To the average supervisor (and Drake's was *very* average) it looked as if he was sitting in rapt attention, taking in each integer flooding his vision. In reality, his mind was elsewhere.

After I take care of the Maternity Ward, I should double back and see if any patients have respawned in the Leukemia Ward. If they haven't, I can toss an incendiary device into the Burns Unit and see who blows up. If that goes well, I should have enough points to earn the Blood Soaked Achievement!

A further buzz indicated that his Mutzachan superior's omnipresent eye had cast his gaze at another hapless middle manager. Drake slouched back in his chair and sighed. He wasn't bad at his job. He couldn't help but be competent. Having been decanted only three months prior, practically the only knowledge rattling around in his head was the implanted managerial skill suite. It's just that the thing he was bred to be good at, didn't interest him.

Technically the Gen-Human species were designed to be fanatically enthusiastic about their assigned field, but as Drake himself was a living testament to, it was extremely difficult to genetically engineer a body's personality. One minor fluctuation in the DNA coding could result in a host of new quirks and mental disorders. It was probably why the species had such an abnormally high rate of schizophrenia.

Jake-DKE-r0865, Drake's co-worker from down the hall, popped his head into the pod.

"Hey," Jake said. "Did you see? I got in the upper twentieth for *Mazian Bubble Bounce* this week. Now that's a feat."

"Great, buddy. Congratulations."

Mazian Bubble Bounce was a game where you tried to keep an amorphous grey blob afloat using a combination of green, red, and blue bubbles, while avoiding random dropping needles. This was a favorite among the DKE series as it depended primarily on muscle memory and required no actual higher brain usage. Some of the others had created a secret leaderboard where they competed for the high score, but Drake didn't partake. He just liked to lazily shoot things.

"When are you gonna join in?" Jake asked. "That way we can challenge each other. It'll be fun. Match our wits."

"I dunno if I want to."

"Ahh you never know what you want," Jake said and left.

What did he want? He wasn't so sure. Something exciting that he could brag about. Something on the edge. Something that others would ooh and ahh over when they heard. Like a hero from the movies, or the *Spiff Blasthandy* Tri-V show. They'd slap him on the shoulder and call him brave, maybe buy him a beer. He'd never had any alcohol, but the vids made it look great. Yeah, that was Drake's dream, as vague as it was.

He snapped to. There had been a noise far far away, one that was distinctly different from the usual hums and buzzes of his artificial environment. He couldn't exactly place it. Then his screen flickered and the near fleshless face of a Zen Rigeln appeared.

Drake knew the species without having met any, they being one of the 12 core races making up the Galactic Alliance. Zens tended to adhere to a religious philosophy of pacifism and healing, codified in a series of interminable rituals and exhausting canons that was of little use to any outsider except as a cure for insomnia. The Zen's had a reputation for being sanctimonious, but this one seemed different.

"Hello," the Zen said in the Standard Trade Dialect. "I don't know you… but I hate you!"

Drake heard the words echoed in the hallway and stepped out to see that every monitor and screen had been hijacked. If this unknown person had managed to send his message to the entire station, it was indeed an impressive hack.

"I hate you because you live. I hate you because you breathe. I hate you because you can think. I hate you because you have ideas other than my own."

All of the overhead lights turned to a warning red and the evacuation alarm boomed, drowning out the rest of the figure's words. The monitors cut in with a yellow circle- the universal symbol for emergency. Drake panicked. He knew the routine, had been drilled on escape procedures, but when imminent atmospheric collapse loomed all discipline deserted him.

He ran down the hall screaming and shoving others out of the way. The hysteria was infectious. Soon the entire section broke down into a free-for-all with Gen-Humans, Mutzachans, Orions, Goola-Goolas and a host of other races all pushing, kicking, tripping, and biting each other to reach the survival bubbles.

Drake had just accidentally knocked another Gen-Human down a flight of stairs when an explosion rocked his section, bowling everyone over. Then what had just been a confused struggle turned into a murderous riot. People clubbed and stabbed whoever was ahead of them. Mutzachans let loose fatal blasts of matrix energy to clear the decks. Sporadic gunfire was heard further down the section.

"Remain calm! Remain calm!" a voice yelled over the intercom.

But the toothpaste was out of the tube. Drake stumbled, his knees nearly buckling with fear, and steadied himself on a desk. He picked up an oblong paperweight and judged that it might be a good weapon. Several voices, overlapping each other, squawked through the monitors.

"Sebe engaging… electrical systems compromised, launching fighters… flux shield holding… configuration unknown, seems to be a hodgepodge of inconsistent parts….."

Was the station under attack? No way. It had to be sabotage. This was the best defended area in the quadrant. They had three battle cruisers in rotation around it at all times. Any assault would be a suicide run. And yet…

White gas vented into the room. Definitely not part of the evacuation procedure. It was some sort of acidic mist that liquefied any flesh it alighted upon. The mist was scrubbed away in seconds by the station's atmospheric conditioners, but the damage had been done. Jake, who had somehow gotten ahead of Drake, lurched before him, screaming. He had taken a spritz dead in the face. His eyes had melted and were running down his cheeks like giant globous tears. Large chunks of meat still clung to his face, attached by thin strands.

It was enough to make a person vomit and Drake was no exception. He heaved his stomach contents onto the floor as a further explosion shook the station. Drake knew that he had to get out of there *now*. He readied his paperweight and…

"Help… help me," Jake hoarsely cried.

… paused. Damn it! He couldn't just leave the guy. He'd known Jake his entire life (all three months of it) and the man deserved better than this. Drake hoisted him up and helped him walk down the hall.

"Hold on buddy," Drake said. "We're almost there." "Drake?"

"Yeah."

Jake said nothing more. Most of his tongue had plopped out of his mouth and smeared down the front of his shirt, yet the jaw continued moving in a foul mimicry of human speech. Drake vomited a second time.

By the time they finally managed to make it down to the evac chamber, most of the section had already ejected. There were a few broken figures lying about, some burned, some bleeding, some trampled, but otherwise it was empty. He boarded the bubble (a device designed only to be a short term solution) and hit the large, idiot proof, eject button.

Chapter 2- Trishmag

Species: Mutzachan

Planet of Origin: Trishmag in the Germinga system

Description: The first of the Alliance races to achieve spaceflight, Mutzachans have developed the ability to store excess energy within their own bodies and direct it externally when needed. A dangerous skill that requires decades of training. They are a long lived race (two thousand years on average), but this is balanced with a correspondingly low birth rate. Despite being considered "the backbone" of the Alliance, there are only an estimated four hundred million Mutzachans in existence.

Freaky Fact: Mutzachans are radiovores, receiving most of their nutrition in the form of radioactive isotopes and minerals. They can eat regular food only after it has been impregnated with radiation. For this reason Mutzachans tend to sit alone in the cafeteria.

***

<Oxtiern, Full Text of Transmission- Brethia Stargate Project>

“Hello. I don’t know you… but I hate you! I hate you because you live. I hate you because you breathe. I hate you because you can think. I hate you because you have ideas other than my own.

“Across the wounded galaxy we fly. From planet to planet, species to species, all under the cold heavenly glow. And if these balls of light, these givers of all life, are nothing but specks in the grand scheme of the cosmos, what does that make you? What is less than a speck?

“But you, in your arrogance, don’t really believe that about yourself. Do you? Your false religion, whichever one it is, has brainwashed you from infancy to think that there is a grand purpose to existence. That every life, no matter how pathetic, has meaning. You were lied to and you willingly lapped up their vomit! The greatest survival skill for any sentient race is delusion.

“I am here to wake you up from your fantasy. I am here to demonstrate that all of your lives, your petty hopes, your dimwitted dreams, can evaporate in a microsecond into the indifference of space… Say, ‘thank you.’”

<End transmission>

“He’s got a pithy way with words,” the mission controller, Malon, said. He paused the data stream

Of the four Mutzachans in the room, three were seated professionally around the desk, quietly contemplating the tragic events of the Brethia Stargate. The fourth, Molphus, was feeding grain pellets to a bright blue bird with three legs. He had been told to stop wasting food, but ignored the order.

Almon settled back into his curvaceous chair, one designed to comfortably support a Mutzachan's massive head. He had been born when Magellan was attempting to circumnavigate the world and felt every millisecond of it as he gazed at the face of the Zen Rigeln leering from the desk monitor. Things should never have gotten this far.

"You understand that we expect a high level of discretion on this assignment," said Malon. He was flashy for a Mutzachan, always decked out in loud colors, completely opposite to the standard cream or muted metallic garments that many of his race preferred. He also had a penchant for wearing radioactive gold rings that he would suck on during any pause in the conversation. "Under no circumstances go into detail about why you are after the target, except to say that he is wanted for murder."

"Yes of course," Almon said quickly, smoothing out the ruffles in his gold robe. That warning was for the other two, not him, and he was anxious to get going. "Let's have the background particulars… please."

The controller hit a few buttons. Molphus wandered over to the desk which was transmitting information across its glass surface. He and Quandle (the fourth Mutzachan) stared intently as the information scrolled up. Almon regarded the two.

They were former students of his, mentored in the art of manipulating energy matrices. While both had been powerful in their abilities, neither had really been suitable personality-wise for Almon's line of work. He hated that he needed them now, but he was unwilling to trust any of his normal associates.

Quandle had been the easy first choice. He was combat trained, though he had never been in an actual battle. He had enlisted in the Mutzachan Defense Core and served as a matrix controller on a cruiser. The weapon systems on such vessels were powered and directed by skilled energy manipulators, their destructive abilities amplified through the ship's systems. He wasn't the most skilled of energy crafters, but had a talent for unleashing blasts of such intensity that made up for a lack of finesse. Plus his loyalty was absolute. That was the important thing.

Molphus had been the trickier choice. He was young by Mutzachan standards, two hundred and sixty five (the equivalent of twenty in human terms) and while powerful, tended to focus on less violent aspects of the matrices. Molphus had specialized in maintaining and developing the ion drives that powered their planet's commercial navy. Due to his inexperience, Almon had been hesitant to recruit him, the boy had never been off planet before, but desperation won out. Molphus would be loyal.

The monitor displayed:

Subject: Oxtiern Lomasi

Race: Zen Rigeln (Tza)

Born: 2237   Proscribed Zen Community: 2245

"He was exiled at the age of eight?" Molphus

asked incredulously. "What could he have possibly done to earn that?"

"That was due to his uncle, Vargeneit, if you remember the story."

Molphus and Quandle shook their heads. Almon sighed. *This younger generation.*

"A viral engineer," he stated matter of factly, "who perfected the G-series plague bomb and tested it in a city on Langoon. Killed fifty thousand sentients in twenty four hours. After three days the death toll reached a quarter of a million."

Molphus was shocked speechless at the cruelty. Quandle took it in stride.

"Langoon is outside of Alliance territory, isn't it?" he asked.

Almon nodded. "That's why they couldn't prosecute. But that didn't stop the Council of the Righteous from branding the uncle a Tza and banishing him from any Rigeln-controlled area. The rest of the family was then kicked out in case they carried the uncle's 'taint'." He spat the last word out with venom.

"So they were destitute?"

"Not exactly. He sold the bomb formula to the Alliance so the family could resettle on another planet, but it wasn't a luxurious life style."

"The Alliance bought that foul device?" asked Molphus.

"Well, it did work."

"But to even consider dealing with such a person…"

"We're not here for an ethics debate," Almon

interrupted. Quandle snickered a little. "Familiarize yourself with the target."

Molphus went back to the bird in a huff, refusing to read anymore. *The target? You mean the person. The subject of our inquiry.* Target was much too violent, too final, a term. It did not sit well with his philosophy. Maybe this Oxtiern person could be taken alive. Maybe he could be rehabilitated. He had been kicked out of his own culture at such a young age, is it any wonder he had turned out maladjusted? Therapy, not bullets, was needed here. Molphus forced another pellet into the bird's mouth.

Almon glanced at the boy. He hadn't meant to be harsh, but knew that Molphus was about to go on one of his pacifist rants about how peace was the goal hidden within the DNA of every sentient being. After a century of tutoring, Almon had never been able to shake him of this idiot belief. The youngster was soon going to get a very harsh wakeup call.

Oxtiern Education Background: Homeschooled until accepted into secondary institute. Graduated Micromegas Technical Institute (2255), Attained Undergrad Degree in Virology from Somnium University (2259), Accepted to School of Bio-engineering at Somnium University (2259). Expelled Somnium University for theft and academic dishonesty (2260).

Oxtiern Military Background: Enlisted Galactic Marines (2261). Assigned to 845th Brigade, Company C, 5th Platoon, Unit H as an M5 rank (Field Medic). Reassigned 5th Platoon Unit Q (Interrogation) as I5 rank (field interrogation) (2264). Promoted to I8 (long term interrogation) (2266). Brought up on charges of excessive torture and murder (2268), exonerated by military court (2269). Dishonorably discharged from service (2270)- reason <REDACTED>.

Oxtiern- Further Activities- <REDACTED>

Known relatives: Vargeneit (uncle, presumed deceased), Twolel (mother, deceased 2264)…

"What's this redacted material?" demanded Quandle, a little too forcefully.

The controller stopped sucking on his gold ring and exchanged a quick glance with Almon. "That's unimportant," he said. "Focus on the objective."

"Are you kidding me?" said Quandle. "Where he went to high school is unimportant. What he's been doing for the last twelve years seems very relevant."

Stay out of it, Almon told himself. *Let the controller handle the situation.*

"If there were any pertinent information in there, you would have it. Be content with the information as it is presented."

"Where did this file come from? Galactic Control? From what I understand, Mutzachan Intelligence has an open door policy with them. A free and total exchange of information. If they're holding back it's a violation of…"

"They're not holding back."

"So it's you then!" Quandle said scornfully. He touched Almon's arm, gently in deference to his mentor's rank. "Can you explain this? What is going on?"

Almon shook his head and closed his eyes,

meditating. The storm would pass.

Away from the argument, Molphus turned on his wrist data pad and flipped through the stored images. The device was a widely used electronic item in the Alliance. It contained all of the user's personal information, communication abilities, credit history, and allowed access to most services in Alliance areas. They were so prevalent that special legislation had been enacted, requiring all Alliance systems to allow uniform access to the organizers.

A three dimensional picture of a Mutzachan female manifested on the pad. Molphus sighed, there was the face of his love. Beauty personified. He loved the way her steel blue eyes perfectly matched the veins running over her broad head, and that the bumps at the back of her scalp were in a similar position as the constellation Fen (a guardian jug filled with cleansing blood from Mutzachan mythology) as seen from the southern hemisphere. They had so much in common, spending hours talking over the latest poetry equations, watching films, and eating the same preparation of radioactive isotopes. Though they had only been courting for twenty years, both of them knew it wouldn't be long before they were life-bonded (*buni* in the Mutzachan language).

She hadn't wanted him to be part of this mission, had shed several tears over the thought of him going. But when Almon contacted him, he felt a duty to… no, that wasn't fair. Duty was the least part of it. He wanted to explore, to taste the air of bizarre worlds, to see aliens in their own environment, and to marvel at their customs. To live outside of the protective shell that was the Mutzachan's home planet of Trishmag. Almon had told him years ago that Trishmag was a bubble, the only true "safe space" in the galaxy. Never having stepped out of that bubble, Molphus felt that his education was incomplete. So he had told her that duty calls. A white lie much more palatable than the truth.

Molphus stared out of the window at the dappled plains of Trishmag, where the ever shifting sands altered their shades from yellow to green to brown as the day progressed. Spiky flaxen stalks of grass, which only grew on vertical surfaces, jutted around the sides of canyons and rock walls. They sprouted up to three meters in some cases and moved towards the sun or any light source when it appeared. Reptilian birds flew past in formation, multihued feathers spiking down their backs. A collection of glowing lizards skittered about in the garden below, each trying to steal food from the others. Continuous streaks of white marked the skyline like errant chalk lines, the leftover residue of ships leaving the planet. All across the horizon, he could see copper bumps of habitation units and larger bulges of offices and manufacturing units - though these days most of that had been out-sourced off world. It was beautiful, tranquil, everything he really needed. Molphus wondered how much he would miss it. How much he would miss her.

He sighed. Trishmag the beautiful. Trishmag the globe of peace. The axis upon which the Alliance spun. Home to the glorious Mutzachan people, who had conquered the heights of reason and in doing so created the apex of civilization. By dint of this recognition of their importance, they claimed the title “Caretakers of the Alliance”- though only amongst themselves, the other races could be so prickly. Each Mutzachan, from the tiniest babe to the greyest elder, knew that without them the Alliance would crumble under infighting and civil wars, allowing the enemy they were at war with to destroy them all. Molphus did not believe in war for whatever cause, but those who were waging it never consulted his opinion.

He snapped back to reality as Quandle shouted a hearty curse.

“Fine, if you want to hobble us right from the beginning…. What about the item that was taken? Can you tell us about that or will it remain another mystery for the ages?”

A golden cylindrical object floated up on the monitor. It was roughly a meter long, ending with a vicious jagged needle on one end and a control knob on the other. The knob, when activated, would project a keyboard containing the 74 characters of the Mutzachan alphabet for entering commands. Apart from this, the only other markings on the device was an identification stamp, for some reason it was written in the human alphabet, X-1813518.

“It’s referred to as the bionucleotide restructurer,” stated the controller. “Its initial purpose was to eliminate any genetic diseases detected in a fetus in a relatively painless way. However, it was soon discovered that it could be used to restructure a sentient’s brain to habitually act in a certain manner or to unhesitatingly follow the commands of a person. We assume that Oxtiern stole it for this last function."

"Interesting device," said Quandle. "You could create a private army in a matter of hours."

"It isn't a fast process. You couldn't whip up a slave force quickly, but it is programmed to be a universal tool. The RNA manipulation sequence for every known sentient species is in there... with the exception of the Andromeni." This last race being made of pure living energy. The only known one of its kind.

"So he broke into one of the most secure bases in the Alliance, an incredibly difficult feat, to steal this device that, while potent, isn't a super weapon..."

Much too risky for any obvious reward, Almon thought. *If it's about money, he has to know that we won't stop trying to kill him. How much cash is worth your life?*

"Then he splashes his face all over the station, so everyone will know it was him. Why? What's his endgame? It can't be just this!"

Almon shivered. *Why indeed? Oxtiern is no fool.* Various scenarios played across his mind, all of them bone chilling.

Quandle continued, "And how did he get into the Brethia base at all? And then to further penetrate into the most protected of areas. Who helped him? He must have had some sophisticated technical assistance. That's where we need to start looking, his associates..."

"No!" Almon emerged from his silence. "We

need to start by identifying the ship that Oxtiern escaped in."

Chapter 3- Hyperspace aboard The Arc of Blood

Species: Zen Rigeln

Planet of Origin: Katrel in the Orionis 29 system

Description:
A mammalian race with blue colored blood, the Zen Rigeln has only a thin layer of surface skin over their thick skulls, giving them a "skeletal" appearance. The prize achievement of the Rigeln society is the development of energy matrices that can manipulate flesh/carbon on a molecular level and thus allow Zens to be excellent physicians. Their primary government is a theocracy and the current ruling philosophical house, the Council of Assizza, has decreed an official policy of total non-violence for all members. Any who disobey this policy are branded as "Tza" (soiled/degraded/shameful) and exiled from Rigeln society.

Freaky Fact: Zens tend to be compulsive nudists. They justify this by stating that the body is a temple of beauty, majestic in form and function. Very few outsiders who see a Zen's naked angular body agree with that sentiment.

***

Drake awoke in pain. Sticky wet pain all over, except his arms which had gone completely numb. He wished that he could slink back into the infinite blackness. But no, it was too late. Reluctantly, he opened his eyes.

He was naked and dangling by his arms from a pipe running across the ceiling. The wire that bound him bit deep into his wrists. It was a dingy metal room, no windows and poor ventilation. There was an acrid rusty bite to the air, which made it unpleasant to breathe. A thin stream of some pale yellow liquid leaked down the wall to his right.

He tested his body. First, right foot and all of the toes. Then left. Good. His fingers, though cold and numb, seemed to respond to his commands. His breathing was heavy, due more to his current position than any internal damage. None of his ribs were cracked. Same with his legs. Genitals… phew all there. Now he had to get out of there, or at least reduce his discomfort.

If he tried, he could just brush the tip of his big toe across the floor, but there was no way to give himself any support and end the pain radiating out of his shoulders. Every slight movement brought on a corresponding throb of agony. Perhaps if he could just…balance his legs somehow on the wall, it would give himself a few blessed pain free seconds. Drake believed he'd seen something like that in a movie once.

Of course that wasn't easy. He had to move …arrgh…slowly...ugh…down the pipe…ahhh… by swinging his body like a pendulum… arrrgh… eating the pain with every thrust… gahh… in case a loud noise would alert some guard…urrgh…it was not easy….ugh.. but little…arrgh…by little… he did it.

Now came the great leap. He readied himself…huff huff…and…ARRRGH! His leg slipped down the wall, yanking his arm, dislocating it at the shoulder. Tears of frustration fell over his face. There was nothing he could do.

What was going to happen to him? Would he be tortured? Would he be raped? Would he be sold into slavery? He had read on a newsfeed that there was still a fair amount of that in the frontier worlds and some Alliance sectors. Worst of all, were they stringing him up for meat? The common definition of cannibalism had been expanded to include the eating of any member of a sentient race, but there were several species that didn't agree with it. Was he going to be some banquet item, fresh food from their plunder? Again, he had heard stories…

A bright light went on over the door to the room. A few minutes later it shuddered open, letting in a dangerous looking assortment of people from a dozen different races. There was no identifying uniform or tag on their clothing, no similarity in equipment, nothing to identify their affiliation, if any. Drake did note that many of them carried metal bars, flaking with rust. They gathered around him, silent, just smiling.

Eventually, an evil looking Orion pushed his way to the front. The race was physiologically similar to humans, except smaller, with pointed ears, and seven fingers on each hand. A thumb graced each side of their palms. This one possessed the added charm of having the worst breath imaginable. A potpourri of rotten gums and cheap booze. He lurched up to Drake and pinched his cheeks between two greasy fingers.

"Awake huh?" he burbled out, obviously drunk beyond reason. "Well, welcome to the hospitality suite of the glorious cruise ship The Arc of Blood. I am the recreation officer, Parg Mildue. Pleasure to meet you."

The others all hooted and slapped their knees at Parg's words. Drake said nothing. What could he say? Maybe he could make a witty crack like all the guys in the films, but right here in the middle of action, it just seemed like an invitation to get his head cracked open. Parg roughly let him go, wiping his hands on a pair of overalls that seemed more stain than fabric. Drake noticed that the Orion's work boots had a fair amount of dried blood crusted on them.

"Now on a more serious note," Parg continued. "I'm afraid that this isn't going to be all that much fun for you. We've all been talkin' and decided that the only fair way to divvy up the loot was by lady luck's choice. So guess what we did?"

Drake remained silent. Parg grabbed a metal bar from the guy next to him and smacked him across the ribs. Pain, oh much more pain. Drake screamed.

"Har har har. Well, I'll tell you. We each picked

a number and rolled a die. Luckily mine came up first. That means the virgin territory that is your anus is mine to furrow."

There was an intense burst of laughter from the crowd when they saw the fear in Drake's eyes. He began to thrash. No...*no*! This was not going to happen to him. No matter what, he would fight, he would struggle, and he would overcome. Wouldn't he?

Parg gave him another whack in stomach.

"Hold on there. Save that energy, punk. You're gonna need it. Like I said, my number came up *first*. But we kept rolling until everyone knew exactly when it was their turn. So, as you can see from the crowd of esteemed gentlemen here," he waved an arm about, encompassing the whole of the scummy mob. "This is going to be a busy afternoon."

Drake howled and shook. His dislocated shoulder was yanked even more out of place. Pain, pain, but fear most of all. He twisted his wrists, hoping that the wire keeping him suspended would cut an artery, ending his life or at least delaying what was coming.

This was the funniest thing in the world to the crowd. They laughed and pointed, eyes watering with the humor of this Gen-Human's plight. A few fell over, holding their sides at the much needed live entertainment.

And when the very last of Drake's energy was spent and the absolute knowledge that he was going to be gang raped fell upon him, he slumped and pissed all over himself. The ultimate act of fear. Another smack, this time across the face. Drake nearly blacked out.

"That won't stop us," Parg snarled, listing a little. "You just need to hold on, because everyone'll tell you a marathon is all about pacing."

"Be careful with his mouth there," someone yelled from the back.

"Shut up!"

Drake looked about, his left eye swelling up from the blow, the metallic tang of blood in his mouth. He scanned the crowd for the tiniest scrap of pity or mercy or basic concern over someone else's distress. He found none. He found the exact opposite.

A string of profanities and a dervish whirl of motion brought a black furred Fott out of the crowd. A genetic joke that had gotten out of hand, the Fott race had been artificially created from the DNA of an Earth rabbit. The joke had spread very quickly however and before anyone knew it they had swept across the Alliance. The species had turned out to be damn hardy and impossible to completely eliminate, despite vigorous attempts by certain Alliance members.

"What's this, Parg?" bawled the Fott in an odd twang. "You pullin' a scam here, boy? Yeah you were! Don't deny it. You wait until I'm occupied checking for lice to start chopping up the sweet meat without me!"

"Shut your stinking face, Jack Mace," yelled Parg, taking a drunken swing at the Fott and missing by several inches. Jack kicked him back with a powerful blow, knocking Parg into the corner behind Drake.

"I suppose y'all know you been cheated?" proclaimed Jack to the crowd, who had begun murmuring ugly ideas amongst themselves. "Yeah y'all picked numbers and rolled, but whose dice were they?"

Jack Mace swung his head around as the idea sunk into the mob. His fur was completely black, except for one small patch at the tip of his left ear. The other tip may have had one in the past, but it had been torn off during some drunken scuffle a decade ago. Apart from some ill-fitting leather jeans, the only thing the Fott wore was an off-white chef's apron, the front pouch of which contained various sharp and dangerous objects that he deemed necessary to conduct daily business on board the ship.

Parg had, with difficulty, gotten back up and stumbled towards the increasingly hostile group. Some of them yelled, others pulled knives, threatening to do all sorts of nasty things with them to the Orion. He waved his arms, trying to calm them down.

"Hey now. Don't go listening to this drug addled short-order cook. Everything's above board."

"Then let 'em see those dice."

"Well, I just don't remember where I put them at this moment…."

A howl of laughing derision rose from the crowd. None of them believed a word of it. Parg looked about, panic started to sink into his booze sodden brain. Realizing that he was one or two slashes away from death, he turned to Drake, eyed him up like a slab of beef, then turned to the crowd.

"If…if there's a problem, we can always try again. I want to be fair." A lot of hoots at that. "Someone else can provide the dice or whatever… on the other guy."

"What other guy?"

"The one we pulled from the pod with this meat." Parg jerked his thumb behind him.

Ridicule. Foul language. More threats.

"Most of that guy's face was a puddle when we dragged them out of there. You know that. We chucked him down the chute to feed the Phentari."

Rest in peace Jake-DKE-r0865. Hope you enjoyed your few months of life.

"Oh yeah… I forgot."

"You think we're all as stupid as you are," barked a no-eared monstrosity with a solid black tattoo across his face and biceps as big as the Orion's head. "Now I got the second place and since you tried to cheat us, I figure it's only fair that you go to the end of the line, till we all had our turn." He raised a hooked blade. "If you got a problem with that, I'll cut out your larynx for ya."

The crowd loudly agreed. Parg backed off, angry but beaten. Jack Mace smirked in evil mirth. He raised a hand.

"Now I think I get a swing too, bein' as I…"

Everyone grew deathly quiet. Not like before when they were having a private laugh, this silence stank of fear. Jack lowered his arm and shrank against the wall. The mob parted and a dark figure of a Zen Rigeln walked in their wake. He wore a lavish black robe with silver stitching that blossomed into a wide circular collar edged in platinum. And his eyes.... Electric blue irises, almost luminescent, that pinned down whomever was caught in its gaze.

The only one not cowed was Parg.

"Get the hell out of here, Skel," he yelled in an alcoholic blather, pointing his finger like an incoherent child. "You weren't parta this. You and that cat were busy spinnin' dials and pushin' buttons while we did the real work. You can just...."

Jack Mace grabbed Parg's arm and pulled him back, fearfully.

"Parg, Parg," he said in a low tone, "that ain't Skel."

No, it wasn't. Drake lifted his head and saw the face of the person who had beamed a message of hate across the entire Brethia Stargate Project. It was worse in real life. This was Oxtiern, though Drake wouldn't learn his name until sometime later. There was something about him, some unnatural element in his chemical makeup that caused a person's animal instincts to kick up in alarm. Everyone in the room knew instantly to be wary.... With one exception.

"How could I tell?" Parg muttered. "All these Zens look the same to me."

Ignoring the drunk, Oxtiern stepped up to Drake, who whimpered a little in spite of himself. He ran a thin finger down Drake's body, taking in every curve and crevice. It was a soft, probing touch of one exploring something unusual. It began with the shoulder bone, circled the areola, flicked down each rib, curved about the pelvis, and ended deep in the inner thigh. Everyone stared. Every breath was held. Even Parg managed to shut up for a few moments.

"Is this one of the refugees from the escape bubbles?" Oxtiern asked to no one in particular.

Everyone turned to Parg, who was now reluctant to answer. Jack Mace pushed him forward a few centimeters.

"Yeah," Parg blustered. He was sobering up fast, something he did not like. "You… you got plenty. Like ten or so. We kept one for ourselves." His voice became louder with a fake bravado that fooled no one. "I figure we earned it."

Oxtiern stepped to the Orion, looming over him, daring Parg to meet his gaze. A challenge not accepted. He lifted his left hand, each fingertip glowed with an azure power. He held it by Parg's cheek. One second, two, three, four. The Orion shook violently, sweat clustered about his temple. The rest of the crowd huddled closer to see what would happen, dark curiosity brewing in their minds. None of them even considered interfering to save a fellow crewmate.

Oxtiern dropped his hand, the power receded from his fingers. Parg fell back limp onto Jack Mace, who pushed him to the floor.

"Yes, of course," the Zen said smoothly. "I have more than enough. Everyone here deserves a bit of recreation."

The tension evaporated. The crowd settled back happy. Their fun wouldn't be interrupted, that's all they really cared about. Oxtiern turned to Drake again and poked his left nipple.

"Odd protuberance."

Jack Mace spoke up hesitantly, "So can we..uh..."

"You know I admire the Gen-Humans," Oxtiern said, ignoring the Fott completely. His voice drifted up high, talking to everyone and no one. "The humans found that they were dying out, having poisoned their own genetic stock, and rather than roll over and die like so many other species, they improved upon the model. Imagine that."

He waved his hands and twirled before the crowd. No one laughed.

"They didn't just say, we need more. They said we need to do it better. Recessive eyesight traits? Fixed that. Too long of a gestation cycle? Fixed that. Various cancers linked to gender? Fixed that. Need to be stronger? Done. Need to be smarter? Done. Need to be faster? Done. Quit wasting time with a nuclear family, parents just screw the kids up. No need for a wasteful education system, stick it in their heads before they first open their eyes. Why bother with a childhood, a person learns their self-worth through their work."

He grabbed Jack Mace by the scruff of his neck and whispered loudly in his broken ear.

"Why don't more species do this? Sure the humans had to run like lap dogs to the Mutzachans to get it done and have been their pawns ever since, but as these two species can interbreed they will eventually become an uber-race, strongest of all. No one else does this. Why?"

He looked at Jack Mace, who blinked stupidly.

"I hear all of this talk of religious ideology and genetic purity and not wanting others tinkering with their DNA, and I can see that. It's been done before, one species making inferior copies of other races to enslave them. But no one else attempts to radically improve themselves as a whole. I would do it to my race in a heartbeat. Burn out all sorts of idiocies and leftover bits of evolutionary debris. I mean do we really need toes? Wouldn't one flexible mass be more efficient?"

He cocked his skull head at Jack Mace. The Fott nodded vigorously, his ears flapping about. Bored, Oxtiern pushed him back and viewed Drake with a more clinical glower.

"Still mistakes are made. This one seems to be an inferior specimen with some weird parts still connected." He stuck his finger in Drake's belly button as deep as it would go. It was not pleasant. "What job was this one conditioned for?"

The mob stared at each other with blank faces.

"Each of these has a primary designation imprinted in a chip in their scalp. You can read it easily enough. It might be interesting… but I will leave you to your sport."

He left, the crowd giving him a respectful channel to exit through. Jack Mace detached the data pad from his wrist and waved it behind Drake's head. The rest began discussing whether to recast the order, or carry on from what they had previously decided.

"Let's see what we got here."

"Why bother?" Parg bitterly picked himself off the floor. "Who cares?"

"I wanna see."

"Then see, just hurry the hell up!"

He pulled back the data pad and pushed a few buttons. His eyes narrowed at the readings, mouthing out each word displayed before speaking it.

"He was a 'Hazardous and Human Waste Specialist Manager'."

Jack's head jerked up and went into whispered conference with Parg. Drake's consciousness kept slipping, black gaps popping into his mind. Only the ache from his shoulders kept him partially awake. Parg came over and slapped him across the face. He waved the data pad in front of Drake.

"Is this true? You're a shit surgeon?"

"What?" Drake was groggy, barely capable of talking beyond a few simple words.

Parg slapped him again.

"Pay attention. It says you're a waste whatever whatever. With septic stuff. Yeah?"

"Uhhh…"

"Can you fix the damn toilets?"

Drake was not actually trained to do this. He supervised those who were responsible for the real work, came up with their schedules, made sure the supplies they needed were ordered… but was he going to say no?

"Absolutely! I did it in my sleep. All the time."

Snip, snip. The wires holding Drake aloft were cut. He dropped like a sack of cement. The cold of the metal floor pressed deep against his cheek. Jack Mace was explaining the situation to the remaining crowd and after a few minutes they all agreed. Being able to take a dump in comfort again was far more important than whatever brief carnal pleasures they could derive from their captive. He was a find.

Parg slapped him in a friendly manner on his dislocated shoulder, sending a spear of agony down Drake's side.

"Congratulations," he said, "you're the newest recruit aboard The Arc of Blood."

Chapter 4- Stilt

Species: Tr'laa (known colloquially as the Arachnids)

Planet of Origin: Officially unknown.

Description: A conglomeration of genetically tied creatures which are invading Alliance space from an unidentified galaxy. The first invasion occurred one hundred and seventy four years ago, causing the extinction of several sentient races. It was only repulsed by the combined efforts of a dozen species. The result was the creation of the Galactic Alliance: A defensive pact to repel the Arachnids if the threat ever reemerged. Thirty years ago it did and the galaxy has been at war ever since. The standard Arachnid warrior stands three meters tall with four legs, two arms, and a thick exoskeleton. They are a deadly foe.

Freaky Fact: When the Arachnids conquer a species, they determine if said race can be molded to fit a need in their own society (soldiers, janitors, technicians, musicians, etc). If so, then the whole of the race is genetically modified and selectively bred to fulfill that one function. If not, the species is exterminated.

***

The planet Xensera is an Alliance frontier colony on the edge of the sector lovingly dubbed The Plains of Desolation. While currently devoid of any naturally evolved creatures, at one point it must have been teeming with life as an incredibly rich assortment of fossil fuels were detected on it, along with a high concentration of rare heavy metals embedded deep in the planet's crust. Researchers could not determine the nature of the extinction event, but whatever occurred had wiped out all life, except for some bacteria spores and a few molds found clustered around volcanic vents deep in the sea bed. Specialized science had allowed life to flourish once again. The terraforming of the planet's soil did not take long.

Commercial exploitation had occurred quickly, especially after the Alliance offered very favorable grants for settlers and tax credits for mega-corps to stimulate expansion in the sector. The planet became the sector leader in the production of plastic, electronics, and other petroleum goods. And while mining and manufacturing remained the planet's bread and butter, nearly every major corporation and signaling agency established a subsector headquarters there. This brought in a host of luxury items and other illicit services that go along with success.

The planet was nicknamed Stilt due to the massive twin tubes connecting its primary cities of Jericho, on the ground, to its counterpart Enginalo, rotating directly above it in low orbit. The first tube served to pump life giving gasses up to the floating city (thus reducing costs), while the second acted to transport goods and personnel from city to city. This was done by utilizing ultra high-G accelerators coupled with state-of-the-art inertial dampeners

Enginalo was initially built to make the transfer of goods from freighter to the surface swifter and more efficient. But after the corporations established themselves, the price of rooms on Enginalo skyrocketed and it became a status symbol to be able to afford the extortionist rates. Later on, after the planet was constituted as a sovereign entity, other cities were founded as commercial mining ventures.

The planet itself was not guarded by the Galactic Navy. It opted to be part of the Colonial Naval Network, a multi-corporation funded fleet mandated to keep the trade routes safe from hostile races, Arachnid scouts, and, the most common nuisance, pirate attacks.

The profits swelled. The population blossomed. Over five million people emigrated from various Alliance worlds to craft a life in this new land of opportunity. Art was commissioned to spruce up the utilitarian functionality of the original building designs. Several Stilt born musicians had become slightly famous with singles on the Core World's music charts. A few films had been financed by the government and a Tri-V show was being produced locally. A corporation had even financed a local Cyball team- the sport of choice in the Alliance- albeit only as a farm team for the popular Merchants of Doom, which operated out of the nearby Harper's World. Things were going good for the people of Stilt.

And then it all ended.

***

Captain Raskor-idan of the 845th Galactic Marine Brigade, Company C, sat behind a barricade in the middle of a broken rubble filled street in the city of Jericho. Or more accurately, what had *once* been Jericho. Most of it was gone now. His men, scattered all about him, fired at the enemy. Screams of pain. Shouts of rage. All the verbal carnage of battle. For the first time in a long long while, he felt satisfied.

Only a week before the captain had been wasting his life away working in admin, running a team that matched DNA swabs of pirate corpses against open warrants on the ridiculous number of criminal databases in the Alliance, then voiding the warrant. The standard aftermath of a raid against the never-ending stream of criminal vermin. It was a task that had seriously caused him to consider suicide. Then suddenly he was placed back into a frontline commission.

Here was a mission worth doing, he thought as he watched a wall of his men assault a barricaded group of Arachnids. Here was a battle worth fighting, worth dying for. It wasn't some piddly raid on a pirate base in a hollowed-out asteroid or eliminating some rebel insurgency with a shaky ideology and more money than sense, as had been too common of late. Here was a true enemy! The darkness come out of the void. The evil which jeopardized every life on every planet. With enough Arachnid corpses, Raskor-idan mused, one could redeem any amount of lost honor.

From what they could tell, there were about thirty Arachnids and others holed up in what had been an underground carpark. Normally Raskor-idan would have fired a position broadcast round into it and directed a precision bombing on the structure, but they had some vague intelligence that there may be a few families being held down there. Orders from Brigade Command disallowed any bombing of places were civilians were suspected of cowering. So in they went, despite being ninety nine percent sure that any non-combatants down there must be dead.

Bullets rattled, pulse cannons blasted spats of superheated plasm, grenades were thrown and thrown over and over again. All to little effect. They had only managed to kill three of the bastards, while taking fifteen casualties themselves. Thus putting a damper on the captain's plans for glory.

But then if it was easy, what would there be to write about? He needed men to sing of his bravery. He knew that this was his last, greatest chance when he had heard the mission briefing for the officers. The general had called them in and played a film, cobbled together from the gun and drone footage available.

"I want to impress upon you the seriousness of this operation," the General had said. "We *will* retake this planet from the Arachnids. Many of you haven't been in the field for a while, so I'm showing you this to remind you of how deadly the enemy is."

The footage played.

The attack had caught the government of Stilt completely off guard. While the early warning systems did alert the defense forces that Arachnid vessels were jumping in, the sheer volume of enemy ships overwhelmed all defenses quickly. Three Arachnid motherships, fifteen destroyers, and thirty five troop carriers appeared. Against this were two defense frigates and a handful of cargo freighters.

The Arachnid destroyers were cruel hulking machines, shaped like a larval cocoon, bristling with weaponry. The design was arranged around a central omega cannon- a weapon that collected a massive amount of negatively charged ions into a force field and then fired the energy through a magnetic flux bottle, creating a concussive beam of incredible force. One shot was capable of breaking smaller ships in half or of irreparably disrupting the flux shields of larger vessels.

The Arachnid troop carrier's main weapon was a huge spiked prong, used to ram a ship and then send out an EMP burst, disrupting all electronics in the victim vessel and preventing the ship from jumping to hyperspace. The prong would then expand, opening a hole in the hull to allow Arachnid troops to board and kill every living thing on board. A few of the freighters were taken this way and the ships directed planet-side into civilian population centers.

Though it was obvious from the outset that they were going to be overwhelmed, Raskor-idan had to say that neither of the Colonial frigates wavered in their duty. *Of course they didn't have much of a chance to*, he mused. The first of them, the Tholl, had its shields knocked out within forty seconds by successive omega blasts, allowing enemy fighters to fly in close and cripple the engines. Then one of the looming motherships, a cylindrical beast almost as long as the orbiting city, cracked it in half with a volley of missile strikes.

The second frigate, the Esoqq, had lasted nearly twice as long. Its shields were down and leaking power from omega fire. Rather than accept an impotent fate, they had suicidally rammed into a mothership, maiming it sufficiently so that it was forced to withdraw.

Now that's an honorable exit, Raskor-idan thought. *The ship captain's family must be so proud.* It was a death he could easily wish for. He fogged up the methane converter strapped to his face, oxygen being poisonous to his race.

The footage paused.

"This next bit is the most disturbing," he said. "I know several of you are from this sector and some of you have relatives there. Remember that retribution is coming."

The film began again. Nuclear devices were launched at each of the stilts, splintering them. The orbiting city engaged emergency thrusters. Massive engines, designed for just such an emergency, jutting out across the bottom of Enginalo like unattended blackheads, stabilized the city's orbit. Unfortunately the weight of the remaining tube structure, still attached to the city's underbelly, dragged it down. The tube ruins were ejected from the city's superstructure, but the damage was already done. Enginalo was going to collide with the planet. The best they could do was to slow the fall and hope some of the population survived.

The orbiting city's defenses had been designed to repel any ships attempting to forcefully board and invade. The architects did not foresee an active attempt to simply demolish the structure outright. Arachnid fighters skimmed beneath the city, knocking out engine after engine. The destroyers lined up and blasted one edge of the city's lip with successive concussive bursts from their omega cannons, pushing the metropolis closer to the planet. Eventually the blasts forced it to flip over, sending it tumbling end over end, crashing into Stilt. Two hundred thousand souls were instantly obliterated in an explosion that was felt three continents over.

Ejection bubbles from the rare few who survived the attacks dotted about the blackened flotsam, helpless as newborn kittens. The remaining Arachnid fighters amused themselves by leisurely puncturing them with precision shots or using their ship's wings to bat them towards the planet to burn up in reentry.

As this was occurring, the ground defensive array was in full swing, firing batteries into the troop transports which were descending from the sky like swarming locusts. But for every transport destroyed, five more successfully landed. The remaining motherships blasted the cities from orbit, clearing away most of the defensive infrastructure, then targeting power stations, water treatment plants, hospitals, communication towers, and any government buildings left.

Before colliding with the planet, the orbiting city had blasted out an emergency beacon through a pinpoint wormhole link to Alliance command. It was a last ditch communication device costing five hundred thousand credits per second. *But who would think of money at that moment*, Raskor-idan thought. It was played to the growling crowd. The transmission mostly consisted of incoherent screaming, but that in itself conveyed enough of a meaning.

A fuse had been lit in the crowd of officers. Mutters and curses abounded. Each envisioned their own city, their own planet, in the destruction of Stilt. They were ready to kill, to order men to their deaths, to accept no surrender.

"This is the enemy!" the General yelled. "This the destroyer of all life. They want to exterminate all our species. It's up to us to make sure that doesn't happen. We are here to save the galaxy."

To Raskor-idan, the future assault was more than that. It was an opportunity, a great stepping stone.

***

Most of the Arachnid forces had moved on by the time the Marines arrived. Only one mothership remained. The Galactic Navy had struck quickly, sending a barrage of thermonuclear missiles into it. Battle cruisers then closed in and ripped a hole in its midsection the size of Norway. Explosive decompression wracked its insides and whole battalions of enemy troops were flushed out to freeze in the void. Pilots reported seeing Arachnids and various support races clinging to walls and broken floors, desperately trying to grab onto a non-existent life line. The mothership fought back, sending one cruiser down in flames, but it was too wounded to continue the attack and retreated. The battered vessel zoomed away with a thousand guns firing after it.

This left only the stranded ground troops to deal with. The Alliance was determined to save whatever civilian population was left, which meant a ground assault and fighting them street by carnage filled street.

The scenes of devastation the marines saw upon entering the cities sickened even the most hardened veteran. Every street corner had piles of corpses. The Arachnids had gone door to door murdering everyone, no matter how young or infirm, and threw their bodies into a central hill. They had killed and killed and killed. Some piles reached up to twice the size of a house. The stench of thousands upon thousands of corpses all putrefying together was unbearable. The order was given for every trooper to don their breather masks. Most the streets had been completely painted over with blood and liquefied organs. Barely an inch of ground remained that was not splattered with gore.

An arena ripe for retribution and personal valor, thought Raskor-idan. But instead of gathering glory, he was bogging down in this choke point, trying to root out an enemy too stubborn to die. Raskor-idan slammed his cybernetic left hand into a wall and winced in pain. He flexed it and marveled yet again at how this lump of metal could so accurately mimic the sensations of an actual hand. His support staff stared at him, waiting for orders. He breathed heavily into the methane converter.

Raskor-idan was a typical Eridani. Tall, with deep yellow skin like aged urine, and flat nostrils pushed against his face in place of a nose. He had a mane of dreadlocks running halfway down his back, dyed ghostly white- marking himself to any other member of his race as one who carried the "white disgrace"- a person that has brought great shame upon his house.

The central government of the Eridani was a combination aristocracy/military dictatorship with a heavy emphasis on the Buddon code, the warrior path. Those who joined the glorious Imperial Naval Echelon were considered the greatest members of society, people destined for prestigious positions and to have their names hammered into the rock of history forever. Raskor-idan was not one of them.

That was why he was on Stilt as a captain in the Galactic Marines. The Alliance Armed Services had been a refuge for Eridani military failures for over a century. Still, every now and then some exceptional Eridani who had distinguished himself in the Alliance forces was, with great fanfare, offered a position in the Eridine services. This had been Raskor-idan's hopes when he enlisted. Seventeen years later it was still only a hope, a fading one.

He crawled away from his cover to find his first sergeant, John Aebisher, being tended to by a field medic. Aebisher had taken a blast from an Arachnid weapon. A hole blackened around the edges was lodged in the torso of his combat armor. The plasi-steel frame was designed to withstand most plasma and bullet strikes, with an ablative lining shining over it to deflect laser fire. Whatever had hit the sergeant was massive.

The medic was sticking him with a body rehabilitation injection, the "miracle drug" which quickened the body's response to damage a hundred fold, stimulating white blood cells and healing most tissue damage in seconds. The military would not be half as effective without it.

Aebisher attempted to rise a little when he saw the captain, but quickly slid back down under the pain. Raskor-idan simply nodded at him, the effort was enough.

"Sergeant, how many of those mobile grenades do we have cached back at the ammo dump?"

"About three hundred, sir."

"Have them all brought up and send them out in a single wave. We'll blast these bastards out yet."

"Yes sir."

Aebisher rose, now mostly healed, and went to follow orders. Aebisher was a Homo Sapien and had enlisted in the Galactic Marines to escape a crap shack lifestyle on the polluted planet Earth. He had been Raskor-idan's first sergeant for three years now and, despite being from an inferior race (though from the Eridani perspective nearly every race was inferior), he had a decent regard for the human's drive and military prowess.

It took a half hour to get the devices ready. Each marine helmet had a light system installed near its brim to allow quick orders for attack, retreat, or hold actions. During that time Raskor-idan had ordered his men to stand down, only firing if one of the creatures emerged. None of them did, thought they sent out plenty of plasma fire. Two more men were downed.

The mobile grenade was a standard military issue plasma grenade with an attachment at the top that sprouted slender spider-like legs. It scuttled to a preset location before detonating.

"All ready sir," Aebisher reported.

"Send them out."

The Alliance troopers braced themselves, ready to spring into action the moment the go light was activated. The Arachnids tried to shoot the grenades, but there were too many. They crawled into the entrance from every conceivable direction and then…

BOOM.

Even with sonic dampeners, the blast was ear splitting. Whatever defenders were at the front of the barricade had been instantly vaporized.

Raskor-idan sent the go light. The men charged in. The subterranean entrance and several levels below filled with bullets, beams, and fire, leaving a trail of squashed corpses behind. As he followed his men, the captain noted that the upper levels were entirely guarded by cannon fodder: grey skinned bony creatures with vestigial wings and hooks instead of hands and feet, and brutish monsters with no facial features, cybernetically modified to allow them to restructure their limbs into nearly any shape they desired.

The bulk of the enemy force was located on the lowest level. They had, once again, barricaded themselves in at the bottom of the last ramp using cement slabs dragged from the upper floors. Five more soldiers were killed in an attempt to rush the defenses. Most of them had bled out after falling to the bottom of the ramp where none of the field medics could get to them. One managed to stabilize himself with healing injections and tried to make a break towards his comrades, but was cut down in seconds.

Raskor-idan personally came down to deal with the annihilation of these bastards, leaving Aebisher up top to organize the evac of anyone who was too wounded for field healing to deal with. He clutched his rifle in his artificial hand. The loss of his hand was a wound he had taken on long ago so that he would never forget the past. However, at some point the past may be forgiven. Perhaps this victory would be the tipping point. Perhaps his people would take him back.

To breach the last level, Raskor-idan had authorized the use of ultra armor assault suits. These bulky mechanized machines were designed to allow a solider to go toe-to-toe with an Arachnid warrior. A pilot was cybernetically implanted into the armor and controlled its massive limbs as he would his own. As effective as they were, the ultra armors were also extremely cost prohibitive and, due to budget cuts, Raskor-idan's company was only issued two of these. To make it worse, both of them were hand-me downs from previous campaigns. They had arrived battered and full of holes. Still, they were better than nothing.

The hold light was issued. Rockets were launched at the barriers, reducing them to rubble. A few more were sent down to soften up whatever was in there. Raskor-idan had given up any pretense of rescuing civilians. Everyone knew it was just a fantasy.

He gave the green light for the ultra armors to advance, with the rest of the troops, himself included, following directly behind. This proved to be his undoing. Most of the Arachnids had retreated to the back of the level. This was to be expected, but Raskor-idan immediately noted two things and knew he had made a mistake.

First, the intelligence he had received was off. There were easily twice the number of Arachnid warriors here. As the head exploded on the soldier standing next to him, he realized that he should have waited, should have sent in a reconnaissance drone.

The second thing was the presence of a large creature in the back, snarling with ferocity. It stood five meters tall, its face covered with hanks of coarse black hair that swallowed all of its features, except for a vicious snarling mouth. Twin tapering thick antenna extended diagonally from its head. The Alliance technicians were unsure, but they had made a guess that these served as a sensory apparatus, a combination of ears and eyes. Its personal battle armor was covered in blood. This was a Maelstorm General. Bred to lead the Arachnid troops into battle. Engineered to withstand the most savage of sieges. They were going to need a bigger gun. A chance the captain would not get.

The Maelstorm General raised its arms. The Arachnid surged. There were a series of bright flashes and, for Raskor-idan, the world went black.

Chapter 5- Trishmag

Black Flag Pirate Clan: A collection of affiliated ships under the tentative banner of a democratically elected Admiral. They are primarily engaged in looting and slavery activities in the frontier sectors of Alliance space, as well as being a plague on many unaligned systems. Black Flag is consistently rated as the most violent and vicious pirate clan by the Alliance Justice System. And with five thousand different clans in operation, you have to be a special kind of evil to gain this distinction. The Arc of Blood is a member of this group.

***

Almon, Quandle, and Molphus examined the camera footage shot by the Sebe, one of the cruisers that had been orbiting the Brethia Stargate Project when Oxtiern struck. They watched the marauding ship drop out of hyperspace and go into an apparent suicide run against the massive cruiser. At the last minute it swung around, skimming along the surface of the Dyson sphere.

"There. Look," said Quandle, stopping the feed.

Almon and Molphus leaned in closer. At the paused moment, they saw an open docking bay and a shuttle half emerged from it.

"That's how he got out," Quandle continued. "By

this time the Project was in a complete panic, everyone escaping. So after picking up Oxtiern, the attack ship stops," he fast forwarded the feed, "to grab a number of escape bubbles. They could have been easily destroyed, so why?"

"I can only imagine," Molphus said. Almon could tell that his heart went out to whoever was captured. The boy needed to toughen up fast.

"Slaves perhaps, to be sold outside the Alliance or to some Phentari world as meat? Maybe they were other collaborators who couldn't get to Oxtiern's shuttle," Quandle offered, to answer his own question.

Almon thought of a few more evil possibilities, then shrugged. It wasn't important.

"Bring up a closer image of the ship," he said.

It was an ugly vessel, seemingly made from ill-fitting parts slapped over each other. It curved in a wide angle around the front, with three engines blasting from behind. A large jagged spike stuck out awkwardly.

"What's that on the front?" Molphus asked.

"It's from an Arachnid ship. It allows for easier boarding," replied Quandle. "Very useful for a pirate vessel."

"And we're sure they *are* pirates?" Almon asked.

Quandle nodded respectfully. On the screen he pulled up the file on the ship from the Pirate Watch Bureau of the Galactic Navy's criminal database.

"I triple checked it," he said, "but the unique configuration left no real doubt. The ship is called The Arc of Blood, part of the Black Flag fleet."

Black Flag, the worst of the worst. It made sense though. Almon knew that Oxtiern had cultivated contacts with them over the years. All part of his duties. All necessary for the cause. *Until they became a liability.* Almon cursed himself yet again. It seemed his whole life was a series of liabilities. Of lies and boxes within boxes.

But when the deceptions of his life were shredded away, layer after carefully cultivated layer, there remained at the center one dark lump of truth. Only *that* had importance. Even his own mission against Oxtiern was secondary.

"Good work," he said to Quandle, who beamed in spite of himself.

No matter how long it had been since he was Almon's student, no matter how much he had achieved in his life, praise from his stoic mentor always brought a flush of joy to Quandle. Almon had been a difficult taskmaster. Any kind word was hard won.

"What sort of people run that thing?" Molphus asked, fascinated by the ugliness of the Arc of Blood.

"No way to tell," Quandle answered. "These pirates have an appalling attrition rate, yet they have no problem filling their ranks with more. These other races always have a high surplus population that slips into criminality. The end result of breeding too much."

Molphus didn't care for that at all, but held his tongue. Quandle was military and had a tendency to look at a problem simply, but mentioning that now would solve nothing.

"Where are they now?" Molphus asked. He didn't know much about Black Flag or other pirate groups. He tended to avoid news dealing with violence or hatred. However, what he did know was all bad. "Where do these types congregate?"

"Excellent question," said Quandle, a little condescendingly. "Pirates move fast. By the time we hear about an attack, they are long gone and most of their havens are well hidden. But we do have this report from the Pirate Watch Bureau of a large number of sightings of Black Flag ships around Myntal-5."

"How many?" Almon asked, his curiosity finally aroused.

"Close to fifty."

"That's it," Almon said, rising. "If the ship or Oxtiern aren't there, it will be our best chance to discover where they are or will be." He addressed Quandle, "Arrange transportation. Nothing ostentatious and not a Mutzachan ship. We don't want to draw attention to ourselves. Myntal-5 is out of the way, near the frontier. Perhaps a decommissioned scouting vessel."

Quandle nodded and left eagerly. Finally some action.

Molphus turned to the elder. He cleared his throat several times, a nervous habit that Almon remembered well. He was preparing himself to confront his mentor and Almon knew exactly what it was about.

"I was issued a laser today," Molphus said. "I'm not qualified on it. I don't know how good I'll be."

"Point at the enemy and pull the trigger," Almon

said flatly, knowing that Molphus meant something else in his statement. "The reason I chose it for you was because a laser has no recoil to throw off your aim."

"How… how are we going to handle it?"

"Depends on *it.* We have to do some reconnaissance, gather intelligence, and look for an opening."

"I see."

Almon drew close to him, their faces level. An outsider might not be able to tell much difference between them, but Molphus noticed distinct sag lines around the other's mouth and grey had begun to set in on the edges of Almon's eyes, a sign of advanced age in a Mutzachan.

"I don't believe that you do," Almon said. "If you get him in your sights, you must attack without hesitation. Because if he spots you, I'll be bringing your corpse back to your lover."

"Aren't we even going to try to arrest him? This mission is sounding more and more like an assassination. I can't abide that."

"This is one of the most dangerous creatures you will ever meet."

"Person."

"Creature. He surrendered the right to be thought of as a person long ago. Let me say again, he will not hesitate to kill or torture you."

"But in all moral conscience we have to allow him the chance to surrender. If he resists then I am in favor of defending myself, but…"

"Put your morals to one side, because it isn't just

your life you're gambling with. It is Quandle's and mine as well."

He left Molphus behind to process that.

***

Almon retired to his quarters. As he entered, the lights automatically sensed his presence and filled the room with a heavenly glow. Several pieces of grav furniture, boards that projected a gravity field upwards, allowing a person to float in perfect comfort, were arranged around a massive screen that dominated the high wall. Currently the scereen was on a mood setting, projecting a series of intersecting lines from different angles which collided to create geometric shapes of absolute uniformity before breaking off to create new shapes. A pleasing sight to the Mutzachan sensibilities.

He wearily entered the bathroom, handing his silver robes to the servitor drone that silently floated up to him. It was past time for his monthly blood cleansing and he was feeling the fatigue. Mutzachans have no kidneys and cleansed their hemoglobin of impurities with a microscopic parasite, called a reed worm, which raced through their veins gobbling up toxins. These creatures grew fat on the Mutzachan's waste and could clog up the bloodstream, causing a heart attack or a stroke, if not expelled.

The tub had been waiting for him, the water's temperature just as he liked it, lukewarm. He settled in with a sigh and waved the drone over. It was round, about a meter in diameter with various appendages needed for cleaning and maintenance. Almon stuck his arm out. The drone injected a needle into him and began siphoning blood. To do a thorough cleanse, three liters had to be taken out and replaced. It took a while. In the olden days, Mutzachans would cut themselves open and manually massage the reed worms out, sometimes dying as a result, but time and invention had improved the ritual to simply be a minor inconvenience.

As the drone fulfilled its function, Almon worried about the task ahead, about what he would be called upon to do. He thought about his companions. He thought about Oxtiern. Would they be able to take him? Alive was not an option, Molphus would just have to come to terms with that. Even their own lives weren't guaranteed. Quandle and Molphus's deaths would be a tragedy, them being so young, but since when did the implacable iceberg face of necessity care about waste?

The blood loss made him lightheaded and his mind drifted. Back a dozen years. Back to a darkened room and a disturbing encounter…

Almon sat, half shrouded in gloom. A thin desk and a terminal in front of him. It displayed a dossier on the Zen Rigeln. Not the one Molphus and Quandle had been shown, the real one. Oxtiern himself was seated in the center of the room, a pillar of light surrounding him. He affected nonchalance, leisurely crossing one leg over the other, pulling long drags of steam from his electronic cigarette. But there were certain twitches in his legs and a jerkiness when he moved his head which betrayed a nervousness lurking underneath. Almon was pleased, he needed to know that he could put the Zen under pressure.

"When you were in the Marines, you were brought up on charges of murder and excessive torture during the course of your duties," Almon began.

"For which I was found not guilty."

"But you and I both know that the verdict was faulty."

Oxtiern did not reply. He simply grinned, encompassing the Mutzachan in his azure eyes.

"Tell me about your interrogations during this time, before you were charged."

Oxtiern settled back, joyful memories flooding his skull.

"This was on Bandraginus 5, you remember the place, a little colony world established by the Humans, modest profit center, very taxable. Then this rebel outfit, The Trawl Liberation Army, begins laundering a ton of credits through them. All of this spilled over to the locals, raising their standard of living. This group gets their own people elected into government. Next thing we know, they're all clamoring for independence from the Alliance. Well, we couldn't have that, so they sent in the Marines."

"What were the aims of this rebel group?"

"I never bothered to find out."

Almon knew. The Trawl Liberation Army were well funded, but more talkers than doers. Their aims were to create their own coalition of planets which would work in a "perfect symmetry, providing for the physical and spiritual needs of the whole in a collective function and a service based economy". They viewed the current Alliance as an unhealthy corporate prostitute. The group was wildly unsuccessful and had since retreated into some dingy hideaway, spending most of their time killing each other in a "purge of the ideologically corrupt".

"Continue on," Almon said.

"We went in, wrecked the place, and the rebels go scurrying off in to the back woods. Of course they can't just roll over and die like decent pests, they have to go on a guerrilla footing. Planting bombs, assassinating generals, disrupting trade. All tediously predictable. It was taking forever to get rid of them. So when a few got captured, I made sure to break them as quickly as possible."

"What methods did you use?"

Oxtiern smiled wider, he was rather enjoying this memory trip.

"Usually we rely on empaths to scrape the information out of a subject's head, particularly when smacking around civilians, but these rebels were trained to withstand that. It could have taken weeks, so I implemented a few techniques that I had developed."

"Which was your favorite?"

"I'd lay one out naked on a slab," Oxtiern chuckled. "Tied down with scratchy restraints that irritated the skin. Next to him, within eyesight, I'd have a tray of surgical gear modified with a few extra curves and hooks. I'd stomp in wearing a blood stained smock. Often they'd lose control of their bowels at the sight.

"Concealed about me would be a juvenile Mazian. You know the race. Sentient blobs that can twist and wriggle into various shapes. Communicate by banging themselves into the ground. Without asking the subject any questions, I'd slice a fat slit into their belly and dive in. The Mazian would slide out of my sleeve and I'd pull it up. The subject would be screaming by now, eyes bulging. I'd tell them that it was their large intestine and I was going to reroute it back into their stomach. The look on their face when they'd thought they'd be shitting inside of themselves…ooooh it was tasty."

He paused, savoring the memory.

"They'd crack soon after that," he added.

"How did you feel after you were charged?" asked Almon.

Oxtiern's face darkened, twisting up in rage and hate.

"How does a person feel when betrayed? Even if it was just for show, it never should've happened! Nowadays I wouldn't piss on a Marine to save his life." He stopped, trying to collect himself, then exploded again. "We were there to do a job! To destroy an enemy. And then they want to throw some kind of stupid morality in there. Kill them, but be gentle about it. Get the information, but be kind to the scum. Our purpose *was* to be violent. Shoot them, burn them, bury them alive, bomb their houses, torch their crops, nuke their cities. It doesn't matter. They'll be just as dead."

"And what about the innocents who get caught in

the middle?" Almon asked. "What do you do for them?"

"Innocence?" Oxtiern laughed, misunderstanding the Mutzachan. "There's no such thing as innocence. It's just a phrase to describe someone who's too ignorant to know how shitty the universe is. Innocence is just ignorance in disguise." "I meant people not involved in the conflict who get hurt."

"That's the price of doing business in war. One guy, ten thousand children, it doesn't matter. The mission is what's important. Letting nothing stop the goal from being attainted. An Arachnid warrior or a doe-eyed newborn, it's all the same. That's what wins wars. Determination!"

Almon reached over to the terminal and typed on it. The word "approved" appeared over Oxtiern's dossier.

Chapter 6- Hyperspace aboard The Arc of Blood

Species: Orion

Planet of Origin: Taos in the Chi Orionos system

Description: The Orion is a fourteen fingered bipedal mammal who, amazingly, has developed along a parallel evolutionary tract as Homo Sapiens. Ouwardly, they are strikingly similar. However, an internal probe quickly shows that the resemblances are only skin deep. They first developed space travel with the unlikely help of the Phentari, when both cultures faced invasion by Eridani forces. They formed the Kwashie Alliance in 1770 C.E. and defeated the Eridani decisively at the Battle of Three Powers above Eridine. Since then the Orions have developed intergalactic travel to "spread their seed across the universe" and ensure their race's survival.

Freaky Fact: A current fashion trend among the

Orions is their discovery of the bagpipes. This occurred after it was noted that the Orion's traditional *bawl* garb, designating family allegiance, was remarkably alike to the Scottish kilt. Curious Orions did some research and came across the instrument, which apparently resonates in the Orion's pointed ears in a much more pleasant manner than any sane human.

***

Life just couldn't stop kicking Drake in the nads. After generously popping his shoulder back in, Parg, Jack Mace and the rest dragged Drake up to the office of the Arc of Blood's first mate. There he was dropped, bloody and naked, before Craw, a castrated Cizerack (a quadruped feline species) with blue and black stripped fur and a wild look, that seemed to Drake as if the feline was sizing him up for a light snack.

Parg, in typical Orion brashness, demanded that Drake be added to the crew immediately or else! That didn't sit well with the first mate and the pair screamed obscenities at each other until Jack Mace broke them up.

Once Drake's particulars were explained, Craw bent over Drake, who was still groveling on the floor. He sniffed at Drake's bloody body, his whiskers twitching.

"This one stinks like a pussy," he declared, his voice sounding as if he'd inhaled a tank of helium. "We don't need any goddamn weaklings here."

"If he was a pussy, he'd be able to give you your balls back," quipped Parg, which did nothing to aid his cause. The other pirates quickly threw him out of the room.

Craw ranted at them for a while, claiming that they were undisciplined vermin that should all be blasted into deep space, but backed down when the others continued to insist upon Drake's claim.

"I'll square it away," he said. "Just get that chip out of his head. I'm not having anything around that can be tracked."

Satisfied, the crew members departed to whatever duties occupied them. Clearly it wasn't cleaning, as nearly every place was dirty with rust and grime. Scavenging insects scuttled brazenly down the metal halls, having no fear of the larger animals. Jack Mace supported Drake as they walked the corridors.

"Don' worry 'bout that cat," he said in a friendly manner, acting as if he hadn't planned on molesting the Gen-Human only twenty minutes ago. "If the Captain hadn't put him in his job, we would've skinned him long ago."

"He really has no balls?"

"Yep."

"Did he loose them fighting?"

"Naw he's an escaped *nall*. Whacha call it? A eunuch, female slave. Not a fit person to lead real males."

Drake remembered something about that. In Cizerack culture, high born females would take male slaves from the lower castes and remove the testes to make them docile. In more barbaric ages, the female would castrate the male with her own teeth, but now science allowed for a much more sanitary mutilation.

Instead of a medical bay, Drake was lead into the ship's kitchen area. It was a dilapidated room with broken down machinery and dinged up cutlery piled about haphazardly. Most space crews were fed with freeze dried food packets that was rehydrated in specialized machines, but pirates, having an irregular flight schedule, were forced to improvise. There was a lot of uncooked food around, culled from God knows where. Nothing was sealed. Nothing was stored properly. Raw meat was thrown onto dirty counter tops and left for days before being prepared. Bits and pieces of decayed food stuck to Drake's feet as he navigated across the stomach churning floor.

Drake was tossed a pair of dirty blue overalls and a t-shirt from a hamper.

"You'll eventually run across some shoes," he was told.

Jack Mace directed Drake to a rickety wooden stool. He felt about the back of Drake's skull, looking for a bump which would indicate the implanted chip.

"Where is the damn thing?"

"Shouldn't we go to the ship's doctor for this?"

"He's more of a drug dealer than a physician. I wouldn' trust that pill head to lance a boil. The only time you wanta see him is if you plan to party wit' a few pharmaceuticals."

He lit up a cigarette made up of black Russian tobacco mixed with ginseng. The whole room stank like a burning onion.

"Well… I'll just cut a slit there and feel aroun'. Maybe I can fish it out."

"The chip's embedded in my skull," he said meekly. "It's not floating around in there."

"How was I supposed to know that? Why didn' you tell me earlier?"

"Well I uhh…"

"Am I supposed to know everything? Godamnit!"

The Fott threw a steel pot against the wall, denting it badly. He paused, thinking. Not a natural skill of his. He flicked the butt of his smoke into a huge basin.

"Maybe we can short it out somehow. Yeah, we'll just run a power cable up to the back of yer head and…"

"That'll electrocute me!"

"We'll put it in lower power or something."

"How are you going to do that?"

"I don't know."

"I don't know either."

The pair stared at each other for a moment, then Jack Mace threw up his hands.

"Ah screw this. We'll just tell 'em we got it done. No one will ever check."

A low buzzer warbled from the ceiling. Jack Mace threw a broken mug at the loudspeaker.

"I hate that friggin' thing. Come on, give me a hand."

"What is that?"

"Chow buzzer. Time to slop the pigs."

The pair ripped open freeze dried food packets

and emptied them into a basin (the same one he had thrown his cigarette in) flooded it with water, topped it with a pressurized heating unit, and waited twenty minutes.

After this, Jack Mace stirred the swill with a huge ladle, occasionally tasting it to make sure it was edible. Every time he bent over, bits of fur and dandruff fell in, which he just ladled over until they disappeared deep into the mixture. The procedure seemed simple enough, but to listen to Jack Mace talk it was the most arduous backbreaking labor since Sisyphus was condemned to eternally roll a boulder uphill.

Roars of hunger and demands for food came from an adjacent cafeteria. The denizens were hungry. A steady rhythm of plates banging on tables rang into the room. Drake helped the Fott shift the steaming basin onto a cart and Jack pushed it jerkily into the next room.

"All right you bastards," he yelled. "Get yer grub and stop whinin'."

Drake peeked in. The room was packed with detritus from every known Alliance race and a few outside of it. Usually pirate clans broke down along racial lines, but Black Flag took whatever scum it could scrape up. All you needed was a killer instinct and a felony conviction. Here they were, squashed together, stinking of weird smells, babbling away in their home tongues, or the Standard Trade Dialect, or Galactic Basic.

Each was openly wearing a weapon or twelve. Like the uniforms, there was no standard issue weapon for a crew member. Most were purchased illegally, scavenged from corpses, or stolen during riots. Many displayed some item of plundered wealth. A gold tooth here, a ruby stud there, one was using a silver plated nose hair trimmer.

Drake shuddered as he gazed at this unwashed mass of galactic vermin. Life was not going to get better.

***

He was right.

Despite being on the crew roster, Drake discovered that he was not fully accepted by the others. He was a bojing, someone who hadn't made his bones, hadn't been battle tested, one who had been shanghaied into service. Even Parg, who was thoroughly disliked, was more accepted than him.

What was worse, Drake was forced to share a room with Parg, as each and every other bastard on board refused to bunk with either of them. The berth was no bigger than a cell, with just enough room for the bunk, two small lockers, and a flexi-screen for entertainment. An aluminum lawn chair with a bright flower pattern was crammed into the far end, looking completely out of place.

"Where did you pick this up?" Drake had asked him.

"Some frontier settlement, I don't remember where. This old biddy had a bunch of stuff cluttering up her patio, but I needed it more so I took it. Old bag had a lot to say about it, had to put a few in her."

"You needed it more?"

"Hey, I gotta sit too!"

Drake let it go.

Parg was the worst of roommates. He suffered from an acid reflux problem, but wouldn't change his diet of junk food and alcohol, causing him to have long bouts of flatulence that hung heavy in the air and lingered much longer than they should. He would take off his clothes whenever possible, wandering around in a pair of skimpy bright orange briefs to the delight of no one. Very often Drake would return from attempting to do some work to find Parg passed out in the lawn chair, his flabby paunch flopped over the briefs, giving him the appearance of being nude. Every time Drake saw him like this, he thought about strangling the Orion on the spot, and not just for the near rape when they first met.

As time went on, Drake found that his job was one quarter shit flushing and three quarters shit taking. Every uncomfortable bowel movement was blamed on him. As such, he was not popular. The only person that he could conceivably call a friend was Jack Mace, who seemed to hate him slightly less than he hated everyone else. They spent hours together, Drake picked up all sorts of tidbits of other worlds and how the pirates operated.

He also got some training in the pirate's argot, an incredibly dense and constantly changing vocabulary assembled from thousands of languages that shifted from clan to clan. He picked up the basics. Any pirate in the clan but on a different ship was a"cousin". The military, police, or private security was called "hod". To squeal or inform to the authorities was to "spit".

"Jel" was the term for the victim of a crime. And so on.

Unfortunately this general dislike for him was compounded by the fact that Drake really didn't know what he was doing. The sewage system onboard was designed so that all garbage ran into a series of tanks on the bottom of the hull. Once filled, a tank was sealed, exposed to space, and the frozen block of filth was hydraulically pushed out. As it turned out, most of the lines were clogged with huge lumps of fecal matter that had accumulated over time, sending abominable smells back out the other end. And if that weren't bad enough, all but one of the tanks was broken, making all waste disposal an overly long process and creating a tremendous backlog.

All of these broken tanks were full, and the only way Drake could think of to deal with the problem was for a team to go outside and pry the block out. He was unsuccessful in getting anyone to help him.

"That's *your* job!" was a phrase he heard over and over again.

No one in upper management would assist him either. He had approached Craw about allocating some manpower, but was snarled away in the feline's high pitched voice.

"Get your own damn thing working. I'm too busy. We all got jobs. Do yours."

Then he had stomped away, a few crew members snickering behind his back.

Drake had even attempted to approach the Captain, an enigmatic human with pale blue eyes and thin lips. He had snuck up to the bridge and saw the man standing before a control panel with Skel, the ship's Zen Rigeln navigation officer, who was explaining something.

"It's just sitting there waiting. Almost begging us," Skel was saying. "I mean why not?"

Drake took two steps onto the bridge and was grabbed by a pair of burly guards who leveled a gun at his face.

"Move and I'll put a hole in the center of your brain"

Skel was still talking, "The men like it when there's some plunder. Something they can hold. So far this trip they've got nothing..."

He broke off and the Captain turned to stare at Drake, finally noticing him being manhandled by the bridge guards.

"Assassin?"

"No weapons, sir."

Skel somehow recognized Drake, though they had never met before. "This is the new shi... plumbing officer, sir" Until that moment Drake had no idea that he was technically ranked as an officer. "He knows, or should know, that he isn't allowed up here."

Drake spoke, his voice cracking. "Sir, I need help with the toilets..."

The Captain turned away. This was a speck beneath his notice. Drake was tossed down a flight of stairs and told to get lost, which he promptly did. It was the last time that he ever spoke to the man.

So what could he really do? The best Drake

could come up with was to go around and stick air fresheners on the bowls (he found a large box of them in a dusty storage room, the profits of some forgotten raid) and dumping boxes of baking soda down the holes so they didn't stink as badly. This worked slightly in some cases, but in others the sludge came right up to the rim.

***

Upon reflection, Drake was surprised that anything worked on the Arc of Blood at all. The ship had been damaged and wrecked many times over the years and was apparently repaired by whatever salvage sort of fit it, giving it a truly odd shape. The bulk of the frame was an ancient light freighter, but gun pods and missile racks had been welded on higgledy piggledy. The rear bottom portion must have been razed and fallen off at some point, for it had been replaced with an inconsistent section of a different style of freighter. The shuttle docks, wrapped around the back side of the ship, were a good three meters off from the corresponding decks inside, meaning that pilots had to keep their wits about them or smash up their shuttle. Only two of the three engines pulsing from the stern were the same type. The third had been ripped off of a derelict Erdani destroyer (an entirely different type of vessel) and stuck out like an enlarged limb. This was all protected by an underpowered flux shield, which had to be manually directed as it couldn't cover the whole ship at one time.

But the pinnacle attraction of this scrounged together ship was the massive spike which curved from its head and was its primary weapon. An item which jutted so prominently from the Arachnid troop carriers.

Drake never quite found out how the Arc of Blood crew had managed to gain the weapon. Some of the stories he was told revolved around a chance encounter with a stray vessel, where the ship was boarded and they had to fight for their lives, claiming the spike as a prize. Parg himself had told of how he led a battalion of pirates bravely against the Arachnid horde, giving the tale a lot less credibility.

Others said that the pirate vessel, in an uncharacteristic spurt of patriotism, joined in on the Alliance side of a battle between the rival forces and was awarded it by the Galactic Navy. A few claimed that they had run across it while illegally looting ships after said battle. Still others had darker theories about the weapon's presence, Jack Mace among them.

"Now gee, how did a ship get an Arachnid weapon and then make it work with incompatible systems?" he said, scratching his broken ear and spitting into a pot.

Drake waited for an answer but the Fott just stared at him inquiringly. Finally he shrugged.

"I don't know."

"You're an idiot," Jack Mace shook his head in anger. "You can't put basic facts together. It's so obvious."

"Then tell me."

"No one on this ship is smart enough to make that weapon work. They got it because the Arachnids gave it to them!"

"What?"

"It's true, on the top deck they're all Arachnid agents. The Captain, that eunuch Craw, Skel, all in their employ. And they gave it to 'em to cause havoc in the shipping lanes and so forth."

With a firm nod Jack Mace went back to stirring some bubbling green concoction on the stove.

"Don't friggin' listen to him," Parg yelled from across the room. He was lying on a metal counter, alternately chugging from a bottle of cooking alcohol and sucking marrow from the bone of an unidentified animal. One to kill the taste of the other. "He doesn't know what he's talking about."

"I know more'n you ever will," the Fott said, riled.

"You weren't aboard yet when they put the thing on."

"Neither were you! That don' mean what I'm sayin' ain't true, boy."

Parg waved him off and chugged some more booze. Jack drew close to Drake, his whiskers tickling the Gen-Human's nose.

"What you don' see is that it's all a scam to weed us out."

"A scam?"

"By the Mutzachans. It's a frigging conspiracy between the Arachnids and them. There is no war!"

Parg propped himself up to listen better. A slow smile grew on his face, and as he grinned a green blob of vegetable matter dangled in the gap between his front teeth.

"They want to wipe out all the other races and leave only them two in command," Jack continued. "Everyone else will be a slave or dead."

Parg emitted a short barking laugh that Jack Mace ignored.

"Think on it. Whenever you hear about some Arachnid massacre, how many Mutzachans get killed in 'em? None. They don' hit them targets. They go after every other race to whittle us down for the Mutzachans to come in and destroy us with a cosmic backstab."

"And why are they doing this?" Drake asked.

"Because they don't want competition. It's why they tried so hard to wipe us Fotts out."

It was true that when the race was first introduced onto several unsuspecting planets by an anarchist rebel group, hunting Fotts for sport had become a new hobby. But Drake didn't remember reading anything about Mutzachans doing that. It was primarily the Eridani and Phentari. Two races which were flip sides of the same evil coin, in Drake's opinion. He related this to Jack Mace.

"That's all part of their plan," was the retort. "Them two races are so violent that the fat heads just have to point 'em in a direction and watch 'em go. That's why they need the Arachnids to finish 'em off. So they don't have to get their precious hands dirty."

"But what about the Humans, and my people, the Gen-Humans? The Mutzachans have been helping them."

"That's cause they're buildin' a slave race. Only y'all are too dumb to see it," he jammed a finger into Drake's chest. "They'll need servants to mow their lawns and clip their toenails after they cause the apocalypse. So, remember that."

Parg slipped off the counter and lurched forward, laughing heartily. He waved the now empty bottle like a conductor with a baton. "Tell him the other one. About the planets blowing up."

Jack Mace threw a bottle of hot sauce that winged him across the temple. Parg fell back and collapsed into a stack of cans containing stewed tomatoes. He lay there groaning. Neither Drake nor Jack helped him.

"Now let me tell you the biggest conspiracy of all," the Fott said. "These Mutzachans, they realized that they can't just completely wipe us out, so they created a virus that can blow up planets."

"A…a virus?"

"Yeah, they built this virus with really big molecules that can infect a planet. These virus molecules go to the planet's core and multiply until it can't be contained. Kinda like when you stick a sealed carbonated drink out in the sun. Then it explodes. It's their ultimate weapon."

"That's so stupid."

Drake was slapped across the face. Hard. Tears sprang into his eyes, half from pain, half from fear. Jack Mace yelled at him, eyes wild. His face took on the impenetrable ferocious mask of the fanatic. Without question he believed every syllable he had just uttered.

"Then you explain to me about Ering Crasb back in '25. It blew up with two billion people on it. Or Ampyria in the Fornax galaxy. Gone. Fifty thousand settlers, none of them Mutzachans, blown to hell. Or Efrafa over in Aedorian space, huh? There was no natural reason for any of them to explode."

Everything Jack Mace said was technically true. All of those planets had broken up with people lost, that was common knowledge. But Drake wasn't as certain as Jack about the cause, especially after he realized...

"Efrafa was uninhabited. So why detonate that one?"

"That's when they were testin' it."

"But it happened after Ering Crasb."

"I'm not the only one to believe this. There are tons of people on the hypernet flows talking about this with an assload of proof. How about Sharron then? Three billion people on that one."

Drake thought for a moment. Sharron... he knew that name. Not on its own, he remembered very little about the planet, but there was something... that was it!

"Sharron didn't explode because of a virus," Drake retaliated loudly, rousing Parg from his stupor. "That maniac Jaquassarious Phentari destroyed it. I saw a documentary about how he did it. He used some sort of weird missiles that burrowed into the planet's core causing an implosion."

Jaquassarious Phentari was the most notorious criminal in the Alliance. He had indeed blown up an entire planet (the specifics of which were somewhat disputed, despite Drake's statement) resulting in him having three billion murder charges leveled against him. Due to his elusive nature, he was tried in absentia and a death sentence issued. There currently was a ten million credit bounty on his head.

His reasons for destroying the planet were unknown. Speculation abounded, but in general the grotesque facts surrounding the crime overwhelmed most people's curiosity as to the motive. It was usually chalked up to a racist stereotype of the malicious character of the Phentari race in general.

"And where'd he get that from?" Jack Mace demanded. "Weird technology. The Phentari don't have anything like that. The Mutzachans developed it and he tested it out for them. He's a Mutzachan agent."

"So the officers of the Arc of Blood, the Arachnids, and Jaquassarious Phentari are all Mutzachan agents. Who isn't one?"

"I'll tell y'all who," Jack Mace said, missing the sarcasm. "You and I. The everyday little guys who will just get blown away. That's why I'll never give in. I'll always keep fightin' the Mutzachan system. That's why I'm on this boat."

"I thought," Parg said, sitting up and pushing the clattering cans off of himself. "You were here because you shotgunned your wife and her lover after you caught them screwing around."

"That's another reason."

Parg and Jack laughed cruelly. Drake joined them, but only to fit in. Once again he began to despair over every aspect of his life. The intercom crackled and Craw's high pitched voice called out.

"Is that shit surgeon with you again, Mace?"

"Yeah."

"Send him down to middle bulk levels, our *guest* is uncomfortable. And we can't have that, can we?"

The bitterness practically dripped from the speaker. Drake sighed and grabbed a toolbox he had managed to obtain. It was mostly for show and contained almost no tools useful on a septic system.

"I'm going," he said, glad for the interruption. Jack Mace's insane theories were starting to make his head hurt.

"Quickly!"

Drake trundled on, walking by several crew members doing repairs. They ignored him as one would a passing housecat. The passenger, Oxtiern, had been set up in a series of rooms which were initially intended for light cargo that needed to be heated. They were away from any of the occupied sections of the ship, which suited everyone fine. With trepidation, Drake entered Oxtiern's rooms.

They were sparsely furnished, containing only a metal cot, a military issue blanket tossed across it, a few personal electronics laid out on a shelf, and the standard flexi-screen plastered on the wall. The flexi-screen was made of a material which allowed it to be rolled up and easily carried, and then stuck to any surface wide enough to accommodate it. Once activated, the screen automatically tuned into any wireless broadcast frequencies available. Most ships usually would have several films or reruns of old shows playing for the crew's amusement, but the Arc of Blood did not.

He heard movement in an adjoining room and peeked in. Oxtiern was there, completely nude, sitting comfortably on a plastic chair amid a scattering of corpses. All of the bodies were Gen-Humans, Drake's fellow batch mates, captured from escape bubbles as he had been. Each of them had died from some severe cranial trauma. Large holes shone from their foreheads like a carved out third eye. But for so much death, there was a distinct lack of blood on the floor. What had happened to it?

Oxtiern was pleased, his mouth stretched out into a skeletal smile. He took a long sip from a glass mug filled with some steaming liquid. Directly in front of him stood another Gen-Human, a female, with features very similar to that of Drake (genetic variation can only go so far). She too had a wound in her head, but much smaller than the others. A trickle of blood leaked down her face and dripped off her chin.

"How do you feel?" Oxtiern asked.

The Gen-Human said nothing. She rocked back and forth slightly, eyes glassy.

"Tell me if you feel well."

"I feel well," she said, her voice flat and dead.

"What would you like to do?" Oxtiern continued.

No answer.

"Would you like to raise your right arm?"

No answer.

"Raise your right arm."

The Gen-Human raised her limb.

"Salute me."

She complied, giving him an Alliance salute. A balled up right fist thumped across the chest.

"Now pick up the gun."

Drake hadn't noticed it before, being distracted by all the carnage. On the other side of Oxtiern was a foldout tray where a revolver and a golden cylindrical object lay. The Gen-Human picked up the weapon.

"Despite what you just said, I imagine that your current state must be an unimaginable hell. So I am going allow you to be released from it. Say 'thank you.'"

"Thank you."

"Shoot yourself in the head."

Without hesitation, she raised the revolver and blew her own brains out, dropping with a sickening schulmp on top of another body. Oxtiern rose, refreshed. His corkscrew genitalia flapping idly between his thighs. Then he saw Drake.

"Ah the strung up meat. Escape from your tormentors? Very resourceful of you."

He drew closer, his bony fingers scratching at his sides, caressing himself. Drake shrank back.

"Did you know that woman there?" asked Oxtiern. "Was she your sister? An old lover? An incestuous twin?"

"N…no."

"Pity. That might've been amusing. The look on your face would've been something to be savored."

Drake couldn't reply. The bottom dropped out of his stomach and his feet had grown cold. Even naked, when most would've been vulnerable, this creature radiated menace. He stuck his toolbox out like some feeble talisman to ward off evil.

And like all talismans, it didn't work. Oxtiern grabbed Drake's wrist in a crushing grip. His teeth gnashed together with a rictus sneer. The Zen's hand suddenly glowed blue. From every part of his body intense pain erupted through Drake. He dropped to his knees.

"I've opened up all your nerve endings," Oxtiern hissed. "Do you like it?"

"No."

The pain intensified. Drake cried out pitifully, a sound ripped from his shredded soul. Oxtiern's lips glistened. His blue eyes drank in every twitch, every gasp, every iota of agony Drake emitted. It was love. A love of pain and on inflicting it.

"Good. Do you want me to stop?"

"Yes...please."

Oxtiern threw the arm away in disdain and walked into the other room, his lust now satisfied.

"I assume you're here to fix the plumbing," he called over his shoulder. "Since you are a turd it only makes sense. Hurry up and get out. It smells terrible."

Drake did his best and skedaddled.

***

When he returned to his room, he found Parg passed out in a fetal position on the bunk. The room stank as the Orion had urinated all over himself in a drunken stupor, a weekly occurrence. Drake was too charged up from his near death experience to sleep. He hated himself for crumbling so quickly under

Oxtiern's grip. He needed to do something to gain back a sense of empowerment.

The flexi-screen was paused on a frame of a brown haired Orion reeling back, blood pouring from his nose and mouth, eyes crossed in a comical manner. Parg had lately been watching pirated episodes of the game show *Take It Like A Man*, where contestants stood on opposite circles and took turns throwing rocks at each other's faces. The first one to cry or get knocked out of the circle was forced to wear a frilly dress and run screaming through a city street. The show was designed to appeal to a very specific demographic niche.

Enough of this crap. Tonight, Drake was going to watch whatever the hell he wanted. He yanked the data tube containing the videos out of the screen and slammed in another he had gotten from a box Parg kept under his bunk. He settled righteously in the lawn chair.

A Human in bright red battle armor appeared on the screen, a glowing sun behind him. The man stood in a heroic pose, his arm pointed out towards the future, towards danger. Danger that he would conquer. How could he not? After all he was…

"SPIIIIIIFFFF BLASTHANDY!" the announcer roared.

Drake sat enraptured. This was his favorite show and Spiff Blasthandy was his fictional idol. He became totally absorbed, wishing he could escape into the world on the screen and banish all memories of his foul life. Why couldn't someone come and take him away from all this?

"Spiff Blasthandy, Secret Agent for Galactic Control. Trained by ninja masters and bestowed by the Mutzachans with the ancient ring of power. He, with his faithful companions, work from their secret base in the heart of the Earth's sun. Their one purpose…"

HOOOONK

"TO DEFEAT THE ARACHNID MENACE WHEREVER IT MAY BE!"

The alarm had come from the corridor. All of the lights turned a solid blue. Battle lighting. Drake jumped up as Parg stirred, all of his righteous fury draining away.

"Boarding parties at the ready. Wave one, report to your breaching stations. Wave two at standby," Craw's voice spilled out over the speakers.

Parg pulled himself up, his paunch flopping over the edge of the mattress. He popped a few oxygen tablets to sober up quickly.

"Damn it," he growled. "You'd think they'd give us some warning. I wouldn'ta drunk so much."

Not very likely.

He grabbed onto Drake's shirt and hauled himself up, then staggered over to the locker to put on his battle gear. He donned a battered old suit of body armor with a faded ablative liner and a built-in gyrostabilizer. This last feature was nominally to correct the user for automatic gunfire kickback, but it was also useful in keeping one from wobbling about too much due to intoxication.

He unplugged his pulse rifle from the wall and checked that it was fully charged. The pulse rifle, while not as effective as a laser or powder weapon at a distance, had a devastating effect at short range. The weapon fired superheated plasma pulses, utilizing a miniature fusion reactor. A few blasts from one of these could burn through most combat armor and melt the poor bastard inside. Of the few things Parg had, this was the one he was careful to maintain. Drake was forbidden from touching it on pain of having his fingers torn off.

Once suited up, Parg left for the staging area inside of the Arachnid spike. Drake followed behind. He was curious about what it would be like. As with the bridge, Drake wasn't allowed into the zone, but the short announcement time caused chaos below decks and he became invisible in the tumult.

One hundred pirates swarmed the staging area, each stepping into a designated square, behind which were straps and padding. This was to cushion the impact as the spike punctured into the victim vessel. Screens channeling the feed from the outside cameras were mounted on pylons so the pirates could watch the ship's advance.

Drake hid behind a few boxes near some mechanical dollies and braced himself as best he could. He had expected a lot of brash talk and loud boasting amongst the boarding party, but they were mute. Each man was strapping himself in, double checking his armor and weapon, or was mentally gearing up for the attack. All bravado was stored away, replaced by a steely determination. Get in, kill, and take their stuff. Here they were at their best, or worst, depending on your viewpoint. Here is where the Black Flag pirate clan gained their reputation.

From what Drake could tell on the monitors, the pirates were about to engage an Orion light freighter that was having engine trouble. They must have sent out a distress call to the Colonial Naval Network, but the pirates had picked it up first. For some reason the Network was falling behind in their duties.

The Arc of Blood dropped out of hyperspace with engines blazing. Standard protocol on exiting hyperspace was to kill all engines to prevent collisions, but a collision was what the pirates wanted.

The impact was teeth rattling. Drake was buried as the unsecured boxes fell on top of him. He heard the roar of the pirates boarding and peeked out. The spike had penetrated into the freighter like a hornet's stinger, then expanded out from the tip, tearing enough room to allow the entire raiding compliment easy access. Red colored sealing foam automatically squirted around the spike's edges to lock in the atmosphere for the boarders.

Drake tiptoed down the spike's gangway and then quickly retreated. There wasn't a battle going on, but a massacre. Whoever tried to resist had been killed quickly. The pirates were in a bloody frenzy, slaughtering anyone who even raised a hand to ward off a blow. He saw a family of Orions kneeling on an empty floor. A pirate walked down the line slitting their throats with a serrated knife, a bored expression on his face. In another room, Parg was spitting plasma onto a screaming eight year old. Down the hall, two more pirates were hacking the arms off a struggling crew member.

Against orders, the second wave of pirates burst into the staging area and on to the other ship, not wanting to miss out on any of the loot. Jack Mace was among them.

"Hurry and grab what you can," he yelled at Drake as he sprinted past. "Daddy needs some new duds."

Drake gave him the thumbs up but held back, nauseous. This wasn't survival. This was plunder, rape, and riot. This wasn't him and never would be. Unless someone held a gun to his head, he wouldn't participate. And as much as Drake hated what was happening, he also knew there was no stopping it. If he tried, he'd just wind up dangling from his wrists again.

Twenty minutes later the pirates started coming back. The cries of the slaughtered innocents died off, replaced by a babble of greedy murderers drooling over the loot they had found and the "sweet meat" captured. Several women and effeminate boys were dragged past him to be chained up below and shared amongst the men. Drake didn't want to contemplate their fate. He went back to his room.

A few cargo items which could help sustain the Arc of Blood were taken on- repair equipment, spare parts, and bulk food stores, etc.- but this had primarily been an assault for personal profit. A grab-what-you-can fest to line the crew's pockets and improve morale.

And it certainly did. Parg came back, pockets full of cash and arms full of swag. He managed to get a case of Jum cola, a few data pads ripped from dead wrists- which could be reprogrammed and sold on the black market easily enough- several bottles of a strong Orion booze called Utoban, and, most amazingly, a set of bagpipes.

"I've always wanted to try out one of these," he exclaimed to Drake, then began laying into the instrument.

As the hideous sounds surrounded him, Drake turned a corner. His hatred and disgust overcame his fear. Right then, he came to the conclusion that he was going to jump ship at the first opportunity, no matter where it was. And hopefully kill Parg on his way out.

Chapter 7- Stilt

Species: Eridani

Planet of Origin: Eridine in the Epislon Eridani system

Description: An aggressive, ritual orientated caste race, with the Buddon (warrior) caste on the top. This tri-sexual, methane breathing species places a high value on personal honor and victory in combat. Despite their eagerness for battle, the Eridani lost the last pre-Alliance war they fought. The combined Phentari and Orion civilizations trounced their military and nearly drove their home planet back into the Stone Age. This has led to a schizophrenic attitude by the Eridani when dealing with alien races, manifesting itself as a constant need to dismiss other species as inferior and yet still prove themselves superior to said races. This explains why Eridani are such staunch supporters of the Alliance, while banning all non-Eridani from their home systems.

Freaky Fact: Eridani warriors have a bad habit of

mutilating themselves whenever they commit what they see as an error. Tradition demands that they lacerate whichever part of the body performed the mistake.

***

Raskor-idan stepped off the troop shuttle that had carried him to Jericho City and stiffly walked towards the Brigade Command camp. Oh yes, he had survived the Maelstorm General's attack, barely. It had taken him a month to recover in the hospital, despite the healing hands of the Zen physicians and frequent rejuvination injections.

But he felt that it might've been better if they had just let him die. He hadn't just failed, hadn't simply been beaten by overwhelming odds on the battlefield. There was no shame in *that*, especially against the Arachnids. No, the indelible stain on his honor came from the fact that he could have won. His men died, the battle lost, because he had been too rash.

His company had taken eighty five percent causalities and the only reason the rest had survived was because Aebisher had ordered their retreat after it was clear that the Arachnids were about to break through.

The Eridani had torn twin scars down his temples in penance for his folly. The pain when he cut into his own face had been intense. In fact, it still throbbed, but his warrior training allowed him to cast it into the back of his mind.

The methane converter chaffed around his

mouth. It was incredibly annoying to have to wear this thing all day. He wished he could tear it off, but that wasn't the death Raskor-idan was looking for.

The Arachnid menace on Stilt had been suppressed. Every known warrior had been rooted out and torched, even the ones that had nearly killed Raskor-idan. He had read the reports while recuperating. They stated that the Maelstorm General and the Arachnid troopers had broken out of the city and attempted to hide in a derelict mine. Being believers in economy, the marines had pumped gas throughout the tunnels and blasted shut every known entrance. If the Arachnids weren't all dead, they probably wished they were. The troops were still left on alert in case there were still a few of the enemy lingering about, but the assault proper was over.

He walked down the rubble filled streets, still stained in red. They stank from the corpses. There simply wasn't enough time to bury them all. Towering above were the once mighty lifts of Stilt, cracked in half, jagged edges rising upwards like two giant tombstones marking the end of this society. For no matter what happened, this planet would be a ghost town in a year's time. Who would want to stay here? Who would risk coming here?

All of the remaining civilians from other cities had been sent to Jericho, the only city left with any working infrastructure, where Brigade Command had set up their headquarters. There still was very little left to the place, close to sixty percent of it had been destroyed. The civilians who had been safely tucked away in the shelters had lost everything. Most of them were being quartered right back in the bunkers. With nothing to do, they drifted around listlessly, staring at what was once their lives. An entire population suffering from PTSD. A few work crews had been formed in an attempt to rebuild, but with practically no power or machinery, there was little that could be done.

Food would be a problem. The crop yield on the planet was never high and when Jericho's twin city fell down from orbit, the explosion sent up a holocaust of particulate matter into the atmosphere, producing a nuclear winter effect across the globe. Surface temperature had already dropped significantly as only half of the normal amount of solar radiation was able to penetrate Stilt's stratosphere. Reports estimated that it would take half a decade for all of the matter to filter back down. Those would be lean years.

Raskor-idan reached the military encampment, which sprawled outward from a primary school that had miraculously only taken a few bullet holes. Here at least was a bustle of activity, as the troops went about their daily duties

Under a large tent, he saw a number of Marine techs taking apart a large cone shaped device. It was roughly four meters tall, with a glass case encompassing the middle section on top of a metal base. It was filled with an unidentified green substance. A number of these devices had been captured in Arachnid fortifications or by corpse piles. Rumors about their functions were scattered all over, as rumors are wont to do in a military camp. Some claimed that they were used to reprogram sentients into being secret Arachnid sleeper agents. Others claimed that they were used to reanimate the corpses into a slave force. The most popular theory was that the devices were giant cuisinarts to liquefy bodies into a protein paste to feed the Arachnid war machine. Who knows? The truth did not interest Raskor-idan much at this point.

He pushed back his ghostly dreadlocks and entered the command building. After identifying himself, he was quickly ushered before the Brigade Colonel. Raskor-idan gave him an Alliance salute.

"Captain," his superior said. "Your orders have come through."

Finally. He wondered where he would be transferred. He could only pray to the high and mighty panthenon of Eridine that he be placed back in action, to the front lines against the Arachnids again. Quite a few troops had already been shifted off planet.

He unfurled the flex screen. It was written in Galactic Basic, a completely artificial language used by the Alliance bureaucracy in all official correspondence, transactions, treaties, and legislation. It was designed to purge any individual idiosyncrasies and idioms native to one species. Thus making it a flat sterile thing, perfect for legal work.

He was ordered to go… nowhere.

Raskor-idan blinked and read it again, as if it the words were going to magically rearrange themselves. They didn't. He handed the flex screen back to the Colonel.

"I know you're disappointed," he began. "But we need good officers here."

The Colonel was a Gen-Human, designed and decanted for the military life, impregnated as a fetus with knowledge of tactics, administration, and textbook leadership techniques. In his fifteen years of life, he had picked up a few more management methods, but they usually fell flat on Raskor-idan. To the Eridani, these Gen-Humans were nothing but bizarre machines, little more than a robot or service drone. It always irked him that he had to answer to one.

"This colony is in a hell of a mess," the Colonel continued. "All of the civil government and most of the police were killed. Chronic water shortages, no electricity, barely enough shelters, food supplies that will run out in two months even with strict rationing, and unless we get the streets cleared of bodies we will have a host of diseases breaking out. Any one of these factors could lead to massive unrest. Taken together, it's almost a certainty. Do you see?"

"Yes sir," Raskor-idan hid the resentment from his voice, but it was plain upon his face.

"We have 1.5 million civilians here. Most are clamoring to be evacuated, but you and I know that won't happen anytime soon. So we will have to create a temporary militia to keep the peace."

Raskor-idan could see where this was going. *Wonderful*, he thought. *I'll be in charge of corralling drunks and beating on parents trying to steal bread to fill their children's empty stomachs.* Not only that, he would have to keep a strict eye on the local idiots recruited to make sure they didn't abuse their power as almost always happened in these situations. The headaches would be never ending, while the true fight was literately worlds away.

He wondered if this was a punishment. His official report on what had happened with the Maelstorm General skewed slightly from reality, painting himself in a positive light. There weren't many left alive to contradict it. So that seemed unlikely, yet…

"You'll have to keep a special eye on the looters, both locals and off-worlders. We have some temporary detection satellites deployed, but they aren't very sophisticated and a knowledgeable criminal could bypass it. Pirates and so forth. So you will need to keep them in check. Especially with the amount of equipment we'll be moving through here."

That caught Raskor-idan's ear.

"Equipment, sir?"

"With so many battle arenas nearby, Marine Command will be storing equipment on-planet to be deployed elsewhere."

They were turning the entire planet into a supply depot. Raskor-idan's heart sank. His assignment was suddenly about much more than whipping some mewling pedestrians into line. Now it was about guarding military equipment, something that Marine Command *really* cared about. Raskor-idan knew that if he actually did a good job policing the civilians, he might not get transferred off Stilt for several years. The supplies must be protected. And if he did a bad job, it meant he was even less likely to get transferred back into action.

"This isn't ideal for you, I know," the Colonel blathered on. "But we all have our parts to play and guarding this place so it doesn't descend into anarchy is as important as fighting the Arachnids. Even the smallest role is important to defeat the enemy."

And oh how those words, meant to inspire, failed completely and utterly. They merely convinced Raskor-idan of the Gen-Human's inferiority. Still it wouldn't do him any good to spit against the wind right then.

"I have a request, sir."

"Yes?"

"I am requesting that first sergeant Aebisher be transferred along with me."

The Colonel scratched his chin, musing.

"If *you* need good officers," Raskor-idan pressed. "*I* need good sergeants. I can't train a militia up from scratch without them."

"All right," the Colonel agreed. "I'll submit the paperwork to have Sergeant Aebisher put back to your command. Take the rest of the day off. You start tomorrow. Dismissed."

***

Raskor-idan settled down in the large tent he had bullied the quartermaster into issuing him. There, away from prying eyes and busy ears, he lay on his bunk, broke down, and cried. Huge tears stained his shirt in large splotches. He was not keeping in step with the path of the Buddon warrior. It was the antithesis of every lesson from his childhood training. He cried anyway.

To him, this glorified guard duty was a death sentence. For seventeen years of his life he had been slogging through the Galactic Marines, taking orders from inferiors, striving for an opportunity to shine. Now, all of that might be gone.

He took a slug from a bottle of bootleg alcohol he had confiscated from some privates. How much more time would he have in the Marines? Perhaps three or four more years. Five max. Then he'd be pushed out into mandatory retirement and probably spend the rest of his days puttering around some old age home, his bitterness cascading into insanity, lashing out at those who came close, until his death came as a relief to anyone who knew him.

If only… if only… That was the mantra which summed up his entire life. He stared at his cybernetic hand, then slammed it into the iron frame of the bed. Another gulp of booze brought to mind a youth. A young male who had the same name, who looked like him, but was a totally different person. This youth had one great story told about him, a tragic one….

There kneeled the young Eridani in the Hall of Lineage, surrounded by all of his cousins, brothers, and sisters. They had been there for a day and a night in ritual preparation for the Gultum Atum- the honor binding- which would be impressed upon them by their uncle, Rosen-idan, the current head of their noble family. It would be a sacred mission for their entire generation, intoned before the spirit of their house. It could be resolved only by success or death.

The hall was an integral part of their house's estate, though now somewhat fallen into disrepair. Twenty meters long and ten across. A glass pane encompassed most of the ceiling, allowing the recipient to walk in the light up to the far end where lay the shrine of the Moglug- the symbolic statue that represented the collective spirit of their house. All the departed souls of the house merged into the ancestor spirit. The Moglug was the only physical contact point between the living and the dead. The statue was a meter tall, cast from steel and with platinum plating. This was not the original. The first one had been solid platinum, twice as high, and decorated with glittering stones. But it had been stolen long ago.

There were thirty seven of them kneeling there, a fortuitous number in Eridani mythology. Each had their heads freshly shaved into the warrior's mohawk. All of them had their hair dyed blue in the style known as the Death Walk, indicating that they had pledged to sacrifice their lives for the cause about to be presented.

Directly opposite the ancestral spirit avatar was a platform fitted with gold plated stools, topped with expensive furs. These were places of honor for the house mogs, the gestating gender of the Eridani. The other two genders, the sug and fug, supplied the egg and sperm through extended sexual tubes into the mog, where the fetus developed. They were the most prized and protected parts of any house. There were twenty stools on the platform, but only six were occupied.

Their uncle rang a gong, signaling the beginning of the liturgy.

"Know then why you are here and understand its gravity," he began.

Raskor-idan only half listened, his head had been filled from infancy with the House's history. Centuries before, their House had stood for wealth and honor. Its members strutted through the corridors of power, issuing orders, and advising the great. They commanded armies, tore enemies apart, and set worlds ablaze. From its foundation with Inquarti-idan in the golden era before space travel, right up to its rapid decline five hundred years ago after the Battle of Three Powers - when nearly all of Eradine was razed and its warrior caste, so beautiful, so proud, were humbled by the foul Orion and Phentari races. A long time ago, but the wound was recut into the hearts of every generation of hopeful warriors. Done to keep the passion alive, the hate ablaze, and to inspire them on to rebuild the House's glory to that of yesteryear.

Finally, they had their chance.

"From before your birth, we elders pledged your lives to the great task of reclaiming our heritage and aloowing the honor of our family name to be reignited. Now, as so many of you have finished your trials and training, it is time to put the plan into motion."

Along the sides of the hall, behind the pillars leading to the shrine, their parents clustered. They looked on at their great sacrifices, their children, with hearts of pride and love. These fine specimens of

Eridani prowess and virtue. The future was assured in their powerful hands. How could they fail?

"You have been given the high purpose to enact our revenge upon the Phentari plunderers and their Orion flunkies. Those monsters who stole everything from our ancestors."

Curses, growls, the bitter venom of primordial hate, came out unbidden from their parents at the name of the Phentari. The young warriors would have followed suit, but the ritual required them to remain silent until their uncle finished.

"During the great shame, when our enemies ran riot in the streets of the holy planet of Eridine, the relics of our founders, even our most holy Moglug, were stolen by the Phentari and desecrated by their profane tentacles.

"Centuries we searched for these artifacts. Their location had long since been hidden, until thirty years ago, when an auction occurred on the Phentari homeworld. Listed among the items were our precious artifacts."

The uncle paused for a moment, collecting his emotions. Even for one who has trained all his life in the art of control, this was so powerful that it threatened to burst the dam around his heart.

"We pursued the legal channels, sued these backward monsters in the Alliance courts for what is rightfully ours. But they said," A gasp emitted from his lips, "in their legal tongue, ripped straight from the Mutzachan's hindquarters, that the theft had occurred well before the foundation of the Alliance. Thus, they had no jurisdiction."

Muttering among the parents. Their uncle shook his head, soundlessly laughing at some joke.

"That's as well as it should be. For we are the Eridani and our way is the blade. For courtesy's sake, we tried the courts, and now it is for you to fulfill your function in life, to complete your duty to the House. We know where the relics are. We know the enemy's defenses. You must simply go and retrieve what is ours."

Their uncle intoned the dusty ritual, booming for all to hear in old Erdi, the language of the golden age of Eridine. He stood before each of the kneeling youths and impressed upon them the Gultum Atum, binding them with words in front of their ancestral spirit to this mission. After this was done, the youths solemnly left to embark on a confiscated Phentari ship and blasted off towards their destiny.

As you may have guessed, it all ended in disaster.

The infiltration went well enough. The warlord's dacha was located on the side of a mountain, near a thick and vicious jungle. The Phentari were ruled by a military junta. This particular warlord was high in the current government's circle, with all of the extra manpower and protection that such a position required on the hostile world of Phena. That meant stealth and surprise were everything.

The cousins landed successfully, bluffing their way past planetary security with a stolen code, and trekked up the mountain. Phena was a methane rich planet, like Eridine, so they had no need for respirators. The plan had been perfected by their elders. Their aunt, Ksubo-Edan the house strategist, had drilled them over and over on it for a year. They had even gone so far as to build a replica of the Phentari stronghold and run simulation after simulation with variable threats added randomly to allow for any contingencies. Each warrior knew his part and his fallback position should the first plan crumble.

But, as they say, no plan survives contact with the enemy. They struck at night, cutting the main power source and jamming all transmissions from the dacha. Wearing stealth suits, which had bafflers to delay detection by sensors, the first of them slipped over the walls and silently killed the perimeter sentries. While the first line stood guard, the second group crept in and disabled a secondary power source located in a small bunker on the dacha's grounds, killing the technicians manning it. A third group then ran through the courtyard and entered the dacha. They put down the guards there and slit the throats of the sleeping servants, most of whom were slaves of different races.

Raskor-idan himself had been part of the first team. He had gleefully hacked into a Phentari guard's neck and stood triumphantly over the creature, laser rifle ready. His job was to keep sentry for any unexpected arrivals at the dacha and to give covering fire should the third group have to retreat. He suppressed a giggle of glee. This was all perfect. Each step they had made was flawless. There was not a single wasted sword stroke or foot fall.

Lights flooded inside the building, startling

Raskor-idan. That was supposed to be impossible with the power sources disabled. Then the firing began. Explosions, laser fire, plasma burps. He looked through his rifle scope, trying to see in through a window, but he couldn't tell what was happening. His instincts pushed him to run in, sword swinging, gun blazing, like a hero from a story. But those were not his orders, not his place in the plan. He had to fight himself down to remain in position.

Then radio silence was broken, indicating an all-is-lost moment. There was static, screams in the background. One of his cousins yelled,

"Abort! Abort! Retreat and regroup."

The cousin roared in rage, amid a torrent of laser fire. The doors and windows shattered and a horde of defense drones shot out. It seems the warlord was more paranoid than the elders had reckoned. He had had a third power source installed inside a panic room that kicked in if the first two failed. From it he could control a state-of-the-art defense system and drive out invaders. True, it was installed to defend himself against his fellow Phentari in the case of a coup d'état, but it worked just as well against the Eridani.

The drones were two meters in diameter, spherical, and bristling with destructive implements. They fired several micro-missiles into the backup generator bunker, annihilating everyone inside. Then started in on the first group standing tall near the gates.

Time slowed for Raskor-idan. His cousins, those he had been raised with, had trained with, had eaten with all his life, the ones he loved and the ones he hated, were swiftly being gunned down. Their blue mohawks turning red in the carnage. He barely had time to fire once, before he saw the enemy's barrels leveled at him.

There was his death directly ahead and he did the opposite of what he had pledged to do. He rejected it! He leapt from his position, the laser fire ripped apart the area he had just been occupying, and ran. He should have stayed, accepted his fate. He was there to do or die, but… but… he did not want to end his life, did not want his legacy to be a footnote about some failed mission from an extinct House.

So he ran all the way down the mountain, a horde of drones behind him. He radioed ahead for the pair of cousins, left behind to guard the ship, to prepare it for takeoff. He burst onto the strip where they had concealed the vessel, deftly weaving back and forth avoiding the fire, and saw one of his last two cousins at the ship hatch waving him on.

"Hurry! Hurry! Urgh…"

A plasma burst hit the cousin square in the face, burning it down to the bone. He fell forward shuddering in pain, the last drops of life shaking from him. Raksor-idan hopped the corpse and yelled for his last remaining cousin to take off, slamming the hatch behind him. The ship rose and blasted into the atmosphere, laser fire thudding into its hull. They slipped into hyperspace the second they were able to.

Raskor-idan sat in the co-pilot's chair. His cousin looked at him, inquiringly.

"Where are they?" the last cousin asked. "The

relics?"

Raskor-idan turned on the subspace coms system, tuning it the frequency predetermined by their uncle to let the family know whether the mission was successful or…

"Failure," Raskor-idan stated impassively into the communicator. "Mission failure."

He cut off the transmission. Nothing more needed to be said. His cousin eyed him suspiciously, silently demanding to know why Raskor-idan was alive, why he had not fallen honorably. But he kept his mouth shut. He sent ship control over to Raskor-idan and walked into the back. A few minutes later, Raskor-idan heard the cousin's body hit the floor, having cut his own throat.

At that moment, the gravity of it all sunk in. He was alone now, completely and utterly. There was nothing to do, nothing to live for. An emptiness opened up inside of him, sucking in all of the heat from his body. What was he to do? What could he do? There had never been a time before when someone had not given him an order, directed his daily routine. When to exercise, when to practice, when to eat, when to sleep, all of these had been spelled out for him. Some might consider Raskor-idan's situation absolute freedom, he could go and do what he wanted, but to him it was a horrible void. A pit of uncertainty.

He nearly followed his cousin down the road of suicide, but the same reason that he ran stilled his hand. He did not want to end here. The emptiness would not go away. Despair flooded him. He flipped the ship onto autopilot and entered the medical bay. First he dyed his hair white, to mark himself with the white disgrace. He was going to own his failure, he would not shy away. Then he hooked himself up to a medical drone, which was designed to keep him alive, and unsheathed his sword.

He stared at it for a moment. The sword was the symbol of the Buddon, the Eridani warrior. Even though it had been replaced by much more useful killing devices, an Eridani always kept it about to show his loyalty to the past. In truth he didn't feel worthy enough to wield it any more. He raised the weapon and, with one massive arc, cut off his right hand.

If he could not pay with his life, at least he could give this. A little recompense for his lost honor, his lost house. The emptiness vanished, replaced by blessed pain, something familiar to Raskor-idan, something he knew how to deal with. He smiled and collapsed into black.

That was when the boy Raskor-idan ended his life and gave birth to the bitter elder crying on his bunk. It seemed he would be a footnote after all. A serial number, lost among thousands of others pulling duty in the Galactic Marines.

He finished the rest of the bottle and curled up on the thin mattress. There he indulged in drunken dreams of revenge and power. Of felling the whole of the Phentari race in a single blow and setting their stinking world ablaze. He succored himself on this like tainted mother's milk. And for a little while the emptiness inside of him subsided just a bit.

Chapter 8- Myntal 5

Species: Misha (known colloquially as Dream Merchants)

Planet of Origin: Vego in the Sculptor system, Andromeda Galaxy

Description: A small demure race with nearly transparent skin and clear blood, the Misha are known for being able to dream of the future and give advice to affect its ebbs and surges. Brain scans have shown that each section of a Misha's brain is chronologically out of phase with the other, meaning each ages at a different rate, culminating in their unique ability. How they developed in this manner is unknown, but some conjecture it is linked to the Motaran Rift- a massive area of space-time disturbance. A side effect of this bizarre evolutionary path is a spaceyness in their character and predilection toward narcolepsy later in life.

Freaky Fact: For some reason the Misha race has a critical shortage of male offspring, with an average of one for every ten females. Out of sheer necessity, the standard family unit on the Misha worlds is a polygamous one. A male can have up to twenty wives, depending on his fortunes.

***

Twenty thousand kilometers from Myntal 5, the mini-freighter carrying Almon, Molphus, and Quandle shunted out of hyperspace. The trio had managed to secure passage aboard an independent trader vessel run by a family of Cizerack who specialized in bringing "luxury" food and beverages (mostly junk food and soft drinks), spare electronics, circuitry and bootleg vids of movies and tri-v shows to frontier worlds, where such material was scarce.

The trip had taken several weeks. While Almon and Quandle spent most of their time locked away training or meditating, Molphus took the opportunity to interact with the quadruped feline race. He took his meals with them, played with their cubs, listened to their stories of other planets, and learned bits and pieces of their language. He was fascinated by their female dominated society and was especially interested in their technology, the Cizeracks being the only known sentient life form to achieve spaceflight without the use of opposable thumbs.

Upon reaching sight of the planet, the Mutzachans were called up to the bridge.

"There's an incredible amount of traffic," the captain told them. "I've never seen anything like it."

Close to two hundred ships of various shapes and sizes, clustered in orbit about the planet. Quandle took over the communication system, zooming in on the ships and checking them against his pad's database on known pirate vessels.

"These all seem to be Black Flag ships," he said. "Their entire fleet must be here. Something's going on."

Obviously, thought Almon. Aloud he said, "Is the Arc of Blood here?"

Quandle continued to scan for several minutes before replying, "Oh yes."

"Good," Almon said. "Get the shuttle ready."

Molphus touched Almon's arm, pulling him aside, while Quandle went to help the Cizeracks with the preparation.

"Why are they all here?" he asked his mentor. "Do you think it has something to do with Oxtiern?"

"It's too much of a coincidence to believe otherwise. The only times they congregate like this are to elect a new admiral or to vote on some massive enterprise. I had hoped that he was coming here to sell the golden needle in a clandestine auction, but that's definitely not the case."

"I see."

"Make sure you leave fully charged," Almon warned. "And keep your gun ready."

The Cizarack used a rig harness attached to their back with two magnetic clamp arms to move their cargo aboard the shuttle. This was controlled by a bit connected to the mouth. After an hour, all of it had been loaded and the family and passengers departed on the vessel. Out of the window, Molphus looked at the Myntal system and its ugly planets.

The Myntal system was a binary star system with eight planets, two of which had been colonized. Myntal 4 was an automated mining operation run by the Erectus Corporation and only accessible for 17 days out of the year due to the gravity pressures of its unusual orbit. During that window, the corporation would swoop in and haul away the minerals its robot minions had reaped.

Its sister planet, where the Mutzachans were hurtling towards, was less inviting. The planet also maintained an irregular orbit. At times its trajectory brought the planet so close to one of the stars, that its oceans of dark sand would have melted into glass if not for the thick toxic atmosphere. One unfiltered breath on Myntal 5 was like smoking an entire carton of cigarettes.

The shuttle landed on a massive platform a kilometer away from the only structure on the planet, the subterranean city of Myntal-Igas-Eridi, which meant “Fall of Eridine” in the Eradani tongue. From there, the shuttle was lowered into an underground hangar and berthed in a gloomy cubical.

The hangar was crowded and loud, filled with armed pirates openly showing Black Flag insignia and tattoos, each of them impatient to get transported into the city so they could take some leave. The Mutzachans hung back in their shuttle, while the Cizerack family unloaded their goods. Molphus noted that they were the only Mutzachans to be seen.

Eventually the local customs officials, burly thugs with silver armbands that proclaimed them to be King’s Men, came over and began haggling with the Cizerack captain. There were no set prices for a trade license. The vendor paid whatever the official felt they could squeeze out of them.

Myntal 5 was currently ruled by a particularly dumpy brute with a vicious trigger finger. He had proclaimed himself king after his gang's hostile takeover of the central fusion plant, back-up generators, and water filtration substations. His rule mostly involved collecting docking fees, issuing trade licenses to the vendors, and keeping the worst elements out of the marketplaces. Other than that, the city was lawless. Murders, rapes, and theft were all too common.

Once their tab was settled, aided by the family throwing in several bottles of booze to the King's Men, the officials then attempted to collect a fee on the Mutzachans as well.

"They're here to buy," the Cizerack captain said. "Not sell."

"Doesn't matter," one of the King's Men replied. He was a broken toothed human with a wide nose and hair that gave off a stale oily stench. "New rules. We got too many coming down. Place is filled near to bursting. Now you gotta purchase a visitor's pass, fifty credits."

"Fifty credits? Are you out of your mind?" Quandle balked. "That's extortion."

"So what if it is? You can get your fat head back on the ship and get the hell out of here. I won't charge you for that."

"It will be okay," Almon intervened, giving Quandle a stern look. "I will pay for all three of us."

He handed over a credit stick that, when connected to another stick, automatically deducted the inputted amount. They were issued three tiny red tickets in exchange. The King's Man stopped after he collected the fee. His beady eyes, peering out through thick hair, seemed to actually see them for the first time.

"We don't get too many Mutzachans around here… or ever really. What's your business on Myntal 5?"

"Shouldn't you have asked that before taking our credits?" Quandle asked irritably. Always a hassle dealing with these races. They were all so damn unorganized. On a Mutzachan colony they would have paid their preset charge and been long gone by now. These creatures were always looking for an extra handout.

"I can still have you kicked out," The King's Man threatened. "I don't care if you've paid."

"We have come," said Almon smoothly, slipping the official a small bag with a hallucinogenic moss that he knew the King's Man race enjoyed. "To purchase some extra IDs and get a few genetic alterations. We heard that you could get this easily enough here."

The King's Man laughed, his thick hair flinging little spots of oil in the process. He stuck the plastic bag in his pocket. "You can change as much as you want. One of your race is going to stick out no matter what!"

"We don't plan on being here very long."

Yells emerged from the group of Black Flag pirates. Several of them had pulled weapons and were threatening to kill everyone within gunshot. The King's Men refused to back down and a scuffle broke out. Fists thudded. Groins were kicked. One pirate whipped around a piece of chain with spikes welded into the links. He lashed it across the face of a King's Man, blinding him.

"Guess I'm not the only one upset about the fifty credits," quipped Quandle.

Weapon's fired, a few pirates fell over. One of them, gut shot, dragged himself along the floor, leaving a dangling trail of intestines and blood behind. A King's Man, a portly Orion, was slashed along across the head and a large slice of his scalp dangled off like a bad toupee. A few more were burnt from a makeshift portable flamethrower a pirate had smuggled on-planet. It was not looking good for the King's Men.

With a roar of glee, a huge scaly figure bounded into the fray. It was close to ten and a half feet tall, with rippling muscles and a thick tail that crashed into the ground after every step. Molphus identified the speicies. *A Ram Python*, a race known for its great strength and stupidity. *Rare to see one out this far.* The Python species had never developed space flight and usually only left their planet after being recruited into the Galactic Marines as shock troopers.

This one was tall even by its race's standards. He whirled around a massive quarterstaff, called a thwack-'em-stick, made of hardened wood with spiked steel tips on each end. The Ram leapt into action with pure abandon, smashing the stick down on a pirate's head, reducing it to mush. He pulled back and hit another pirate, shattering all the ribs on that side and rupturing several organs. A third was spiked in the stomach, leaving him gasping for breath and trying desperately to clog up the large hole now in his midsection with a jacket.

"Who is that?" Molphus asked, aghast at the violence.

The broken toothed human laughed. "That there's Ika Dhole. Anyone who steps outta line answers to him."

A few of the pirates began firing at Ika Dhole with pistols, but none of them penetrated the Ram's scaly hide. They regretted it instantly. One was hit twice with a whirling one-two motion, ripping his jaw from his face. The Ram then dropped the stick and grabbed the second pirate with both hands around his head, lifted him up, and squeezed. He stood there for a moment, his arms straining, the pirate's legs and arms flapping about impotently, until there was a loud crack like a huge walnut being shelled. The pirate's limbs went limp. Ika Dhole threw him away and guffawed. The remaining pirates scattered.

"Well, that's settled," the human said. "Enjoy your visit."

The Mutzachans helped the feline family load their goods onto a monorail system and took the trip into Myntal-Igas-Eridi.

The underground city was originally an Eridani mining boom town, established to extract much needed thorium, silver, and iridium deposits. These were quickly drained and the settlement abandoned, only to be taken over alternatively by pirates, mercenary bands, and various groups of scum. Each had briefly wrestled control from the other until the current "king" managed to stabilize the area somewhat.

Upon first viewing the city, what struck Molphus was the sense of space. He had expected it to be a claustrophobic series of narrow tunnels and dingy holes, but this was not the case. The majority of the city had been scooped out in one massive canyonous extraction, a hundred meters down, and then topped with a heavy tungsten steel frame ceiling. The undercarriage of this was covered in immense sun-lamp arrays, circuited at standard hours to give residents the feeling of time and regularity.

A prepubescent Orion female ran up to them trying to hawk her wares, knock-off designer jewelry dangling from her four thumbs. Molphus had always marveled at this odd genetic quirk of the Orions, the double thumbs on each hand. He wondered at what the selection pressure could have been to allow this trait to become dominant in the race's hominid ancestors. Why did four thumbs become better than two?

"Come on," the youth barked. "These'll put some color in that drab you're wearing."

Quandle pushed her away rudely. The girl made an obscene gesture and zipped off. Almon called the other two together.

"Our Cizerack friends have agreed to make a few discrete inquiries."

Molphus's eyebrows raised.

"Nothing too dangerous," Almon assured him. "Just whatever gossip turns up. They're in a better position to find Oxtiern than we are."

There were many free standing buildings left from the mining days and the city had been expanded only slightly. New dwellings were carved out of rock and then propped up with portable wall units, steel beams, and other bits of debris from space ships. No manufacturing plants existed on Myntal 5, so a steady trade of junk peddlers and salvage ships arose. They did well pushing off the bits of pieces of stuff no one else wanted onto the denizens of the city.

Almon hustled them into the marketplace. They stepped onto an electric trolley car, powered from the municipal fusion reactor, whose lines crisscrossed all over the city. Originally designed to haul rock, it was modified for personnel transport by more industrious leaders than the current batch. Molphus stared out at the bizarre sights of the underground metropolis.

The city was alive! A vast free port full of bartering, trading, and boozing. While there were plenty of mundane facilities, the specialty of the house were those services deemed illegal under Alliance laws: DNA masking, ID falsification, unregistered cloning, unlicensed slaving, restricted animal auctions, prohibited cybernetic deals, fencing, assassination services, and outlawed weapon sales.

The trolley sped up. Living, breathing sentients from races he had barely been aware of shot into view. Squat, purple skinned Goola-Goolas tinkering with sections of space junk; globous, grey Mazians with no distinct shape of their own; thin, greenish blue Chatilians known for their dangerous empathic abilities; hulking, insectoid Sarands who could build beautiful dwellings out of sand mixed with a resin that they secreted; cannibalistic, four-tentacled Phentari proudly displaying their colored capes that advertised them as assassins for hire; scavenging, salamander-like Aeodronians, looking for an unguarded stall to steal from; silicone-based Gemini bartering for unusual crystals, which they slurped down over rocky lips; and annoying bowling pin shaped Pacians scurrying around on six spindly legs, babbling nonsense at whomever would listen. All these mixed with the standard assortment of Humans, Orions, Zen Rigelns, Cizeracks, Fotts, and Eridani made for those most eclectic menagerie of wonder to Molphus's eyes

The trolley shuddered to a stop. The Cizerack family hurried to their rented area in the food market with Almon and Quandle behind them. Molphus lingered behind. He was amazed and a little dumbstruck. It was so different from life on Trishmag. Everything was odd. Never before had he been the alien, to be the person who others stared at and whispered about.

What curiosities did they have to show him? What new ideas, thoughts, and philosophies could they impart? A thousand new tastes. Ten thousand new paths to spirituality and enlightenment.

"Get your fat faggot head out of the way, asshole," a drunk foul mouthed Orion yelled at him.

Molphus recoiled, drawing his grey robes about him. He had literally in his life never encountered such uncalled for rudeness and could not figure out how to respond. The Orion was flanked by a black furred Fott and a sandy haired Gen-Human, who was staring at a picture of a large woman on his data pad.

"You think because you're a fucking Mutzachan you just own the goddamned street?"

"No… I …I…."

"Oh, I'm so smart, I'm so important. Never mind I could kick the living shit out of you without trying," the Orion sneered. The Fott behind him simply stared with intense hatred. "You cock lickers think you run everything? Not here, you don't!"

The Orion was getting more and more riled. Molphus did not understand him. Such unbridled evil at a complete stranger. It beggared all logic. The Fott snickered and whispered something into the drunk's ear.

"My friend says you're about to try to boss me around because you think you're better than me." The Orion drew closer, poking a stained finger into Molpus's chest. "Is that right, shit scum? You think you're better than me?"

"No…I…."

The Orion punched him in the side of the head, knocking him over into some discarded offal. He loomed over Molphus, still waggling his finger.

"Damn right you're not. You and your whole piece of shit race are pests preying off our hard work!"

The Fott brayed with an incredibly grating laugh, full of hate and mockery. The Orion spat on the Mutzachan. Molphus could feel the power crackling beneath his palms. Never before had he felt such a desire to unleash his destructive matrices, to burn holes in this filthy stupid face before him, to melt his kidneys, to send an electrical surge through his heart, to utterly destroy another living being. He could do it *so* easily. On this alien world, this was the most alien of feelings.

Then his mind clicked. The rational centers of his brain squeezed off any emotions. He noticed the Black Flag tattoos on the Orion, and reckoned that were he to strike back, a horde of pirates would descend on his, Quandle's, and Almon's head. The mission would fail and he would likely be killed.

So he remained silent and let the Orion have his little victory.

The assailant and his stooges, after laughing a little more, moved on. The Gen-Human who hadn't until this point said anything, smiled apologetically as he went past then turned his full attention back to the pictures on his data pad.

Molphus ran to catch up with the others but got lost in the crush of bodies and the zoo of kiosks.

The Cizeracks had set up their stall in an area designated strictly for foodstuffs and perishables. Pungent spices, ground from the roots of plants of a hundred worlds, mixed together into an unholy stench. Vacuum sealed cuts of meat from unidentified animals hung prominently about. Their blood, red, green, blue, and clear, still glistening on the flanks. Milk and other fluids from beasts were offered in plastic jugs labeled in the Standard Trade Dialect.

Not that the labeling made any difference. Molphus picked up a purple jug labeled

"Horrokroshcu Kidney Venom." Of course you still needed to know what a Horrokroshcu was to understand why you'd purchase poison from its kidney.

Other dealers peddled dietary items designed for the space farer. Freeze-dried and dehydrated nuggets of all sorts of fruits and vegetables. Mineral rich powders, more easily inhaled than ingested. Synthetic slimes, engineered for each race, which gave a body all the nutrition needed for a day in one tasteless ball of gunk.

Molphus finally found his companions at the end of the market. Almon took him aside and examined the bruise the Orion had left on Molphus' face. He flinched. Though Molphus knew that he had acted correctly, the incident still had its teeth sunk deep into the Mutzachan's pride.

"What happened?" the elder asked.

"Nothing, some pirates."

"Are they still alive?"

"Yes, and unhurt."

Quandle snorted.

"He did the right thing," Almon admonished Quandle. "We don't need a load of corpses popping up just yet. Not until we locate Oxtiern. Let's find a place to get the lay of the land."

The trio found a table in a crowded bistro where the ceiling had begun to crumble, adding an unwelcome flavoring to everyone's order. Every other table was taken up by pirates who were yelling, bragging, caterwauling half remembered songs, and harassing the waitresses for sexual favors. This was good. It meant that the Mutzachan's conversation was unlikely to be overheard.

The bistro's services weren't designed to cater to Mutzachans, not unusual on a frontier world. They had come prepared for this. Each ordered a can of Krunchy Kola and dropped in gel tablets filled with radioactive serum. Part of the standard traveling kit recommended by the Mutzachan Tourist Board.

As they slurped, a Pascian bumbled up to the table. It was a short oblong shaped creature, very bottom heavy, with two googly eyes and a slit for a mouth. The head and torso was one streamlined mass. Eight spindly legs stuck out beneath its frame, each pumping hard to maintain momentum. Two thin pincher arms waved about, trying to touch and feel everything.

Pascains became a universal constant on Alliance planets about a century earlier. No one, including the species itself, knew where they were from or how they had arrived in Alliance space. The few scholars who bothered to look into the matter concluded that a different race had shipped them in, as the Pascian's didn't seem to have any technical knowledge beyond the Bronze Age.

The creature bumped into Quandle's leg. It slid its claw hands over him. Gender was impossible to tell on the creature, if indeed they had more than one gender.

"This is nice fabric," it said in the Standard Trade Dialect. "I like good fabric that is strong, but it stains too easily. Don't you hate fabric that stains?"

Quandle kicked the creature away. It wheeled

backwards into a pirate, who cursed and punched it into another table, who subsequently kicked it again into another pirate. And so on, until the proprietor grabbed the Pascian and threw it out of the bar.

Quandle laughed about that. Molphus fretted that creature might be hurt. Almon was uninterested, typing away on his data pad. Quandle touched him on the shoulder.

"So I was right," Quandle said. "There is more to Oxtiern's plan. He's planning a raid."

"Of course he is," snapped Almon. "But where? And why?"

"For profit," Molphus said. "That's the only logical…"

"For the pirates, yes," Almon said, rubbing his cheeks which had begun to ache. "But not Oxtiern. Money doesn't interest him. It's not his…style, to use a vulgar phrase."

"How do you know that?" demanded Quandle.

Almon deflected the question with an irritated wave.

"I know him," he said, as if that explained it all. "He will be ostentatious and loud, but he doesn't have a profit motive."

"Perhaps he's changed."

"He hasn't changed!"

Molphus watched Quandle fume. He knew that his companion didn't like secrets. It was the briefing all over again. Quandle wanted the answer to a question that he wasn't quite sure of, and Almon was hording the knowledge inside his head. Molphus wasn't as bothered. Almon was the Mutzachan that the youngster respected most in the galaxy. He had to trust that the elder had good reasons, nagging doubts or not.

"The why doesn't matter, I suppose," Quandle said eventually. "If we can stop him here then all of his plans will probably fall through, especially if it hinges on him using the golden needle."

"Quite so," agreed Molphus. "Still, we have to find him."

"I've been leafing through the services offered on the local hypernet links," Almon fiddled with his data pad. "Amongst all of the immoral and fraudulent facilities, there is a gem wallowing in obscurity."

He showed it to Molphus, who crossed his eyes, the Mutzachan gesture for skepticism.

"A dream merchant?" he murmured.

***

Oovurla D'puppup, the local Misha Dream Merchant, sat by himself in his small rooms. They were located in the poor area of the city, made from old exploratory shafts that had been expanded into compartments. Far away from the productive members of society (those who buy and sell incessantly, to accumulate more wealth to buy and sell), the rooms were used to house the working class of the city, along with the junkies, alcoholics, and terminally ill.

He had hung thick violet drapes around the walls to give the illusion of warmth, and had several layers of damaged rugs and industrial padding stretched across the floor, so it would be at least tolerable for the Misha to walk about barefoot as he liked to do. Doing anything else seemed too much of a hassle to the languid dreamer.

Business was sluggish, but then so was D'puppup. A person who wanted to rent his ability to peek behind the blank curtain of the future had to seek him out. Advertising was such a bore. Better to stretch out here inhaling from his guslu pipe, which sent blasts of rainbow flavored steam over his sensitive palate.

Behind him was a glazed ceramic idol of a three-armed Misha with an exaggerated head and its eyes sewn shut. It was Lom, the Guardian of Dead Dreams, to which D'puppup occasionally offered a half-hearted prayer.

He put the pipe away and leisurely sucked up a liquid solution of cheese, fruits, and meat from a plastic bag. It was part of his payment from a human woman who had come an hour earlier to see if the boy she had recently met was truly in love with her or was he just going to use her for sex.

For such mundane cases, D'puppup didn't bother to use his power. He pretended to go into a trance and told the woman what she wanted to hear. She looked as if she needed some happiness. So he rolled his eyes into the back of his head and mumbled in a practiced singsong voice.

"Once together, you shall not be apart. In body, in thought, in soul. Soul meets soul when flesh mingles with flesh. Love, money, happiness. A new life opens if you can cast aside fear to grasp it."

That was pretty damn good, D'puppup thought. The woman was content, paying him with a few credits, some food packets, and doing his laundry. That last one was the most appreciated, a huge pile of his soiled clothes had been building up for a while. So tedious. Why couldn't they all just self-clean?

Three Mutzachans entered his room, an unprecedented sight on this rock. So much so that it actually caused D'puppup to raise a thin eyebrow. Their presence was a bad omen. Unbidden, they drew up stools and clustered around the table where the Misha sat.

"Greetings Misha," the eldest said. "We are not disturbing you, are we?"

He felt like telling them to go so that he could keep on slurping his lunch in peace, but it might take a lot of effort to get rid of them now that they had seated themselves, so he simply shrugged.

"Where do you hail from?" the eldest continued.

"Vego."

"Ah. What city? What prefecture?"

"Ygam in the Oms prefecture."

What did this little grey person want? If they were bounty hunters, they had found the wrong Misha. Bad luck had brought him to Myntal 5, nothing more. A genetic scan would prove that he had no warrants.

"Ygam," the elder said softly. "Now there's a city I know. There was a pleasant little park I went to for relaxation. It had half a kilometer of water fountains which exploded at their summit into blue and green and indigo balls that floated about before bursting. Quite a sight."

This actually perked D'puppup up. He knew the park! Had played there with his sisters as a child.

"There was a statue of a Misha in the middle of the fountain, raised up and cast in white gold. What was it of?" The Mutzachan tapped his temples.

"It was Oblems, shown with his right arm raised and exploding into light. An old representation of the sun."

"Your god of the sun."

"In the age of unenlightenment," D'puppup yawned. "My former planet is a galaxy away. What were you doing there? We didn't get a lot of Alliance traffic."

"I was there gathering intelligence on the Krakeds," the elder said.

The other two Mutzachans stared at him. The youngest's jaw actually dropped at that statement.

The Krakeds were a vicious race of quadrupeds with hand-like feet and long necks that ended in stalk-like mouth and eyes. Rumored to actually be a servant race of the Arachnids, they had been invading the seven Misha-controlled worlds for the last decade in what they called the War of Nightmares. It was this war that had made D'puppup a refugee.

Was the old Mutzachan lying? Was he trying to prey on the Misha's feelings? Or had he actually been there for whatever reason?

"How can I help you?"

"I know your people and I know your power."

D'puppup nodded. No revelation there, many sentients did.

"I also know that sometimes your race needs a little help." The elder dropped a hypo-shot on the table. "Our need is great and very specific. We want you to be precise."

D'puppup picked up the hypo, knowing exactly what it was. Di-methyl-sodium pentalate. Once injected, the drug pushes a Misha into a deeper trance state, giving the dreamer's vision much more clarity. It also leaves the user nauseous for days and causes a rash to break out under the armpits and behind the knees.

"This is…"

"Necessary."

"Extra," D'puppup sighed. It was going to be an exhausting day.

"Three thousand credits."

"Done."

The Misha said that quicker than expected, surprising even him, but he needed the money. His landlord didn't accept clean laundry for rent, so he would put up with a rash for a few days. He injected the solution into his heart and felt it working within seconds.

"What do you seek?" D'puppup intoned.

"We wish to know the whereabouts of a Tza Zen Rigeln named Oxtiern. We wish to know his plans. We wish to know if his plans will succeed. He is in the city, but we do not know where."

D'puppup swooned, feeling his mind taking one step back from his body. All physical sensations muted and coalesced, converting to a mild stream of warmth. Colors altered, becoming their polar opposite as his mind rolled over and rose above the fourth dimensional super-solid which pedestrians call "time". Things tripled as the second-before and the second-after the concept of "now" focused. Then it tripled again, and again, and again, as the wormskin resonance which each person leaves across the super-solid revealed itself. The past and the future occurred simultaneously. Then, now, and will-be lost all meaning.

His mind rotated again in the direction called "oehf", for which no other language has a parallel concept. The closest translation in English being "inward out". He exploded across the world, entering a realm of cold light and warm darkness. He waited for a sound, a murmur from beyond.

When the Misha realized that their gods were nothing but stories, they did not discard the idea. Instead they repackaged them as mental concepts. The gods of old became rudders and sign posts for the dreamers to navigate the beyond and inwards. For their journey was as much about their own mental control as it was about the conceptual territory they crossed.

In the dark, D'Puppup heard his self-appointed patron, The Guardian of Dead Dreams. The first voice in the shapelessness of the universe. The last voice that will be heard in the scattering of absolute destruction. The gurgling of the first pregnancy in the first womb. The violent death rattle of the last living creature. He caught its call and found answers in the melody.

"A thread is being plucked by this Oxtiern which

stretches back to the time before time was a concept. Not the first creation, but the first great destruction, when the stars exploded and all matter was smashed back into atoms. Life was destroyed except for the black birds and their overlords. He stands in the square on the circle, naked before himself, making ready to enlist the Lords of Filth into his scheme to destroy those who caused his great ache, his eternal wound, his love of hate. He will take a passage unto passage and stir a fetal ancient. If his hand is not taken from the thread it will rip a hole in the tapestry of civilization and everything will fall under a sound. A sound that extinguishes all others. Rul. Rul. Rul."

The elder Mutzachan stood up furiously, flame exploding from his eyes.

Chapter 9- Myntal 5

Species: Ram Python

Planet of Origin: Pythos in the Mu Virginis System

Description: A reptilian biped of resounding physical strength, the Ram and its cousin race, the Python Lizard, never evolved technologically beyond the Iron Age. The race has a somewhat unfair reputation for stupidity and an attraction to shiny objects. Initially the reptilians were denied representation on the Council of Timar, but as the military began to depend more and more on the Pythos races, the Rams and Lizards (in a rare display of solidarity) held a general strike until both were admitted as full member races with council privileges.

Freaky Fact: The Ram Python is a highly emotional race due to an overabundance of the adrenaline derivative, danjuine. After becoming enraged, when they cannot release their tension on another creature, a Ram will go off by themselves and fiercely dig holes in the ground, ripping up huge chunks of earth with their bare hands.

***

Several weeks ago Drake would have called himself the most miserable person in the Universe. Now, he was certainly the happiest. For among this ramshackle dead colony, this rat's nest of the socially diseased and morally delinquent, a rose had grown up from the manure. Yes, it's true. Drake was in love!

Since this was his first love, it was the most important thing to have ever happened in the whole of history. Suns die out, planets shatter, civilizations rise and fall, whole races are extinguished, none of that burned as brightly as his love for Annette. It was impossible for another person to understand the intensity of emotion exploding inside of him. How could they? No one had ever felt anything as real as this.

It was all just dumb luck that he had even met her. After the Arc of Blood had docked in orbit, a number of pirates were sent planetside to help secure the meeting area. Every ship from the Black Flag Fleet sent twenty at first, but that soon increased steadily to help bully and steal whatever the pirates demanded.

Being a bojing, someone pressed into service, Drake was initially denied access to the surface in case he tried to jump ship. While this most certainly was his plan, he managed to convince Craw to let him come down on the pretext of obtaining some specialized equipment necessary to fix the toilets.

"What kind of equipment?" the four legged feline asked in his disturbing voice.

"A xamsior XY-2 pump, a number 8 vomihal rig, and a whole bunch of homiline henson clips. You know, the ones with the double wide guards on the rims."

This was all gibberish Drake had made up, but Craw nodded knowingly, pretending like a clueless motorist at the mechanic.

"Yes, we've been down on some of that stuff for a while now."

Drake disciplined a giggle about to escape his belly.

"I'll send down for it," Craw said. "One of our groups can scrounge something up."

Drake had learned, if nothing else during his tenure on the pirate ship, that when playing a con, boldness and self-assuredness sold it more than anything else.

"Are you going to trust those idiots to put together some highly sophisticated gear? They can barely figure out how to pick their own noses. Who are you gonna send? Parg?"

"And you know better, do you?"

"Well, maybe if Skel goes down I can give him the technical requirements. He can handle it. I'm sure the crew will be happier knowing that he's making sure the septic system is running smoothly."

By now Drake knew of the rivalry between the

two officers. Both mistrusted and disliked the other. And while Skel was considered competent by the crew, though he had little to do with them, Craw was universally spit on by the Arc of Blood pirates. It was all done behind the feline's back, but he knew. A feather in Skel's cap meant much less for Craw.

Down he went into this underground city. At first he felt a little at home, having spent most of his life in the enclosed atmosphere of the Brethia Stargate Project, but that soon wore off. The Mutzachan-run project had been full of efficient people focused on one ultimate goal, this was a place for the rudderless to wash up.

Being outside of Alliance control, the sort of people who dwelled here were the burnouts of every other society. Career felons, hopeless drunks, people abandoned on failed settlements, bottomed-out prospectors, criminals on the run, and sentients who grew up on these dingy frontier worlds and had never known any other way of life.

The crew bunked in a derelict warehouse after chasing off a bunch of squatters. Parg and Jack Mace had also weaseled themselves into the landing party, presumably because Craw was happy to get rid of them for a few days.

They had spent the first couple of nights doing nothing. At least to Drake it was nothing, Parg saw it differently.

"We gotta show the tats and spunk," he said, delving into pirate argot. "Let 'em know that Black Flag and the Arc of Blood are about."

This meant nothing more than walking around,

harassing people, flexing, and being a belligerent jerk- which were perhaps Parg's only skills. He was not alone in this, several others from each ship were doing the same thing, leading to many conflicts with the King's Men and the local slobs.

Usually he only did this after drinking three quarts of alcohol, then he would badger Jack Mace and Drake into following him around, Parg being incapable of making a stand on his own. It was after one particular vicious encounter, involving several dozen pirates, an assortment of King's Men, and a Fott merchant selling knockoff designer shampoo, that Drake first saw her.

She had been corralled into doing laundry for the pirates in his building. From the moment she appeared, loading piles of dirty shirts and soiled underwear into a wire cart with a shovel, he was transfixed.

She was wide, very wide, weighing close to three hundred pounds, with lumps of arm flesh that jiggled wildly whenever she swung her shovel. Her legs and ankles had fused together into a solid mass of muscular pudding, and her torso rippled over and over itself in folds of flesh. Her triple chin melted down into her neck and on the nape Drake saw a rounded button of hard flesh from which jutted three spiky hairs.

Drake had literally never seen another human like her.

He was amazed, curious, fascinated at the differences and similarities in their bodies. He wanted to know more. When she left, he followed, eventually daring to approach as she was wheeling the load to the sulfuric spring intake area where she plied her trade.

"Hi," he said breathlessly. "I'm Drake."

She turned a suspicious eye. A lifetime of muddling about on frontier rocks, dealing with the sort of scrabbling hard-nosed sentients who populated them, made her instantly question any friendly act.

She did not reply.

"So, um, what's your name?"

"Annette," she said cautiously.

"Um, so like, how are you doing?"

"I'm fine," she said and turned away.

Drake blinked. He had no idea what to say beyond this. His heart hammered, likely to split. Man, she was different. An incredibly awkward silence followed.

He edged closer, watching her sort the huge pile of disgusting clothes into several smaller ones before placing them into industrial cleaners- the salvage of a galactic gunship some thousand light years away. Annette for her part ignored him, giving Drake only the large slab of meat that was her back to stare at. Sometime afterwards he left, embarrassed by his lack of finesse.

But let's never say of our man Drake that he gave up once his interest was prickled. A few days later he showed up again with a gift, a rare bottle of Krunchy Kola ("It's Crunchy but a Cola! How Do they Do It?"), and offered to share it with her. Well, she would be foolish to pass up on such a treat and, after making sure he drank from the bottle first, plopped herself down and listened to him trying to make small talk. With as much success as before.

Still Drake managed to get close enough to touch her a little and feel her sweaty flesh. That gave him the thrill of his life. Her skin was so different, so exotic and enticing. He masturbated furiously that night at its memory, placing a pillow over his face to drown out Parg's deafening snores. It was part of the cosmic irony of life that Annette would have to clean those same sheets which Drake had soiled in her honor.

The next day he took her another treat, a Yummie Bar in delicious red flavor. Then another the following day, a hunk of Gujja candy, processed from the pulp of an Orion plant. And another after that and so on.

Each time he tried to engage her, talk to her, spark some kind of emotional reaction or at least a physical interest. Being too inexperienced to know better, Drake couldn't think of anything to talk about except his own interests. Annette rarely replied, but Drake became so giddy whenever he was near her that he couldn't help babbling on.

"So, like, if the plumbing system doesn't work properly, then the whole ship could shut down. That's why my job is so important. I'm very respected."

Or

"My favorite episode was when Spiff Blasthandy was captured by the Arachnids and they were torturing his colon, but he escapes and his ring of power given to him by the Mutzachans speaks for the first time. It was very dramatic."

Or

"He snores constantly, brushes his teeth with booze, eats with his mouth open so little chunks spray everywhere, and he likes to spit whenever he's walking next to someone. When I lived on the starbase, it was clean and we had drones to make sure it was antiseptic and if you didn't like someone, you could easily put in a transfer request and never be associated with them again. And then he yells at me for stuff like putting my boots too close to his or walking around while he's watching one of his stupid game shows…."

This is not to say that Annette was a cold person, but Drake's attentions made her nervous. She was in her late 30s, very much worn down from toil. Here was this younger (she didn't realize just how much younger) beautiful man, much more handsome than anyone who had pursued her before, who claimed to be in love, who brought her tokens of his affections, and who was nicer to her than anyone had ever been.

But as a magna cum laude graduate of the school of hard knocks, she could not escape her suspicions that Drake was just going to use and abuse her, like all of the others. Thus she maintained her frigid wall.

It wasn't until Drake started helping her with her job, accompanying her when she collected clothes and washing them, for no pay, that she softened a bit.

Maybe, she thought, *maybe he's being truthful…*

***

It was the night cycle and the canopy light array burned low. Most of the honest merchants (well, honest for this place) had turned in, but the bars were in full swing, clogged with Black Flag pirates embracing alcoholic oblivion. Plenty more roamed the streets waylaying anyone they came across, vandalizing as they pleased, and causing general mayhem.

The King's Men announced that they would begin having night patrols, something they had not done in the past, to keep the peace. But it was a bandage on a gaping head wound. The King himself had retreated into his heavily fortified bunker in the fusion plant and most of his men had followed suit. Officially they acted if they were still in charge, but the pirates had de facto carte blanche for the time being. It was hoped that things would quiet down once the liquor dried up.

Not that all of the King's Men hid away. Some were just too stupid and stubborn. Of these, Ika Dhole was the ring leader. He and a hand-picked team of thugs pounded on any pirates who fell into their grasp. The thick muscled reptilian was a source of terror and inspiration to his own men. Alone he had hospitalized thirty two pirates and killed fourteen others. Word had gotten around in the pirate's quarters, "Stay clear of the lizard."

Ika Dhole was with four of his fellows, the only ones he could bully out that night. It had been pleasant so far. They had come across three young pirates wearing white, beating on an incoherent lush. Ika Dhole pounced upon them, crippling three and hitting the last so hard that his heart exploded. The blood was still slick on his twack-'em-stick. He licked a slurp off of the end. Salty.

It had been a busy day. A fire in one of the habitation areas had eaten up a lot of attention. At least fifty people had suffered from smoke inhalation, and with no medical attention available for them, things were tense. Most blamed the pirates, but a few claimed that some Mutzachans had started it. Ika Dhole didn't believe that for a moment. Everyone used the Mutzachans as scapegoats, usually when they themselves were to blame.

The group was patrolling by some makeshift shacks, made from portable walls units and steel sections blowtorched from a spaceship interior. Travelers could rent them out by the day or hour as needed. One of the men pulled up short.

"Wait," he said, "There's…"

Attack! Rapid laser fire poured out the dark alcoves between shacks. One of the King's Men was sprayed up his body- left knee, thigh, groin, abdomen, lung, right shoulder. Down he went. Another was nearly cut in half across his torso. He slumped against a shack, feeling the heat from the blasted flesh rise up inside of his body as his life leaked out. The other two bolted, much to Ika Dhole's ire. One was gunned down with a spray up his spinal column, while the other managed to get away, taking only one shot to his lower arm.

Black Flag pirates emerged from the alcoves, holding laser and plamsa rifles at the Ram Python. Ika Dhole noted vaguely that none of the pirates had shot at him. One of them stepped up, the insignia on his flak jacket marked him as part of the Arc of Blood crew. He pointed a gleaming maser at the reptilian.

"Are you gonna be a good boy and come along?" he sneered. "Or are we all gonna have some fun?"

He was answered with a dead-on blow from the thwack-'em-stick that pulverized his nose and bruised his brain. Ika Dhole would have his fun no matter what! He flailed about, sweeping the legs out from under one pirate and poking another in the ribs, cracking them.

An electronet was thrown over him. It was a weapon created to subdue raging Rams made of thick steel cables that conducted enough electricity to crisp most races, but would only render Ika Dhole unconscious.

Power crackled. Ika Dhole's muscles tensed. He fought…fought…as hard…as he could… but….collapsed into blackness. His last thought before passing out was of blood.

***

Oxtiern stood naked, examining himself in the mirror, practicing his speech over and over. He added new phrases, shunting off old words, replacing bits that he had a hard time wrapping his tongue around. The pitch had to be perfect. Unlike the rabble beneath them, the officer classes of the Black Flag Fleet tended not to be complete idiots. But that didn't mean they would be receptive to new ideas.

"Behold, I show you a mystery," he said, quoting

a line from the Zen Rigeln sacred texts. "We shall not all comprehend, but we shall all be changed."

He had been billeted in a circular building connected to an old box theater, where the Eridani used to perform amateur musical theatricals in the Yol style. The actors would wear painted red faces and could not gesture with their arms. Words had to be enough. That was back when the city was alive, not a parasite ridden corpse. The building was easily capable of seating two hundred, but even then it would be standing room only when Oxtiern gave his presentation.

"Peace, brother skin, peace," he intoned to himself, dipping into an old Zen meditation mantra. "Your discomfort will pass. Tension is an illusion, a construct of the mind, and now the mind says *peace*."

There were groans from behind him, the large figure lying on the floor would not be quiet. He shut them out. It was all part of the process and he had to concentrate. This was the most pivotal point. To convince the whole of the Black Flag to go on his venture. He had to make it seem possible, but not simplify it too much. They would see through that. He had to appeal to their sense of adventure, to their vanity. For this would be the biggest pirate raid in recorded memory. The greatest heist. Something for the history books, with all of their names remembered forever. Something like that.

For Oxtiern it would be the greatest revenge. His evil way of demonstrating to the whole of the Zen Rigeln people the lunacy of their pacifist doctrine. That its ultimate end would be their own death and enslavement. And by the Gods from Beyond, he would enjoy doing it!

He was sure that once twenty million of their own people lay dead, the Zen's ruling philosophical houses would fall. And that prefix assigned to his family name, that of Tza (soiled/degraded/shameful), would fade away into obscurity as the Zens embraced hatred and violence. Then all that he had had to endure for his entire life, the degradation from being branded into that untouchable caste of Zen society for the crime of being born into the wrong family, would be paid back a million fold. Oxtiern's great vengeance.

His limbs shook. Were he to fail… were he to fail…

Movement behind him. The door to his room opened. Oxtiern grabbed for a weapon and turned, but it was just the bloated laundress come to collect and… oh, ho, ho! The little shit surgeon. Such a tasty morsel.

The pair stopped, gaping at his nudity and the large reptilian figure sprawled out on the floor. It was Ika Dhole quivering on the carpet. His eyes were open, twisting back and forth, pleading for release. Buried into his skull was the golden needle. It was so deep that it appeared as if its cylindrical body was simply resting on the Ram Python's head.

"The problem with this thing," said Oxtiern, flicking the golden needle with his big toe, "is that it takes so damn long to work its magic. Still, the Ram has a relatively small brain so it cuts the time in half."

"What are you doing to him?" the shit surgeon asked. Oxteirn could never remember his name.

"I'm making him mine. In brain and body, if not soul."

He grabbed hold of the boy and dragged the shit surgeon near, hugging him close.

"If it isn't my favorite turd flusher," Oxtiern whispered to the Gen-Human and licked his face. "You always know how to satisfy."

Oxtiern's palms glowed blue as he activated his race's ability to manipulate flesh and bone. Pain ripped through the boy once again. Oxtiern could taste the agony as the Gen-Human cried out. The woman cried out too, only in horror, adding extra spice to the mix. The Tza Zen lifted one blue finger and pressed it deep into the corner of his victim's mouth. Flesh sizzled and charred. A blast of smoke puffed off his cheek and stung the struggling Gen-Human's eyes. Oxtiern pulled the finger along the boy's face, creating a deep furrow in the flesh. The trench turned downward, in imitation of a frown. Then he repeated the process on the other side, only curving upwards like a smile.

"Look at this," Oxtiern crooned. "Comedy and tragedy combined."

The boy went limp. Fun over. Oxtiern threw the body onto the still shrieking laundress's cart. He slapped her across the face.

"Shut up, slut," he ordered. "Get this trash out of here."

The woman quickly obeyed and Oxtiern turned back to the mirror, completely relaxed. That was more refreshing than a shot of booze. He was ready to face the world now

Chapter 10- Myntal 5

The Motaran Rift: A colossal chaotic tear in the fabric of space/time, one hundred lightyears across. Inside of it, the laws of physics are in constant retreat, causing massive time dilation effects (wherein a ship may emerge after a day to find that several months had passed), sporadic generation of wormholes to other parts of the universe, and disruptions in the causal nexus (wherein a ship may find itself damaged before it had been shot). The effects are not limited to its central area and have been linked to other distortion effects across the galaxy, such as the appearance of Shade Worlds.

The cause of the Motaran Rift is unknown. It has been determined that the anomaly was generated by artificial means. Because of this, the Rift is surrounded by the usual assortment of conspiracy theories and paranoid babble that such things attract. It had once been rumored that the Rift was a staging area for the Arachnids, but this has since been disproven. If there is a purpose behind it, the reason must be linked to a more sinister foe.

***

Quandle and Molphus pulled Almon from the burning Dream Merchant's room, the elder practically weeping electricity. Neither had ever seen their mentor lose control of his talents so utterly. D'puppup was in a bad state, taking the full blast of Almon's wild energy release. His burning body had blown back, setting the velvet drapes and carpeting ablaze as he fell. There was probably little that could be done for him, but Molphus dove back into the room anyway to rescue the charred wreckage of the Misha.

No emergency systems had ever been installed in this area of the city so the hallways quickly became choked with smoke and concerned citizens. People began screaming and a general panic ensued. Quandle supported Almon. Molphus half carried, half dragged D'puppup into the crowd.

"Rul. Rul. Rul," Almon kept murmuring, sparks shooting between his knuckles with each intonation.

The people running away from the fire crashed into a wall of rubberneckers. The two groups dissolved into a general mayhem of pushing and shoving. The Mutzachans took refuge in an open rental shack. Molphus put D'puppup on the thin cot provided by the owners. His breathing was shallow and full of gurgling, as liquids filled up his lungs. Mercifully, the Misha was comatose. Had he been conscious, the burns covering most of his body would have caused excruciating pain. Molphus doubted he would last through the night.

Almon had quieted down and sat in the dirt. He leaned, against the metal wall watching people run back and forth outside of the open door. Quandle squatted across from him, scrutinizing his old mentor's face.

All of the nagging doubts and little inconsistences had begun coming together. He had believed that the mission had come from the

Mutzachan Intelligence Service and that Almon was a longtime agent. The fact that he and Molphus were brought in under the guise that the service was having "personnel issues" sounded odd at the time, but Quandle had accepted it, trusting his old mentor and not knowing much about the inner workings of the Mutzachan espionage service himself. Of course now, the explanation felt hollow.

Then there were the inconsistencies with the miraculous Oxtiern. This Tza Zen Rigeln who could waltz into top secret areas and steal from them with outrageous brashness. Who could pull together an entire pirate fleet to listen to his words. Who had large chunks of his life deleted and denied by the government. Who could put together a plan so audacious that it caused Almon, the most unflappable person Quandle had ever met, to lose control.

The lynchpin of Quandle's reflections was the revelation of Almon's past on the Misha homeworld. The telling detail was his admittance of gathering intelligence on the Krakeds, a race holding almost no interest to the Mutzachan government, in a galaxy that their race had no real dealings with.

However, there were others who did have an interest in the Misha. Who were *very* concerned about what the Krakeds were up to and about their possible allegiance to the invading Arachnid forces. Who would have placed agents in a forlorn galaxy to assemble what intelligence lines they could.

"We're beyond this ruse that you used to get us here," Quandle began. "I think we've earned a few truths."

Almon stared back at him, his guts cold as ice. He could hardly refuse.

"You aren't part of Mutzachan Intelligence, that's easily determined. But this is still an officially sanctioned mission, correct? I mean you do work for an espionage agency."

Almon said nothing. His face tensed. Would they soon learn the truth? Could they discern it? Molphus sat down next to the gurgling Misha, absently rubbing the wounded creature's hand as he became absorbed by the confrontation.

"You're part of Galactic Control," Quandle stated.

Almon almost laughed in his face. It was the logical leap to make. Galactic Control was the Alliance's intelligence arm. A long limb it was too, gathering up and suppling information to every other part of the vast galactic bureaucracy. It would be the obvious deduction from Quandle's perspective. Almost certain money. It just happened to be wrong.

"Yes I am," he lied.

Molphus gasped, feeling as if he had been physically slapped. Did no one ever tell the truth?

"Why the deception? We would've helped regardless," he asked.

"I didn't have clearance," Almon replied.

"But if you were an agent from…."

Quandle interrupted, "He's not just some agent. Maybe in the past he was, but due to his age and experience, I'd be willing to bet he's a case supervisor running his own team. Perhaps he's even in charge of a department."

Everything Quandle had said was technically true, it was only wrong in its context, but Almon didn't bother to correct him.

"One of these agents was Oxtiern," Quandle continued, his face glittering with pride as he outsmarted his mentor. "And he has gone rogue. You need our help putting him back in his box before he causes whatever destruction he has planned."

"Oh yes," Almon said. It still wasn't a lie, just not the whole truth.

"Why did you need us?" Molphus demanded. "Galactic Control has so many resources."

"Don't you see? He doesn't trust anyone else that he works with. If the Zen went bad, then maybe they all would. He probably recruited each one of them personally. He was probably scouting us out for a position with Galactic Control all the time he was mentoring us."

High marks for Quandle in deductive reasoning, Almon mused. Had they been back in school he would have gone to the head of the class. Quandle was supremely happy in his find, but Molphus looked sad, betrayed. Some childlike innocent belief about his mentor had been ripped away and pissed on by a horrible fact. Perhaps innocence was simply ignorance after all.

"Is that true?" Molphus asked meekly. This irritated Almon beyond reason. Time for him to grow up.

"I rejected you both for indoctrination into my association. Neither of you seemed as if you would have the interest or aptitude to be a member."

The two younger Mutzachans drunk this in, turning it over in their minds to determine if they should be insulted by Almon's statement. Eventually they both decided that their egos were unbruised.

"So then," Quandle asked. "What is Rul?"

Rul, the black spot planted at the center of his soul. The name itself was nothing, but the concept behind it was so profound that the grasping of it fundamentally altered one's perception of the universe, of survival, of what could and could not be done in a civilized society.

Almon stopped thinking. He saw these two wallowing in their ignorance, awash in innocence. Would he take that from them? Would he indoctrinate them into the cult as it were? If he did, he was damning them to become a part of it. They would have no choice, either by force or conscience. No! He wouldn't. He couldn't.

He shook his head. They didn't need to know.

Quandle reacted violently, a green spark igniting in the depths of his eyes, which he suppressed with some difficulty. Molphus became further downtrodden. Neither understood that Almon's refusal was an act of mercy.

Silence spawned in the hut for a time, until Molphus blurted, "Does it have something to do with the Motaran Rift?"

Almon started. How did he make that leap of logic?

"What makes you say that?"

"It's … just…"

Quandle stopped him.

“Answer the question,” Quandle commanded of Almon.

“Yes,” Almon said, “in a roundabout way it does, or might be. Now how did you deduce that, Molphus?”

The younger Mutzachan guestured to D’puppup.

“Something he said. The substance of his vision sounded much more cryptic than is usual for the Misha. Until I realized that what he said might not have been cryptic at all. ‘Not the first creation, but the first great destruction. When the stars exploded and all matter was smashed back into atoms.’ At first I thought it may have been a metaphor for the First Arachnid Invasion, then I remembered my physics history and realized it was a reference to the Proto 1 Scattering, thriteen billion years ago.”

The Proto 1 Scattering, as it is labeled in the Mutzachan universal cosmology, was the explosive destruction of the first stars. The supermassive stellar factories (five hundred times larger than any star recorded today) that rose and fell half a billion years after the Big Bang. It blasted the heavier elements into deep space and helped give definition to the conical shape of the universe. Those which hadn’t gone supernova (or pan-instability supernovae to be technical) had collapsed into massive black holes, such as the one at the center of the Milky Way.

“The only thing we know that still exists from that time is the Motaran Rift,” concluded Molphus.

“Very good,” Almon said, impressed. “Instead of wasting your time working on ion drives, you should have gone into game theory. We might have even recruited you."

Quandle was confused, "How does…"

"I'm not answering any more questions. You've figured out quite a bit, but the reality is you are still not cleared to know everything." Almon stood up. "These things you want to know are peripheral to the mission. If we stop Oxtiern then all of this other nonsense does not need to come out."

Silence.

"All right, I'll give you a choice," he continued. "If either of you wish to back out, feel free to do so. There will be no recriminations. Nothing will go on your records. I will not think less of you. Just raise your hand and walk away."

The younger pair exchanged glances. This wasn't much of a choice. They were on an alien world. Walking away likely meant they would be stranded. Both kept their hands down.

Almon's data pad lit up. He looked at his wrist. It was a communication from the Cizerack family they had arrived with. He scrolled through the text.

"Now that's interesting. They've learned where the assembly of Black Flag captains is going to be held. If we can't find him before then, we will have to eliminate Oxtiern at the meeting. The last of the fleet is expected in four days. We have until then."

***

Drake was sprawled out naked on a thin mattress in Annette's dwelling, a threadbare blanket draped leisurely over his midsection. He was sated, relaxed, drained of energy and a half pint of sexual juices. He looked over his body, watching the sweat slowly drying off his skin. A little blob of perspiration was stubbornly perched on an erect nipple.

Annette shifted about on the other side of the room, pulling a massive pair of overalls up her bulky frame. Her rooms (a living space and a toilet) were part of a hardened sand complex originally designated to house miners back when the city was an Eridani excavation concern. The walls were perpetually slick and cold, a chaotic yellow and brown pattern raced over them. When the door was closed, all sounds of the city outside were silenced.

Drake could easily have stayed in the room with Annette forever. Until this time, his life had been incomplete in a way he had never understood. The standard byproduct of having so recently lost his virginity.

He touched the scars on his face. They were still tender, though the pain had gone down considerably in the week since he had been disfigured. The first few days had been unbearable. His face had practically radiated heat as his body worked overtime to heal the wounds.

Strangely enough, it was this attack which broke Annette's hard shell. She stayed with him for two days, dressing his wounds, cooling his head, and feeding him broth with clumps of vegetable matter in it. On the third day, his strength had recovered a bit and she gave him a rag bath, wiping down his lithe body with efficiency and dedication.

She wasn't gentle about it. Roughly scrubbing out the grime that had set into his skin due to his tour aboard the Arc of Blood. Back and forth she rubbed, until the skin gleamed raw and shiny. Despite the harsh treatment, her slightest touch aroused him uncontrollably. On her part, she couldn't help but sneak glances at his erect penis, the head shining the deepest purple like a signal beacon. She grew moist at the thought of him.

One day while working down his frame, she tried to skirt around his genitals. His hand shot out, grabbing her meaty wrist. This was the boldest he had ever been, driven on by irrepressible cravings. Their eyes met. Warm desire rolled off them both, mixing together into a potent aphrodisiac. The gaze lasted for a second, then they broke, collapsing into each other. Grasping flesh, rolling tongues, hot lips tasting deep. Like the feeding frenzy of a predatory animal.

The first time didn't last long. One, two, three, ooooooh! But what a fantastic few seconds it was. He simply lay there afterwards transfixed by emotion as she gratefully accepted his semen deep into her body. It was beautiful. An act of communion. The only religious experience he had ever had. He looked at her face, full of vulnerability and surrender. Their lips crushed together.

The next few days had been devoured by sexual exploration. He spent hours sightseeing through her folds, sucking at her breasts, nibbling at the large mole on the back of her neck, and licking the stubborn hairs that spiked from it. He ventured deep into her sex, washing his face in her musty cream, probing its mysteries with his fingers, and cultivating orgasm after wonderful orgasm.

As for Annette, she couldn't get enough of caressing his muscles, nuzzling his hair, and placing him in her mouth. When they made love, a new horizon opened up before her. Pleasure, like she had never had before. Her previous sexual encounters had all been furious pounding, an empty respite from toil while she let some jerk have his way, often with him saying afterwards how disgusted he was about having to stoop to having sex with someone of her girth. With Drake it was something more, something beautiful, and her body responded accordingly.

In-between these erotic fumblings, they rarely talked. They asked nothing of each other's past. An understanding had passed between them. She was Drake's woman now and he was there to stay. Both were so content that nothing else was needed. They groaned together, sweated together, came together. In the end, they lay helplessly entwined, drinking in the other's smells.

Heaven. There was no other way to describe it.

But now she was planning to go out. The real world and its dreary demands had come banging at their door. Annette finished dressing and sighed.

"I'll probably be all day," she said apologetically.

A whole day until they could be naked together again? An epoch! How would he survive?

"I'll help you out," Drake said eagerly, leaping from the mattress. "If we split collecting the loads, then we will be able to…"

He caressed her rippling buttocks. She shivered

with excitement.

"Can you collect the loads from your pirate friend's barracks?" she asked.

"They're not my friends!"

"I'm sorry, I forgot. But can you get them? They're always the worst and it would save so much time."

He hesitated, rubbing his scars. What would they say about them? What jokes would they make? Would they question his courage? Or his manhood?

Oh, who cares. He was done with them anyhow. He had mentally jumped ship. The plan was to spend the rest of his life here with Annette, making love and doing laundry. Let them fix their own damn toilets.

"Of course I will," he said. "I'd do anything for you."

This sappy statement pierced Annette's heart. They embraced and left.

The squealing wail of bagpipes spilled out of the Arc of Blood crew quarters, meaning the last person Drake wanted to see was in attendance. He pushed the laundry cart in as quietly as he could, hoping to reach the mountain of reeking clothes without incident. That wasn't in the cards, Parg and Jack Mace seemed to sense his presence almost immediately and descended on him.

"What the hell happened to you?" Parg laughed. He was naked except for his orange briefs and the bagpipes slung across his shoulder. The pipes banged lightly against his paunch.

"I don't know if I should laugh or cry," Jack Mace quipped. His fur was matted and snarled.

Crumbs and dried liquor clung to it.

"I got into a fight."

"Yeah right," Parg laughed again. "You mean you got jumped. Which crew did it?"

"Never mind."

"Nah," Jack Mace said. "We can't let that go. It ain't about you, it's us. If someone from another ship did this, we gotta sort it out. Else it will get around that the Arc of Blood is weak and everyone will gang up on us."

Parg grabbed the back of Drake's neck.

"So spit," he said, delving into pirate talk, as he did whenever violence loomed. "We got reps to back up."

"It wasn't another crew."

"Oh great," Parg said, losing interest. Drake shook off his calloused hand. "Leave it to you. City full of cousins to back you up, everyone scared shitless of us, and you still managed to get your ass kicked."

"And kicked hard," Jack Mace said, examining Drake's burns more closely. "These are deep. Someone took their time here."

"I don't want to talk about it."

The pair shared another evil laugh and Drake pushed the cart over to the pile of clothes. He took a small shovel out and began loading it up.

"What the fuck are you doing?" Parg yelled.

Jack Mace ran over and grabbed the shovel from Drake. He mockingly threatened to hit him with it.

"We got a fat bitch to do this," the Fott said.

"Yeah well…I was…"

"What?" yelled Parg again.

"I was just helping Annette out."

"Who is that?"

"It's the laundry broad," said Jack Mace, leering at Drake. His tongue waggled at the Gen-Human. "Drake's got himself a slop wife."

Slop wife was pirate slang for a woman that a pirate took up with during an extended stay. Typically they were discarded once the ship left port.

Parg came closer. "I think he's the wife. Why you doing her work?"

Drake ignored him and grabbed the shovel back from the laughing Jack Mace.

Parg wouldn't let up. "Doing the bitch work," he said. "If I knew that was your inclination, then maybe we *would've* taken our turns through these double doors."

He slapped Drake's ass.

Drake swung the shovel, trying to sink its dull edge into Parg's face. The Orion was too nimble however and fell back, tripping over some loose sheets and plopped into the pile of clothes. His bagpipes blasted out a short squawk. Other pirates, who had clustered around, laughed raucously at the sight. Parg got up and laughed as well, trying to make it seem all in good fun, but Drake could tell that inside he was seething.

"Well anyway, have your fun porking the slop wife, but don't make any plans," Jack Mace said. "The big meeting is tonight. By tomorrow, we'll probably be off planet. So have your last screw and be ready."

"The dump is practically dry," Parg snarled. "Can't wait to jump off this shit pile."

He walked away, bellowing through his bagpipes. No one could tell if he was good or bad at it. Jack Mace stuffed a pair of socks, stiff from dried sweat, in his ears. Drake didn't bother to finish loading the clothing. He slipped the cart out of the barracks, then raced back to Annette's apartment. He went inside and pulled out a ski mask and some burglar's tools from the closet.

Annette had acquired these items after she surprised a thief rifling her rooms. She had knocked the man over and sat on his face, her fat folds smothering him quickly. The laundress had kept the items as a keepsake and sold the body as food to some Phentari making a pit stop.

He hefted a titanium crowbar with relish. If Oxtiern was making his presentation then it would be the perfect time for some revenge. Drake wasn't delusional enough to think that he could take the Tza Zen on mano-a-mano, but he could do some damage to his possessions. Maybe break that golden needle in half.

With so many people angry at the pirates, it was unlikely that Drake would be fingered. There were plenty of patsies. He laughed at the thought of smashing something valuable. The idea felt good. It warmed his heart.

Time to give some back.

Chapter 11- Myntal 5

Shade World: A planet which appears to be in orbit around a star, but cannot actually be reached by normal physical means. A ship attempting to land on a shade world would simply pass through as if the planet were an illusion. Mutzachan scientists have linked the phenomena to the Motaran Rift. The planets themselves are a reflection of another part of space/time caused by a quantum ribbon rippling from the Rift. Special wormholes have been found in deep space which allows travel to a shade world. One such conduit exists in orbit around the moon of Stilt.

***

The time had come. The captains of the Black Flag Fleet were assembled. The city was lousy with pirate crews. Remarkably, except for a few minor scuffles, all violence had been directed towards the locals and the King's Men. The latter having completely abandoned any attempt to maintain order after Ika Dhole's disappearance. They hid away in their fortified bunkers praying the pirates would leave quickly.

This lack of violence between crews was a minor miracle, but it couldn't last. One wrong word or punch could set off a feud that might last decades, if not splinter the clan. There had been several smaller groups formed that way, spun off from Black Flag over petty arguments, distribution of booty, or (most common) some captain being butt-hurt that he wasn't elected admiral.

One splinter clan, the Knives of Vandred, began over an argument between two captains about a small crate of green plastic cups. The cousin ships had raided a freighter together, splitting the loot down the line with only the crate left over. Both captains, afraid of looking weak in the eyes of their crews, refused to give in over this useless item. The deadlock ended with a ship to ship fight. The Vandred scuttled the other vessel, looted it, and then careened off to another galaxy, before the wrath of the other Black Flag captains could descend upon them. There were no formal laws among the pirates, but that sort of thing wasn't done to another clan member.

Now the booze was drunk, the whores were saddle sore, and every vendor that was able to, had departed. This left the pirates with no recreation. It was only a matter of time until one crew started fighting another.

Every captain that could be was present. A few ships were involved in raids which they refused to abort. A couple had such bad blood with another captain that the two could not be in the same port together. One ship, the Swooshpatpat, commanded by a blobulous Mazian, had been attacked by Galactic Navy destroyers in the Plains of Desolation sector and fled into the Kathamarse Abyss, a quarantined no man's region. They were presumed lost.

Dri of Atch, the current Black Flag admiral, walked onto the stage followed by Oxtiern. He was a

Python Lizard, the amphibious cousin race to the Ram Python. He was dressed in silver and black, bearing the red sash the Admiral always wore in times of official business. Oxtiern had chosen a very simple white outfit, contrasting everyone else, to make sure he stood out and that all eyes would be drawn to him.

The Zen took in the enormity of the crowd. An assembly of hungry carnivores, each easily capable of committing any crime conceivable. But only he, Oxtiern, could have pulled off this great vengeance.

Peace, brother skin, peace, he intoned silently.

Some of the captains were yawning, bored before the presentation had begun. Others were angry that they had been called to this rock for unclear reasons. Many stared with intense concentration, sensing a big job in the works. They had already begun salivating over their imagined loot. And all of them, no matter their inclination, stared directly at him.

Peace, brother skin, peace.

A tri-screen had been erected on the back of the stage, amplified for maximum projection, through which he would present the logistics of the operation. Each captain was given a clicker that would electronically record their vote after the presentation. Oxtiern had briefly considered adding his own contribution to the algorithm to weigh the votes in his favor, but in the end rejected it. If the pirates found out, or even suspected, everything would be over. His life and his chosen raison d'etre.

Peace, brother skin, peace.

If they refused... if they refused it was all over.

What would he do? Where would his life go? Maybe he could slip across to Kraked or Xarian space, or even the Aeodronians if he got desperate, and sell the golden needle to them. Spend the rest of his life as a refugee with a bullseye on the back of his skull. Of course, even if he succeeded he still might have to go down that path, but then it wouldn't matter. He would happily die ten seconds after achieving his goal. His victory, his revenge, and his historic infamy completed. The rest would be a minor epilogue. But first they had to accept.

Peace, brother skin, peace.

Dri of Atch was speaking now, introducing Oxtiern, listing off his credentials for those who had no idea. Some of it was fake, some was exaggerated, some horrifically real. Oxtiern suppressed a glob of vomit that had bobbed up his throat.

What was this? Stage fright? He chastised himself.

You've charged headlong into combat, cut out the vital organs of every sentient race, spat in the face of your near-omnipotent superiors, and yet you go weak-kneed at the thought of making a speech to a bunch of lowlifes! Get ahold of yourself! Your uncle was Vargeneit, the Slayer of Langoon. Fifty thousand lay dead at his feet. What would he think of your cowardice?

Memories of a punishing childhood splashed over Oxtiern's mind. The pain room, the blind box, the razor beds, the burning decks. His uncle hid broken glass in his food to make him wary, fired gunshots over his head to inure the young Oxtiern to the sounds of violence. He forever trained the Zen to be strong, to eat despair, to see that pain and pleasure were the same thing, as was love and hate. His education was long complete. Would he now fumble with the goal in sight?

His mind raced. Random weirdness kept popping up. *I have set my life upon a cast. And I will stand the hazard of the die.* What culture had composed those lines? He couldn't remember. It translated very well into the Zen Rigeln languages...

"And now, here is Oxtiern," Dri of Atch concluded, "who will give you the full details on the raid."

Peace....

Oxtiern took center stage, a thin line of nervous sweat clustered at his temples. He remotely flipped on the tri-screen. A three dimensional image of a planet, its satellites, and orbiting defenses glowed above the stage.

Pause. Pause. Panic! *Swallow the fear.* He closed his eyes and opened them again.

"Katrel," he said, his voice firm and steady. "Homeworld of the Zen Rigelns and one of the cornerstones of the Galactic Alliance. A place of peace, wealth, and harmony."

He stopped and grinned evilly.

"Who'd like to knock it over?"

***

The area around the old Yol theater was thick with pirates. Each of the captains had brought a few bully boys along who were told to wait outside and be ready, "in case anything happens". They lounged about swapping lies, shooting dice, checking and rechecking their guns. A few listened to music or watched pirated movies on their data pads.

Drake had scammed an Arc of Blood jacket from the laundry pile and blended in. The other guards paid him no attention, except for a few glances and snorts. They were clustered mostly at the front and back entrances with almost none by the smaller door of the circular building attached to the theater. The one where Oxtiern was staying.

He slipped up to the door. The only pirates about were an alcoholic human pouring what smelled like aftershave down his gullet and a pair of short purple skinned Goola-Goolas discussing the merits of the latest season of *Aetlantean Stardoor Squad*- a sci-fi drama of a group of rough and ready military types jumping through the stardoors left by the mysterious Aetlantean species. Drake sneered, *Spiff Blashandy* was a way better show.

The locks were 60 years old at least. Back on the Brethia Stargate Project, where the security systems were state-of-the-art, Drake and his assigned friends would sometimes amuse themselves by attempting to bypass the systems and secure zones in their pods. Compared to them, this was an antique. He slipped a few probes into it and sent a charge down the key pad, disrupting the identifier coding. He pushed in a blank keycard and the door clicked open.

Around the corner walked an Orion, wearing pirate leathers and steel-toed boots. His face was a disaster of scars and burn tissue. Both of his pointed ears were clipped down. It was impossible to tell if he had been handsome or ugly in his youth and just as impossible to tell his age. He pointed at Drake's face.

"Wat you got dem, cousin?"

Drake had been pressed into service long enough to pick up most of the lingo, one of the benefits of hanging out with Jack Mace. He fingered the burned furrows.

"Dat little hod present. Made angry when I wouldn't spit."

"Hod" meant police or the equivalent. "Spit" was to talk or squeal about something.

"Dat some pent up cholly wuzzles, cousin. Wat pull they needed spit?"

"Cholly wuzzles", while a cuddly sounding phrase, was in fact an incredibly foul idiom dredged from one of the Orion languages. It meant someone who had a proclivity to commit fellatio on dead farm animals. Drake had a hard time believing that the practice was common enough that the Orions felt the need to give it its own phrase, but there it was.

Drake replied, stuffing as much slang into the sentence as he could. "Chop up gut tuck [forced organ harvesting]. Jel bigface spurt [the victim was an important person's child]. The hod were squeezed, so they squeezed me. Wat I know?"

This was a dance, a series of recognition codes. Pirates rarely talked this way inside of a crew. It was a way for a person to verify someone else was part of the same clan. Such methods were especially needed in a larger clan like this one, where it would be much easier for an outsider to slip in and get lost in the crowd. The slang tended to shift from clan to clan, sometimes only slightly, sometimes it was an entirely new language.

"Bad, bad. Wat did it happen?"

One of the weirdest aspects of the Black Flag lingo, a language bursting with extra adjectives and nouns, was the replacing of all question words (what, who, where, when, why) with the singular "wat". No scholar could explain how it happened. It was simply another instance of the illiterate driving the language, leaving the academics to play catch up.

"Dumb Earth. They got nothing, though there was something to get."

"Wat did? Tell, tell!"

"Old boys, good boys [friends, career criminals] ran the gut tuck business. I just helped with grabbing the dump [finding a place] and keeping it clean [making sure it was secure]. I didn't cut. I just watched. Still the hod had a hard time understanding that no means no. They got slurrip [torture under interrogation, from the Phentari language]."

"Yeah they will."

They both laughed heartily. Drake couldn't tell if the Orion bought the story, but it was standard for a pirate to exaggerate their misdeeds, so he wasn't too worried. The main thing was that he believed Drake was a Black Flag member.

Drake entered the building. The rooms were made of the same sand-hardened resin as Annette's apartment. He slipped the mask over his face. It might be redundant now that he'd been seen outside, but it made him feel powerful. He pulled the crowbar from its hiding spot in his pants leg, and strutted around the rooms looking for something to smash.

There wasn't much. He flipped over Oxtiern's laundry basket and booted the clothes about. A pair of underwear got caught around his foot. He kicked it off and it settled on a light fixture.

"Take that you skull-faced fuck," Drake murmured.

There was no sign of the golden needle, so Drake messed up the Tza Zen's toiletries. Throwing his soap in the toilet, squeezing out the toothpaste, wiping his ass crack with the brush. That made him feel good. He ripped a flexi-screen off the wall and poured water all over it, shorting it out. The screen popped and fizzled. A thin acrid whiff of ozone circled up to the ceiling. Even better.

He scanned about for more things to destroy. He ripped up a few books in the Zen language, scattering the pages all over the room. Then on small table, buried under various pieces of scratch paper, he discovered a data tablet. It seems that the Zen had been in such a hurry that he had forgotten to set the security protocol on the tablet's screen.

A topographical map of a planet called Passage was displayed on it. Mildly curious, Drake tapped on the screen, zooming in. It was a barren rock. Near lifeless except for bare bones fungi, jelly fish, slime molds, mollusks, and trilobite type creatures, most of which hadn't bothered to crawl out of the ocean yet. The atmosphere was composed primarily of methane, ammonia, water vapor, and hydrogen sulfate. Not at all hospitable to most forms of sentient life.

One area was marked in red with the legend "Rul Excavation". It was a large fissure that snaked out from the base of a mountain. The map indicated that it ran deep into the planet's mantle.

What was the significance of this place? It certainly didn't look any different than a million other balls of earth swinging around suns. Drake felt that he should know, but he had been designed to handle managerial issues and paper pushing. The construction company never bothered to decant him with any skill sets relating to geology.

Suddenly the tablet turned black and locked up. The phrase, "unknown genetic sequence" appeared on it in Galactic Basic. A secondary security protocol. Damn. The machine had registered his DNA sequence when he dragged his finger across it. The program probably wouldn't be able to determine Drake's identity, but it would certainly note that a Gen-Human had been playing with it. That brought suspicion almost to Drake's door.

He smashed the tablet against the wall, then ground the circuitry beneath his feet, digging in deep with the heel to make sure it was irreparable. That'd take care of any records.

Something entered the room. Drake caught sight of a hulking figure in his periphery. Ika Dhole. There were no signs of damage to his head. For once Oxtiern must have used his native powers to heal instead of harm. He flexed his huge reptilian muscles and flung his thwack-'em-stick back and forth from hand to massive hand. The look on his face was not inviting.

***

"The creature itself is constructed of organic material with an incredible mixture of superdense alloys supporting the brain, which is located in the dead center of the body. Thus, it is capable of generating its own gravitation pull, equivalent to a small moon."

Oxtiern zoomed in the image projected above the crowd. A massive spherical creature floated in the depths of space. It had no features except for two red slits curving downward across its northern hemisphere. Orbiting it were two smaller orbs. He highlighted them with a laser pointer.

"These two act as appendages and are made up primarily of malleable organic material, which the creature can manipulate by gravitational pressure into whatever shape needed. They are incredibly effective."

His tone was very technical here. He had spent hours shaping his speech to sound authoritarian.

"With this weapon in play, our work will be relatively easy. The fetus will maneuver into the orbit of Katrel and destroy their defensive satellites. Even young as it is, the creature will still be more than a match for them. Its gravitational field will actually cause many of them to smash into its dermis and be rendered ineffective."

Hypocrites, thought Oxtiern. *They talk of pacifism, but still arm themselves to the teeth.* But he knew full well that, in deference to their doctrines, all of the defenses surrounding the Zen homeworld were automated, controlled completely by an artificial intelligence designed by the Alliance military. This was so no individual Zen Rigeln was forced to part from their sacred philosophy.

"The creature will then descend into the planet's gravity well. The effect of this act alone will be devastating, the equivalent of a storm of comets hitting the surface. Massive seismic shockwaves will damage infrastructure, cause earthquakes across several continents, and disrupt all planetary communications."

With the exception of a pinpoint wormhole link, but he didn't feel the need to mention that. A simulation of the event was projected for the assembly to see. Even a conservative death and destruction calculation was impressive. Several of the audience gasped. Others applauded in appreciation. He was winning them over. Oxtiern could taste it.

"This is only the beginning. Assuming the fetus survives this long, it will continue on its rampage, destroying city after city, crushing anything in its path. All simulations conclude that it will eventually be destroyed or disabled by the Zen's innate manipulation of carbon, but they will be in complete disarray. All we need do is swoop in during the aftermath, looting until our greed is content."

A bald Eridani captain with an artificial jaw and synthesized voice box stood up. His jacket patches marked him as captain of The Princess Karina's Revenge.

"What is that thing?" he squawked in an artificial voice.

"That is a Rul."

***

The three Mutzachans were spotted by a few guards walking down the deserted lane towards the Yol theater. They were spread out across the street, each flexing their fingers before them. The odd sight quickly made the rounds. Mutzachans? Here? An ill omen. What could they want?

Five of their bravest went out to meet them. Armor fastened. Weapons powered up. They died the quickest.

"Watch out boys," one of them yelled. "These things can shit energy out of their bodies. They're always armed."

"Along with being damned fuggly," another yelled, and they all enjoyed a last laugh.

Thick blasts of electricity broke from the Mutzachan's hands, burning the pirates down to the marrow.

The three raised their hands, simultaneously generating energy flux shields to ward off the retaliatory fire from the other pirates. An eclectic variety of lasers, bullets, flaming fluids, superheated plasm, and supercooled solutions bounced off. Some of it ricocheting back into pirates.

One Orion was gut shot by his own bullet. Another one, a human, was splashed on the arm by the fluids. He thrashed about, screeching pitifully, and accidentally banged the limb against a wall, shattering it into ten thousand pieces.

On command, the two outer Mutzachans closed quarters with the middle, the eldest, protecting him with their flux shields. The middle one knelt, pressing his hands together as if in prayer. As he unfurled them, a immense omega pulse, a blast of concussive energy, was let loose. It ripped down the street, tossing pirates about as if they were made of cardboard. The entire group lay prone, trying to figure out what just happened. One smaller pirate, a Cizerack, the runt of his litter, had actually been knocked onto the roof of the theater.

The younger ones dropped their shields. The elder rose. Once again they raised their hands, only this time they laid down a field of unholy nuclear fire across the doomed pirates. Fifty men burned, their last curses and pleas melding together like the final wail of a dying leviathan. Eyes blistered. Skin blackened. Bones cracked. Puddles of melted fat pooled everywhere.

When the screams died down to mere gurgling and then nothing, the trio stopped and looked upon their work. One of them went and leaned against a wall, placing his large head in his hands. A lone sob cut across the silence.

***

The captains sat whispering to each other. Was what they had heard real? Oxtiern's description of the Rul and what it meant was overwhelming. Could it be true? Sounded like a tall tale. A nightmare relic of some lost mythology.

They were starting to doubt. Oxtiern flashed his blue eyes at the Black Flag admiral. Dri of Atch took center stage.

"This thing is real, let me assure you," he said in a watery voice. "Oxtiern has shown me the proof. We know exactly where it is located."

"And where is that?" the captain of the Arc of Blood asked loudly. He knew that his ship would be the one who had to take the Zen there.

"A shade world named Passage," Oxtiern replied. "Its actual location is believed to be in Nezzurs Spiral, but its reflection resonates in the Plains of Desolation sector."

Nezzurs Spiral was a galaxy located an unimaginable distance away. No one present had ever visited it. No one could. Even with the Alliance's most advanced technology it would take long past the life span of any species to reach its edge.

"The wormhole conduit to Passage was discovered orbiting the moon of the Xensera, also called Stilt. That's our next stop."

"And how can you constrain it?" an Orion, captain of the Blue Sun, blurted out. "If you told the truth the damn thing sounds un-fucking-controllable."

"With this," Oxtiern produced the golden needle. He used the tri-screen to project its image to the crowd. "It's a Mutzachan device called the bionucleotide restructurer. Its function is to reorganize a creature's brain to obey any commands."

Mutzachan technology! That impressed the captains. Though nearly everyone present despised and feared the race, believing them to be a galactic illuminati, they also held a superstitious awe about what the species could accomplish. If they could control the Alliance, why couldn't they invent a golden mind rewriter?

"And you are sure this thing will work?" asked the captain of the Arc of Blood.

"It's a slow process. It will take about two months to finish. But yes, the fetal Rul will be completely and utterly our slave."

***

Ika Dhole twirled his weapon as if it were a baton. His eyes were glassy, unreasonable. A thin line of drool dripped from his scaly lips. The whole of his face was contorted. Not quite in anger, Drake noticed, more like an imitation of it. As if the Ram Python knew that he was supposed to feel the emotion, but couldn't actually muster it up.

"It's not what it looks like," Drake blurted.

Ika Dhole made no reply. His arm shot out. Drake ducked, slipping on the papers he had scattered about. The thwack-'em-stick broke a chunk out of the wall directly behind where Drake's head had been. No quarter would be given here. From his prone position, he swung the titanium crowbar up in between Ika Dhole legs. He laughed, anticipating the Ram's inevitable groan of intense pain.

This didn't happen. Drake's education had also been incomplete on alien anatomy. He was unaware that the Ram Pythons genitalia retracts when not in use. All he accomplished was to give the Ram a slight bruise on his upper thigh. Now some genuine emotion entered the Ram's face, mirth. He had his prey down and was about to pin him to the floor like an insect on a card.

He struck. Drake rolled out of the way, unable to gain his footing. Ika Dhole stuck again, bringing his weapon straight down like a giant plunger. Drake dodged away again. A third attack, another dodge.

It was only a matter of time, Drake knew. He couldn't keep this up forever and the Ram didn't seem to be getting tired. After the next impaling attempt, he threw the crowbar at Ika Dhole's face. The Ram jerked back reflexively, blocking the bar with his forearm.

Drake bolted, putting all of his energy into hurtling across the room and out to safety. Time slowed with each footfall. One step. Breathe. Two steps. Breathe. Three steps. Almost there. Four steps. Five. Six. Within arm's reach. Pain!

Ika Dhole had recovered and tossed his quarter staff like a spear. The blunt metal tip smashed into Drake's side breaking three ribs, crack crack crack. The blow actually propelled him forward. He wheezed, too much in shock to actually feel the pain yet, and opened the door, bloody foam frothing in his mouth.

Drake staggered out into a firefight and knocked over a Mutzachan who was generating lasers from his fingertips. Ika Dhole roared behind him.

***

Another objection. This time from the captain of the Phentari vessel Slioshotanizi (which translated inelegantly to "The Ritual De-Limbers")."I don't care how much damage this thing does. We're still gonna need more, some significant firepower to pull off our end. Pacifism will only go so far when your house is being broken into."

Let's hope that's the case, thought Oxtiern. Out loud he said, "Dri of Atch and I have anticipated this." He pulled an image of a planet up on the tri-screen. "The planet Stilt, where we are heading anyway, was devastated by the recent Arachnid assault on the sector. As such, the few facilities left have been converted into a military depot and transit point for gear."

"I've been there before," someone murmured in the crowd. "Nice place."

Was a nice place. The image changed to that of the technical details of a suit of ultra-armor used by the Galactic Marines. Egg shaped and enormous, the armor sported personal missile systems, lasers, pulse weaponry, and a whirling diamond tipped circular saws for cutting an enemy to pieces. A battlelord's dream. The captains drank in this beautiful killing machine, imagining what they could do with it.

"This is military issue ultra armor, coveted by all those who relish slaughter. We have information that a consignment of one thousand of these has recently been transferred to Stilt. They are eventually destined for Casada where the fighting is currently strongest. If we act quickly, we can scoop them all up."

Muttering again. Pondering. Slight fear. This was all getting a bit too big for some of them. Wasn't there a nice retirement home they could pillage?

"It would only take three ships," Oxtiern added.

"Only three?" the Orion captain of the Blue Sun asked in a sneering tone.

That one's a nay. But his defiance was an opportunity to show the other Captains that Oxtiern could take command.

"The planet is a disaster area under military jurisdiction with a large stranded civilian population whose needs are barely being met. It's manned by a skeleton garrison being used mostly for book keeping, supplies, and crowd control. A lightning raid will give us the advantage with little chance of them having time to retaliate."

"But to do that, you'd need to know the precise location of the ultra armor suits," objected the Blue Sun captain.

"That's easily arraigned. We have an asset in play on the planet." *Though he does not know it yet.* "We will get the information."

Nods. Satisfactory mumbles. The plan had merit to many of them.

The Blue Sun captain would not relent, "I'm still not sure…,"

"Sit down and shut up," roared the Cizerack captain of the Manjanungo (which unartfully translated to "Alleged Sentients"). The massive feline's tail twitched in a threatening manner. "You've made your little dumb ass complaints and failed. Stop being a nall and grow some testes or whatever it is you people have."

"Right," A human wearing a bad wig, captain of Markuss's Corpse, rose, "I'm satisfied. I vote yea. This is one for the books. No way I'm going to pass it up."

Many of the others began nodding. Sensing the mood, Dri of Atch stepped back up. His amphibious breathing flaps fluttered at his neck. Was that for nervousness or anticipation, Oxtiern wondered. He knew next to nothing of the Python Lizard race.

"You all have your devices. Vote now."

A whirlwind of clicks. The votes began to tally. Oxtiern held his breath.

***

The Mutzachans robes were stained with blood all the way up to their waists. The treads of their boots were clogged with gore.

How is this my life? Molphus wondered as he sliced a laser across a pirate's face, cutting clean through his brain pan. The top part of his head fell off, landing upside down. The brains inside quivered like a bowl of obscene jello.

Had it only been three months since he left home?

The fighting hadn't ended with the burning wreckage of the fifty pirates. That was the just the first wave, those who happened to be in front.

Molphus had had to dry his eyes quick and step over the puddles of liquefied people, when the pirates on the other side of the building attacked.

Fire, fire, and more fire. Almon didn't have enough stored energy to generate another omega pulse, so they were forced to use piecemeal tactics.

The Mutzachans raised flux shields with one hand and fired energy blasts with the other. One, two, three. Down the pirates went. Lasers cut into torsos. Lightning scorched organs. Limbs were sliced off. Teeth shattered. To the left, to the right, pirates dropped. Screams, screams everywhere.

Quandle, more skilled than Molphus at the violent arts, generated a thick concentrated beam of energy in the center of his palm and punched a fist sized hole through five pirates at once. They fell on either side, drooping like weeping willow branches, their singed intestines slipping out and becoming entangled like a horror show Gordian Knot.

Molphus was beginning to feel sluggish. They had planned a day and a night for this. Spending the last eighteen hours in mediation, hollowing themselves out, becoming essentially walking power reservoirs. It was an ancient matrix for when one had to absorb vast quantities of energy. They had tapped into the municipal power lines and drained as much as they could. Lights had dimmed across the underground city. Many residents had worried that it was a sign of catastrophic system failure and had begun hording their nuts.

Ten, eleven, twelve.

Three months… The last night before he left

Trishmag he had spent with his fiancée sitting on a sandy hill, relaxing in a tepid breeze. A bottle of irradiated wine was shared and they tested each other's knowledge of the stars, creating new constellations to amuse themselves. They both knew that the star positions were an optical illusion, but the spirits had made them silly. On that hill, each had pledged their fidelity to the other. They gazed into each other's eyes, wrapped in a serene tenderness that seemed to spiral out from galactic zero point and take in all the civilized worlds.

Twenty two. Twenty three. Twenty four.

Now he was an active participant in a slaughter which his brain could scarcely register. It was a dream. He was outside of himself looking at this clockwork mass murderer who wore his face. What kind of morals did he have? How could he live with himself?

Twenty eight. Twenty nine. Thirty.

The street squished beneath Molphus's feet. He kept walking, absorbing, firing. Near him, Quandle laughed. Never before had he been allowed to let loosc like this, to show all of these other species why the Mutzachans were the pinnacle of creation. It was a side of his classmate that Molphus had always suspected was there. He generated a laser, firing it into the eye of an Orion pirate, burning a clear channel out the back of his head.

Thirty seven. Thirty eight. Thirty nine.

The pirates had deserted the streets, either running away or taking up defensive positions on rooftops and around corners. Quadle laughed heartily at the scurrying vermin, firing wildly into the fleeing pirate's backs. Almon said nothing, his face rigid and determined. Molphus could almost read his mind.

He was thinking, *this isn't why we're here.*

***

Click, click, click. The final vote was in. Oxtiern closed his eyes, too nervous to look. It wasn't until Dri of Atch slapped him on the shoulder and congratulated him, that Oxtiern glanced at the tally.

Eighty six percent in favor. A damn good majority. He nearly fainted. It was going to happen! Then a yawn hit him. All the nervous energy left, replaced with exhaustion. He needed a nap.

A human pirate, part of Dri of Atch's command ship The Ram Splitter, rushed up. He tried to whisper to the Admiral, but Oxtiern overheard.

"Sir, there's an incident outside."

***

Almon calculated their remaining energy reserves. They had pushed the pirates back, but had used way too much doing it. At this rate, he might have to tap into his reserve, the amount he had determined he needed to put that one perfect shot into Oxtiern's face. A blast large enough to ensure his brain's total destruction.

They had deliberately not engaged the front entrance, reckoning that it would be congested with pirates. Forcing their way through the back would be the quickest way to Oxtiern. However, the sheer number of dead was slowing them down, making the walk difficult.

For all of his initial sobs and shakiness, Molphus was doing well, Almon noted with satisfaction. Growing pains could be a difficult thing, but the youth had adapted. Quandle was enjoying himself *too* much. He was losing focus. Allowing the sensation of energy exploding through his body to distract him.

Then it happened. From a supposedly secure side door, a masked pirate wearing Arc of Blood markings stumbled out, knocking Quandle over. Immediately behind him, an enraged Ram Python bounded out swinging his race's signature quarterstaff. The pirate rolled away, but Quandle made the mistake of trying to rise (rather than just shooting) and slipped in some blood. Thus giving the Ram time to strike. As the thwack-'em-stick smashed down on his head, Quandle managed to let loose one last burst of power, burning a hole in the reptillian's shoulder.

Molphus screamed, dropping his flux shield. Almon, shaken, fought to maintain control. He blasted at the creature, driving it back, leaving its quarterstaff buried in Quandle's head. Then he fired two shots into the masked pirate's back, who had been dragging himself down the street. The pirate slumped over, adding to the corpse pile.

Almon ran to Quandle's still body, hoping that some miracle had been performed, that he was just stunned. The truth quickly slapped Almon in the face. The quarterstaff was embedded deep in the Mutzachan's head, its metal tip completely obscured.

The skull had caved in. His features were unrecognizable. Both arms stood up at the elbows, reaching for the obscured sky with grasping fingers.

Unfortunately, the battlefield leaves no one time to mourn. Gunfire rattled down from a roof. Molphus, now bathed in cold sweat, barely raised his flux shield in time. Several bullets shook up the cadaver at his feet. A tiny spat of blood bounced up and hit his forehead, then dribbled down into his left eye. Almon's reactions, hampered by age, were not so quick. He took three bullets in the leg. One hit him directly in the foot and a spray of translucent blood spurt up.

Was this it? Was this the end of Almon? *No.* He would crawl in and raze the building around him. Cut a few structural supports and it would all come tumbling down. He'd bury them all in the lowest depths of hell. Suddenly Molphus's arms were around him. At first, Almon thought he was trying to help him stand, but then he sensed the kinetic buildup beneath his feet and realized the truth.

"Damn it, no!" he struggled. "We've got to kill him. Now is our chance."

He was too weak to resist. If there had been a chance, it was wasted. The energy was released, propelling the pair high up into the sky, nearly scraping against the light array dangling from the city's metal canopy. Molphus slowed them down on the decent with successive blasts of counter thrusts, depleting the last of his reserves. Still they landed rough.

The battle was over. Stalemate.

***

Oxtiern listened intently to the report from outside. Mutzachans! Mutzachan here! He knew who it was. He knew. Some cronies of Almon, sent to murder them all.

They had spent too much time on this rock. Assembling the captains had taken too long. Had they done a hyperlink conference, like he had suggested, this wouldn't have happened, but Dri of Atch had explained that the captains would find that disrespectful for reasons Oxtiern couldn't fathom.

"Admiral, I think we need to vacate this dump. All crews. These Mutzachans could be just the beginning."

"I agree," said Dri of Atch in his watery voice. "We can't waste time with a bunch of idiots going trophy hunting on some revenge kick."

"And have that special cargo of mine shipped down from the Arc of Blood. It will keep any would be attackers too busy trying to survive to harm us."

"What is it?"

"An old family heirloom."

Chapter 12 – Stilt

The Plains of Desolation: This sector of the Milky Way consists of thrity eight populated star systems. Through it runs The Highway - a highly traveled trade route of closely clustered systems. It begins on one end with Xensera, traveling through the Alliance hubs of Harper's World and New Hope, spins off to several other minor colonies, before ending at the frozen Phentari slave world of Jillael. Twenty eight parsecs long (868 trillion kilometers), the Highway was established to aid ships in navigating around the Lorrelen and Kathamarse Abysses, vast areas of black with sinister reputations for gulping down vessels. The exact number of ships lost has been exaggerated by the sensationalistic media, but it is well known that several exploratory ships from the Galactic Navy have disappeared in both areas.

Also nearby is the potentially dangerous Aeodronian Protectorate: Four planets colonized by the Aeodronian, a red scabby reptilian race with triple forked tongues, whose dermis is made up of large mucus covered plates. They have resisted every effort to join the Alliance or open up trade negotiations. Several member species have taken this as a sign that they were in league with the Arachnids and have called for an invasion of Aeodronrian space, but these motions have been tabled until the current Arachnid incursion is dealt with.

***

Life had not been rewarding for Raskor-idan. He felt even lower than when he had broken down in his tent. The trial of keeping an idle and newly poor civilian population in check was a monster, especially to one who had trained his entire life to kill those who defied him. He was not meant to be a policeman.

Worst was the mountainous chain of paperwork that poured in from all quarters. Everyone demanded reports on equipment, manpower, incidents, lack of incidents, etc. Often he would be up all night filling in petty details on garbage he couldn't care less about, slaving away until his eyes turned as red as rust.It hadn't started out too bad. The government of Stilt had been officially dissolved by the Alliance and executive authority handed over to the Galactic Marines. The current occupying general, a human, was appointed as military governor. This gave him wide ranging powers in dealing with a fiercely democratic people.

"Things are looking up," Raskor-idan had remarked to Acbisher. "We can start running an efficient operation here."

"If you say so, sir," answered Aebisher, who was cynical about every policy decision issued from military command.

"It will be when we get these people to come round. It's for their own good."

"Yes sir, I'm sure all of the senior citizens and five year olds will be goose stepping in no time."

"What would you prefer? Anarchy?"

"We already have that. Anarchy with paperwork. The only thing keeping these people in check is that we have more guns than they do."

That bit of foreshadowing rolled into reality almost immediately. The day the decree was broadcast to the trapped civilians, riots broke out in nearly every shelter. Part of the problem had been the presentation. They had simply read out the decree by the Alliance, which was so full of bureaucratic and legal jargon that most of the population couldn't follow it. The interpretation that sprung up amongst the refugees was that they had been abandoned on the planet and were under the absolute authority of the military. Wild rumors ran amok: Stories that they were all going to be sold to a Phentari colony for food, or to an Eridani planet for cheap slave labor, or that they were going to be killed because the Alliance didn't want to foot the bill for their care.

"We will not be slaves," they chanted.

It took three days for the unrest to die down. Raskor-idan had been deployed in full riot gear, along with nearly every available soldier. He took the opportunity to release some tension by cracking a few skulls in complete autonomy. It was better than a stress ball. Once they had been calmed down, and it was explained that all civilians would eventually be relocated safely off planet, Raskor-idan was deployed to his new position.

He was currently a block captain in Jericho, tasked with scouting the ruins, enforcing curfew, shutting down the large number of illegal stills that had popped up, and preventing looting. His main problem was that the powers-that-be had neglected to assign any soldiers to assist him in fulfilling his duties. Most of those who were combat ready had been shipped off-planet to the new front line, forcing him to recruit heavily from the refugee population.

The men volunteering for this new civilian police force weren't civic minded heroes, salivating to sacrifice their lives for the good of the body politic. Any one like that had been blown away by the Arachnid invasion. The majority who tried to join were sociopathic losers and military rejects with something to prove, eager to gird their fragile egos with some petty power. Or else they were sleazy grafters, out to shake down the refugees of their last pennies. Like blood hungry vultures they flocked, clamoring for a gun and a badge.

All criminal records had been obliterated, along with the rest of the information networks. So, unless an applicant had been genetically tagged for a crime off world, it was impossible to weed out career felons, rapists, or murderers.

He had been assigned this duty after an altercation with several refugees who were complaining about the water quality, which admittedly was very poor. After assuring the spokesman for the refugees, in his gruff Eridani manner, that everything would be taken care of, the man kept whining, growing angrier, and even striking the table in front of Raskor-idan. This would not do.

"Sir, I am ordering you to go back to your bunk."

"Or what? I'm not one of your idiot soldiers, Captain. You can't order me around."

"You are under military jurisdiction and I outrank you."

"Outrank me? I'm an Alliance citizen with rights. I'm not going to be bullied by some fascist Eridani washout."

It went downhill from there. The man was left with very few teeth. Raskor-idan received a black mark on his record and was transferred to the patrol section. An area that wouldn't bring him into contact with people who weren't breaking the law.

Later, he contemplated on the man's remarks and wondered if someone had been talking about him. Was there a rumor running around the camps? Or maybe it was his dyed hair that gave him away? Perhaps it was just the stereotype that all Eridani in the Alliance military had been rejected from their home planet's forces.

In any case, he had no business mollycoddling a pack of moaners and whiners whom he couldn't discipline. It was a waste of time. If they couldn't fend for themselves, they should be cast out. Were he in charge, Raskor-idan would close all of the camps, cut off supplies, and drive the civilians out into the wilderness. Or put them to some practical use, serving the enlisted men, fixing their meals, building them better barracks, and so forth. That's what would have happened if the Eridani Imperial Navy had taken the planet.

***

Several days later he was sitting in the front cabin of a rumbling armored patrol carrier. It was a beast of a machine, capable of carrying up to twenty troopers, with a sizable pulse cannon mounted atop. The design never took into account a need for air conditioning, so ventilation slits, which doubled as gun ports, had been cut into its sides. He had laid down the rule that every patrol had to be led by at least two regular marines to keep the civilian volunteers in line. But being understaffed with regular marine units, Raskor-idan was forced to go on patrol himself.

Aebisher, seated across from him, perked up. "Something the matter, sir?" he asked. They had known each other long enough for him to be able to pick up on Raskor-idan's moods.

"No, sergeant. Just contemplating."

"If it's about that civilian…"

"No, no."

In truth, it wasn't. The idea that this would be the rest of career had settled in and he was overcome by a general sense of ennui, with a hint of bitterness. He was certainly drinking a lot more.

"Just wondering if I should have ever joined up," he said. *And should I have taken the honorable route of suicide with my siblings and cousins?*

Then he stopped himself. Eridani commanders didn't make small talk with underlings. It was a lapse in personal discipline. One among many lately. But then, did it matter? What had discipline ever brought him?

He looked at Aebisher. The human was a little

slow. Not stupid, but he didn't think much beyond the moment. Good sergeant material. After years of serving together he knew almost nothing about the man beyond his service record. Maybe his background was even worse. Someone else's misery could cheer him up.

"Where are you from again, sergeant?"

"Western New York."

"That's a bacteriological wasteland isn't it?"

Raskor-idan didn't know that for sure, but when dealing with the planet Earth it was usually a safe bet.

"Well," Aebisher lapsed into old memories, "the Mutzachans have cleaned most of it up, but it's still pretty hairy. A lot of still-borns, no jobs, nothing much happens. I joined up the minute I could. Never looked back."

"I see."

"And at the end of all this, I get a nice little pension and can retire wherever the hell I want."

"Are you going to go back then?"

"No way. Parents are dead. Most of my pals are gone. They either joined up or are in jail… or dead themselves. Naw, I'm gonna find a nice warm sandy place to go senile in and stay drunk for about ten years."

So he's happy with things. That revelation did not lift the Eridani's mood. He actually felt a bit of scorn for the human. Imagine being so degraded as a species that this life was a mighty leap forward.

Both of them were wearing standard galactic marine battle armor with their rank insignia emblazoned on the chest plate. At Raskor-idan's side was a plasma rifle, specially souped up to spit much larger blasts - completely against factory recommendations. Across his back was slung his Buddon blade, the same sword he had used to cut off his hand in penance all those years ago. It was dull and rusty, useless in battle. Raskor-idan hadn't tended to it in years. He kept it as a reminder, just as he did with his severed hand and his white hair.

Aebisher sat inspecting his weapons. He preferred powder weaponry of the kind he had learned to use back home. He carefully put down a long barreled automatic shotgun and began to inspect a large caliber revolver. Raskor-idan had chided him in the past of his reliance on such an archaic firearms. In the Eridani's opinion, powder weapons were a peasant's weapon, something only fit for the lower classes. Nothing a true warrior should bother with.

"If it's down to the wire and I got to use my side piece, I want to make damn sure that it won't jam up," Aebisher had retorted.

"Perhaps a more efficient weapon. Such as a laser?"

"Those break down too. Now with my gun, it's all click, pull, bang. Safe and simple."

The captain couldn't argue the logic.

He fiddled with his own gun and peered through a slot at the men in the back. He had forbade them to talk on patrol so they shuffled their feet, played with their helmets, or stared straight ahead. Raskor-idan had nothing but contempt for them.

They were on their way to what was once the warehouse district on the east side of Jericho, near to where the broken tubes of Stilt still loomed over the city. The recently launched satellite signaling feeds had caught a glimmer of a ship dropping into orbit on the other side of the planet and launching several shuttles before departing. Telemetry suggested that the ship might be hiding on the other side of Stilt's moon. The shuttles had flown down, riding along the nape of the earth to deflect radar detection. If they were heading for Jericho City, then the best looting spot would be the warehouse district.

"Coming up, sir," the driver said.

Raskor-idan nodded to Aebisher.

"Weapons ready," the sergeant announced to the men. "I don't want anyone getting trigger happy out there. No one is to shoot unless fired upon first. This is a police action. You're not superheroes battling an arch-villain. Just round them up and we'll cuff them."

They rolled up quickly on the warehouses. The shuttles were parked by several ruined buildings, the cargo hatches open. Orions were running about. Some loading containers, others hauling them out of the buildings. The slack-jawed losers hadn't bothered to post guards, perhaps believing that the area was secluded enough to escape notice, and were completely surprised by the armed men piling out the transport. A few drew hand weapons, but a shot over their heads from Aebisher and the sheer number of pulse rifles pointed at them, convinced the looters to surrender.

"Line them against the wall," Raskor-idan ordered, then went to inspect the cargo containers the Orions were trying to loot.

It was mostly circuitry, electronics, flexi-screens, and so forth. He looked at the prisoners slouching against the wall, most wearing some pirate insignia. Orions, a filthy race of thieves and junkies. One of the two species that had destroyed his family's legacy. There they were, picking their teeth, laughing amongst themselves in their doggerel language, sneering at all decency and honor. This race of scum. What did they ever contribute to the Alliance? Or the universe? He'd had their kind under his command and they were always a problem. Degenerates. There was just something indecent about the entire race.

It was well known that their home planet of Taos was essentially a functional anarchy with close to four hundred different political parties clogging up their senate. Meaning that even the most insignificant piece of legislation had to endure years of debate, alterations, and filibusters. Then, as often as not, the new bill was ignored by the rest of the population. Three times within the last hundred years Galactic Marines had to be dispatched to the Orion home planet just to maintain general order.

Four hundred political parties? Raskor-idan shook his head. *Why would they need more than one?* And there was only a singular party on Eridine - though technically one might refer to it as a faction than party. Their maxim was: One Eridani nation, one people, one direction. All moving in unison towards the brilliant future and the Eridani's ultimate domination of the galaxy. Or at least it had been brilliant until the coming of the Orions and the Phentari.

They did make good cannon fodder though. The captain would give them that. No Orion under his command had ever survived the experience. In his mind they had served their purpose by soaking up bullets that might have killed worthwhile people.

Now this group would be hauled off to waste everyone's time and gobble up precious food and water.

"Hey, hurry the fuck up," one of them yelled. "I need the toilet. Gotta make a fall of Eridine."

The Orion made the appropriate noises to go with the insult, gesturing obscenely to complete the image. All of the looters laughed. Raskor-idan noted that the jokester was wearing a black t-shirt with a pink skull on it which bore the legend "Pimp all Eridani". A fire was kindled in the captain's mind, polluting it with rage.

"Weapons ready," he ordered.

The men quickly complied. Each finger lightly rested on a trigger. Aebisher, his shotgun trained on the Orion in the black t-shirt, looked inquiringly at his commander. Why was the captain ordering this? Had he spotted something that Aebisher missed?

Raskor-idan hesitated, barely keeping himself in check. The order was on the tip of his tongue. Would he plunge over? It would be so easy….

"He's a big talker," the t-shirted Orion sneered a little too forcefully, trying unsuccessfully to cover up that he'd made a fall of Eridine in his pants. "All these Eridani talk their honor shit, but can't stand up when the hammer comes down."

That did it.

"Fire!"

No one pulled their triggers. The men were nervous. A little graft was one thing, but this was just straight up slaughter. Raskor-idan, red heat bleeding in his brain, stepped behind Aebisher and barked into his ear.

"Fire, damn it!"

The sergeant's military instincts were dug in deep. His superior's loud command jerked his finger. The Orion's head became a mesh of red paste and white bone. A second later all of the men had followed suit, emptying their weapons into the helpless Orions.

After it was over, they stood around staring at the carnage they had created. No one bragged. No one displayed any swagger. If anything they were scared. This was a war crime.

Raskor-idan called in for a meat wagon to pick up the bodies.

***

The next day, Raskor-idan was sitting before his Gen-Human colonel, relaxing as best he could in front of his superior's desk, though the cheap plastic chair provided made that difficult. The matter before him was supposedly important, it could potentially end in a court-marshal hearing, but the Eridani just couldn't work up the energy to care. All tension had evaporated from his body, like he'd just had a deep massage. Honestly, he hadn't felt this good in years.

The Colonel shuffled papers, clicked on his

screen, harrumphed a few times, and basically ignored the captain's presence. An old trick to demonstrate authority. Was this technique part of his implanted commissioned officer skill suite, the Captain wondered, or something he had picked up along the way?

"So," the Colonel began. "You state that these looters…"

"Presented a clear threat to the lives of my men, sir," the Eridani said, barely concealing the smugness in his voice. He knew how to juke the system. "They acted absolutely appropriately considering the situation."

"But was it a threat to yourself?" the Colonel asked stone-faced.

That was an unexpected jibe at Raskor-idan's ego. Would he admit that he had been scared? It was against every bit of his training since birth. Fear was never acknowledged. To the ideal Eridani, fear did not exist. It was part of the makeup of lesser races. But he wouldn't hand the man any ammunition, so….

"Yes, sir. I felt that my life, as well as those of my men, were in imminent danger. Hence the correct decision to engage the enemy with lethal force."

"They weren't 'the enemy' captain. They were civilian criminals who needed to be brought in for due process."

"What's the difference… sir? I was there to bring these men in, they resisted. That makes them the enemy by any definition I recognize."

"I understand that your culture has a … different outlook on these things, but you've been enlisted in the Alliance military long enough to know the protocol on handling civilian cases."

"Sir, I'm not sure where this is going," A complete lie. "You have my sergeant's and the men's incident reports and I'm going to assume you've received them."

Of course he had. After they'd finish scraping the corpses off the ground, one of the first things Aebisher did was to get reports from all of the men. While doing so, he impressed upon them the horrors of military prisons and forced labor camps, things that they might have to experience if they were found guilty of murder. They had all quickly fallen into line.

"Yes, I have and they all bear out your statement in general, but there are some very specific inconsistencies which do not jibe. Such as who fired first and so on."

"Well, we can't all be blessed with the perfect eidetic memory of the Gen-Human race…sir."

"Near eidetic. 0.965 on the Oskowitz scale," the Colonel corrected. "But even with the limitations of other races, the inconsistencies here are…"

"I don't see the problem, sir."

"You don't?"

"The punishment for looting in a military area is execution. And there is no doubt that these Orions were guilty. So if they were slated to die in any case, what's the problem?"

"It is completely different. One act is lawful, the other isn't."

"Sounds like a semantic difference to me, sir.

Two definitions for the same thing."

"Captain, I must warn you that I may have to recommend this to a military tribunal and your attitude will be noted."

This bottle born Gen-Human was grating hard on Raskor-idan's nerves. A military tribunal in a sector at war was about the biggest joke there was. Especially when the so-called victims were obvious scum like the Orions had been. When a trial occurred it was usually just for show in case some politician decided to try and advance their career by wingeing about military atrocities. The toothless threat meant about as little as his career did at that point.

Raskor-idan leaned in close.

"Well sir. You do as you feel best. I'm sure your exercise in word play will be given Command's absolute attention."

The Colonel, used to ass lickers, didn't know how to take that. He responded with the feeble, "At the very least you will get black mark on your record." *Oh horror!* "And I'm putting you and your sergeant on restricted duties until the matter is resolved."

Which could be years considering the backlog of cases being racked up in The Plains of Desolation sector alone. Raskor-idan rose and gave a quick Alliance salute. The meeting was over whether the Colonel wanted it to be or not. He left the building whistling an old Eridani hymn. There would be no self-chastisement for him tonight. This was a victory, even if his superiors refused to see it.

Chapter 13 – Stilt

Species: Homo Sapien Sapiens (colloquially called Humans)

Planet of Origin: Earth in the Sol system.

Description: The Human race is in a rapid decline due to prolonged use of nuclear, biological, and chromosomal weaponry which has poisoned their genetic stock. Fertility rates decrease, while unviable fetuses bearing an incredible number of regressive traits are growing. Huge tracts of their home planet are uninhabitable. Research is being conducted by various Earth agencies and the Mutzachan Biologic Conglomerate to arrest this downfall. It is estimated that within five to six generations the Human species will be so reduced in population, that it will be unable to maintain itself as a power in the Alliance. These predictions lead to the development of the Gen-Human. This has caused many to believe that the Humans are simply puppets of the Mutzachan race.

Freaky Fact: Take a look in the mirror and tell me

what you see.

***

Restricted duties for Raskor-idan and his sergeant meant being shipped off to immigration control, a bureaucratic post tasked with transitioning the civilian population off planet: either to other colonies, their species' home planets, or any place willing to take them.

"Not exactly a stepping stone," Aebisher had quipped. "More a puddle of quicksand."

They took the survivor's details, processed it across the hypernet, and arranged transport for the lucky few. Unfortunately, due to a chronic manpower shortage and the ferocity of the fighting in the sector, only seven men were allocated to this office, which slowed everything to a crawl.

Initially they had used the surviving ships of the Colonial Naval Network to transport the refugees, but they had all been recently drafted into service by the Galactic Navy to engage the invading Arachnids. The only seats they could find afterwards were piecemeal on passing cargo freighters or escaping civilian vessels.

The captain in charge of immigration control was another broken Eridani who had taken a bolt of electrified steel in his brain. This gifted him with regular uncontrollable seizures, which the medics could not cure, making him useless for frontline command. He was stuck in this position until his pension matured. Of the other six: three were disciplinary cases, two were chronic alcoholics, and the last was a near illiterate.

One would think that the two captains, both being Eridanis trapped in an alien culture, would get along, but that didn't happen. Captain Sammas-ican took one look at his counterpart's dyed white dreadlocks, penance scars, and self-severed cybernetic hand and spat on the ground in disgust. Raskor-idan knew why. He looked at the other's naturally brown hair, trimmed tight into a Mohawk, and saw the lack of self-mutilation. He knew that whatever had brought the Captain into Alliance service, it had nothing to do with being a near exile from Eridani society, as he was.

"I won't work with this cowardly scum," Sammas-ican roared.

Raskor-idan wasn't upset by the insult. He understood perfectly. Still, custom demanded that he at least make a token effort to defend his honor. So he upended the other's desk, scattering the contents about the makeshift office.

"If you wish retribution," Raskor-idan said coldly. "I am willing to meet you on the field of honor and battle to the death."

The other Eridani became so filled with apoplectic rage that it triggered a seizure. He fell to the ground, face flushed blood red, and rattled about. Froth spat from his mouth.

Realizing that the situation between the two would only get worse, the Colonel took quick steps. Immigration control was split into two sections. The mission of Raskor-idan's new unit was to vet the credentials of any incoming civilians or non-military government officials. A joke more than anything. Who would visit a ruined ghost of a planet on the edge of a battle zone?

"At least we won't be up late doing paperwork anymore," said Aebisher.

The pair were banished to a crumbling basement on the other side of the base, fitted only with a few pencils and a cast-off terminal. They spent their days watching their fingernails grow and playing video games on their personal devices. Aebisher managed to occupy himself by trying to rid the building of a scavenging insect horde that had infested the walls of the upper floor. But no matter how many hundreds he gassed, they bred even faster. Eventually he gave up.

Raskor-idan was becoming quite skilled at *Mazian Bubble Bounce*. He found its mindless simplicity soothing, spending hour after hour perfecting the art of keeping the grey blob afloat as needles rained down. When the game was on, the world tuned out, and his universe curved into a collection of multi-hued pixels where the answer to every problem was a click on the screen. He played it so much that the game's jingly music began to haunt his dreams.

Then one day the unthinkable happened. Just as he was about to perform a difficult maneuver involving three green bubbles and a spinning rainbow disk, an order flashed across his tablet. An immigration request for two civilians to land on Stilt. The interruption caused him to misfire and ended the game. He flipped onto the paperwork, half expecting it to be an idiotic joke.

It wasn't.

The application was for a Zen Rigeln and his Ram Python assistant traveling under diplomatic insignia from the Canton of Labor, part of the Zen Rigeln home government of Katrel. The Ram was ludicrously listed as a "cultural attaché". What caught his attention most was that under *purpose of visit*, the dignitary had typed, "business considerations and to visit my old friend Raskor-idan". He didn't recognize the names on either application, but the credentials passed the authentication check on both the military database and DNA profiles.

"What the hell kind of business could they have here?" asked Aebisher after he had read the request. "There's no industry, no farming, no livestock. Maybe they want a deal on broken glass and gravel."

"Or they're trying to secure the mineral rights, now that the planet's government has been dissolved."

Aebisher scratched his chin. "I don't see what the Zen government would want with them. There's nothing unique here. It would cost more to transport them back to Katrel than they could make in profit."

"The Zen government isn't interested in profits," Raskor-idan said with respect in his voice. "They are a deeply spiritual people."

He did have respect for them. The pacifist dogma of their ruling body was a not an easy road to take. While it was almost exactly opposite of his own upbringing, he admired the dedication it took to maintain their stance. Granted it was only possible due to every other race's willingness to protect them during the Arachnid invasion, but it was incredibly brave to stand firm in the face of genetic annihilation. That was something he could admire, even with the race's well-deserved reputation for sanctimoniousness. There was only one Zen he had ever met who didn't fit the bill, but that was a horror story for another day.

"So who is this guy? Why does he want to see you?"

"I have absolutely no idea."

The pair signed out a vehicle from the motor pool and drove to where the diplomats had been quartered. The building had once been a thirteen story hotel, designed to satiate the desires of middle managers and low level executives. The Arachnid bombardment had sheered it off at the third floor, adding to the mammoth piles of rubble all around. The foundation was cracked, water damage had destroyed most of the furniture, plaster dust was everywhere, and spider web cracks ran up and down every wall and ceiling. It had been selected because it was isolated from any other occupied area. The brass did not want non-military snoops wandering about the base, especially some political type here on dubious business.

A room on the first floor had been hastily policed up to accommodate the visitors. There was no heating, food, or water, except for a few bottles supplied from the refugee camp. All power came from a small generator that had been quickly screwed into the building's wiring. A passive aggressive gesture from the military governor. *Don't get too comfortable.*

Inside the room, they found Oxtiern lounging on a ruined couch. A Ram Python was standing near him, staring at a blank wall. Oxtiern sat up when they entered.

"Lieutenant," he said.

"It's captain now." The Eridani turned to Aebisher. "Wait outside sergeant."

"Are you sure sir?"

"Completely. Stay by the door. If I need you, I'll yell."

After Aebisher left, Raskor-idan seated himself in a plastic chair across from the Zen. Neither spoke for a minute.

Oxtiern, Oxtiern. He mused. *Not a reunion I'd have wished for.* The Zen had been attached to his unit as a field medic back in the day, though he had enjoyed using his powers to rip the meat off of enemies and infect them with horrific diseases much more than healing. He remembered that one of Oxtiern's favorite tricks was to burrow holes in captured soldiers, then necrotize the dermis around the wound, accelerating the decay with his abilities. He had reveled in the victim's screams as limb after limb dropped dead in the front of the captive, the flesh rapidly rotting off the bone.

They had been deployed on several campaigns together. Rooting out rebels on Lothal, dealing with an infestation of hairy-backed monsters created by the illegal genetics dealers of ARM (the same delightful people who produced the Fott race), thwarting Arachnid scouts on Klendathu, hunting Alliance traitors on Harpers World, and burning out pirate clan after pirate clan from hidden bases and stolen orbital platforms.

Attrition rates had been high in those days. Raskor-idan had persistently pushed for the most dangerous assignments, the better to heap military honors on his name. Somehow, the Zen Rigeln always managed to survive. Oxtiern had been good at his job, despite the sadism, so the captain had put up with him… for a while.

The breaking point came when Oxtiern captured a pirate and infected both his legs with accelerated gangrene. He then started a pool with the other troops, betting on which side would reach the torso first. After he'd discovered this, Raskor-idan decided he'd had enough. He filled out the paperwork recommending that Oxtiern be promoted and transferred to the interrogation division, where his atrocious hobbies might be put to some good use. Later, he'd heard that there had been an official inquiry around the Zen, but couldn't remember the details.

Oxtiern took a golden cylindrical object with a thick needle on one end out of a bag and placed it flat on the coffee table between them. The Eridani didn't react, he was too busy remembering the foul smells from the pirate's legs. He assumed it was some sort of torture device.

"So you've changed your name?"

"Briefly. I'll go back to the old one soon

enough."

"I could have you arrested for this. Forging credentials is a serious crime. Diplomatic ones even more so. Ten years hard labor, easy."

Oxtiern smiled. *Probably the least of his current crop of crimes*, Raskor-idan reckoned.

"If you did that you wouldn't be able to hear why I've come. It's in your best interest to listen."

Was that a threat or an offer? "How so?"

"I hear you've taken quite a tumble. Immigration control on a wasteland planet. What a useless non-job. For an Eridani warrior it must be intolerable."

No denying that truth, but he knew that Oxtiern was just buttering him up for some appalling pitch. Why wasn't he dead yet? Why hadn't he been locked away for life?

"How did you hear about that?"

"It doesn't matter. You're still wearing the white disgrace." He pointed at Raskor-idan's hair. "Haven't redeemed yourself yet? The military hasn't been the path to advancement you'd hoped? At this rate, that will be the epitaph on your tombstone."

Raskor-idan focused on the golden needle. Its shiny surface allured him. He thought he could spot Human symbols running down its base. Was it some piece of stolen military equipment? A great deal of the Alliance military hardware manufacturing was outsourced to Earth and other impoverished Human colonies as part of a welfare make-work program to aid their floundering economy. One of the perks of sucking up to the Mutzachans.

"Things must be weighing on you," Oxtiern

continued. "An undistinguished career in the service of an uncaring bureaucracy. This isn't Eridine where they honor their fallen soldiers, where even the lowliest Buddon warrior can hold their head up high."

He said nothing. Wouldn't even blink. His muscles gave no tell as to his true thoughts. Oxtiern took the silence as an opportunity.

"In this army, what are you? A number in a long list of numbers. Once you're out or dead, what happens to your legacy? It's deleted and replaced by another number. One less piece of meat for the machine."

Still no reaction.

"What if I could inject some meaning into your life again? A venture of great audacity. Something that will sing throughout the galaxy. Maybe it will even be enough for them to remove the white disgrace from your head."

Raskor-idan chuckled. The white disgrace wasn't something done to him. It was self-imposed, demanded by honor. A debt to his race that needed to be redeemed. Oxtiern's ignorance of this exposed his base nature. He couldn't conceive of anyone announcing failure so publicly. None but the Eridani could. Raskor-idan had always found the concept of honor in every other Alliance race lacking. Even Aebisher, despite his bravery, could never truly grasp the idea.

"Think of it," continued Oxtiern, misinterpreting the Eridani's laugh. "All your sins forgiven. Welcomed back to your planet with laurels and accolades."

He was pouring it on thick. It was an intoxicating idea, but then the smell of the pirate's leg returned. Whatever Oxtiern was offering, honor would not be a part of it.

"I don't think I can help you."

Oxtiern blinked.

"But you haven't even heard the deal yet."

'That's true, but I still can't offer you anything."

The wall behind him shook. Bits of plaster fell off the ceiling. The Ram Python had punched a large hole in the wall, exposing the wires and struts beneath. The blow had been so powerful that the lights flickered under the impact.

"You'll have to forgive him," the Zen said smoothly. "He's recently lost his favorite toy. It makes him a bit edgy."

Raskor-idan waved it away. A nuisance, nothing. But he began to calculate whether he should shoot Oxtiern or the Ram first if it came to violence.

"If you won't sign on, maybe I can offer you a little something to aid you in your old age. Military pensions aren't much to retire on and it seems you're not going to die gloriously in battle."

It was at this moment Raskor-idan had a revelation. All his doubts about his past, his questions about duty, the validity of his discipline, were struck down by the sneering words from Oxtiern's foul lips. He knew that whatever happened to him, he would not sink as low as the Zen. Having tarnished honor was better than none at all. Perhaps he *was* being an idiot for clinging to his heritage, but he'd rather be a fool than an amoral monster spreading his disease across the galaxy.

"How much?"

"Seventy thousand for a little bit of information."

"That's a lot for a little."

"A consignment of ultra armor is being stored here before being dispatched to the front lines. I need the exact location, the type of security systems in the storage facility, and the number of personnel deployed to that area. Specific races of those on duty would be useful as well."

The conceit of this Zen. How dare he. How *dare* he. Did he honestly believe that everyone was as corrupt as himself? Raskor-idan raised his cybernetic hand and clenched it into a fist. Oxtiern groaned. He'd heard this one before.

"Do you remember how this hand was severed?"

"Yeah. You chopped it off in a fit of buyer's remorse."

He ran his hand over the wounds he had carved into his temple.

"These lacerations are honor touched. Part of the life of the Buddon warrior tradition. And while I failed to live up to its standards, I have never abandoned it."

Oxtiern laughed long and loudly, right in the Eridani's face.

"To think that I would throw it all away for some petty personal profit...."

"You people and your delusions. You act like you're in some movie where the celestial audience is judging how you act. There's no scoreboard tallying up your honor points. No one cares about you. No one gives the least damn about your pathetic life. Ten minutes after you croak, you will be forgotten. Time to wake up!"

Oxtiern snatched the golden needle off the table and waved it at the other's head.

"I thought I would try this the easy way for old time's sake," the Zen said menacingly. "But you are going to join me whether you like it or not. Even better, your imaginary honor won't be stained because you don't have a choice. Say, 'thank you'."

The Zen gestured to the Ram Python, who grabbed at Raskor-idan. The Eridani had seen this coming and, lightning quick, knocked the chair over. He dodged across the room, as the Ram grabbed a fistful of air, banging his shin hard on the coffee table. Raskor-idan, in one fluid motion, unholstered his weapon and aimed it at the Zen's head.

Oxtiern laughed and the Ram leapt in front of Raskor-idan blocking the shot, his hands twitching for a fight. He shot Ika Dhole twice in the stomach, but it barely slowed the reptile down. The Ram landed a right fist across Raskor-idan's face. Fireworks exploded in his head. He could see nothing but little indigo spots of light. The Eridani heard his own face break open, felt the floor crash around him, tasted metallic blood. The methane converter which allowed him to breathe cracked, life giving gas escaped. He wheezed, sucking in as much as he could.

Up, up, up solider! The enemy is on you. Kill them all.

His vision cleared slightly. Oxtiern stood over him. One of his hands rested on the Ram Python's arm, blue power flowed into the other creature, sealing up flesh, causing platelets to cluster faster, stopping the errant blood loss. The reptile's twin stomach wounds curled up and vanished before Raskor-idan's eyes. In his other hand lay the golden needle. Oxtiern looked down at him.

"Now it's time for an attitude adjustment."

"Aebisher," yelled Raskor-idan.

The door kicked open and the sergeant was inside in a heartbeat. He leveled his shotgun at Oxtiern's head.

"No diplomatic immunity from a slug in the skull," Aebisher snarled.

The Zen hesitated. He took his hand off of Ika Dhole.

"Try me. Please try me," the sergeant taunted.

He backed off, pulling the Ram with him. The reptile didn't understand at first. He stood there drooling at Aebisher, his beady red eyes slavering with a desire to break and maim. Finally, Oxtiern kicked him and the Ram retreated.

"Get up, sir. Now."

Raskor-idan, his head still rattled, teetered weakly to his feet. The lack of methane debilitated him further. He could barely think. To rise, he had to grab onto a broken light fixture and pull himself fully erect. His face was puffing up. The left eye was completely swollen and the right still had imaginary lights dancing before it. Moving his jaw even slightly sent a deep ache through the rest of his head.

Hefting the shotgun in one hand, Aebisher slid the other around his captain and pulled him through the door. Raskor-idan was grateful for this, though he'd never admit it. Had he gone more than three steps on his own, he would have collapsed.

"Get off the planet," the Eridani yelled as he limped away. "If I see you again Oxtiern, I will kill you!"

Chapter 14 – The Arc of Blood, orbiting the moon of Stilt

Species: Fott

Planet of Origin: None or Earth- Depending on your perspective

Description: The species was cultivated from the Earth rabbit by the Anarchist Rebellion Movement (ARM)- a renegade scientific organization which develops illegal genetic weaponry and acts as the middle man in arms deals for various terrorist outfits. Realizing they had created a sentient race that propagated at the same rate as their ancestor species, ARM spread the Fotts across a hundred planets. They then had their lawyers represent the species in Alliance courts to gain them rights as a full member race. This was to help the group gain influence in the highest Alliance decisions, but also acted as an advertisement for ARM, demonstrating just how good they were at their jobs.

Freaky Fact: Fotts do not support the theory of a central government. Rather, they believe that they cannot be governed by anyone other than themselves. Many hypothesize that this trait was encoded in their genetic makeup, but others dismiss it as ludicrous. They begrudgingly accept Alliance rule and exploit as many Alliance resources as they can legally obtain. Then ask for more.

***

First love, young love. Denied! Drake was the living image of misery. He moped about refusing to talk to anyone, then secluded himself in empty cargo bins and had long crying jags. In-between, he wrote painfully bad poems about love and emptiness and darkness.

Parg and Jack Mace got ahold of one of these and read it aloud over the ship's communication system.

"Here's a little ditty written by our resident scar-faced bojing, Drake," Parg slurred into the speaker.

"Our love was a brief stop meshed in a brief
moment,
Of pure bliss, desire, and delight.
As we parted in the darkness to other worlds
I remember your body vividly, fondly..."

Drake raced to find the pair but they were too well hidden. Loud laughter rolled from the bunk holes and dank nooks where the other pirates amused themselves. There was a brief pause while the pair burst into sadistic hooting. Jack Mace took over as Parg couldn't stop his cackling.

"Your face with wide flaps

Your spicy scent as I lie ever so close to
you,
And your large lips,
I tasted heaven within you...
Could we have stayed a moment longer?
Instead of heading into the cold emptiness
of vast space,
Save a kiss for me my love,
For I will find those lips again even if it
takes me forevermore..."

More laughter. Mocking insults were yelled at him as he ran down the halls. It was too much. Just too much. Tears streamed down his face. His pain had been ripped open for all these scum to mock. He found a dark hole, a disused crew locker room, and lay down in a corner.

Drake had been near death when the pirates dragged his body back up to the Arc of Blood. He had tried to fight them off as they put him on the shuttle. He needed to stay behind, be with Annette, but the shots from the Mutzachans had burned deep and the four cracked ribs made him feeble. He could barely grasp onto consciousness, much less fight off the hands carrying him.

"Why bother with this one?" Drake dimly heard a pirate say, as they dumped him onto a metal bench. "He's a goner."

"Toilets ain't gonna fix themselves," was the reply.

Yes, leave me, Drake thought. *Let me die in Annette's pillowly arms*. Then the world went black for an eternity.

When he woke, he was in the Arc of Blood's infirmary. The ships "doctor", an incredibly gaunt human, was shuffling about. His assistant/lover was sitting on the floor against a wall, passed out in a drug stupor. Several needles dangled out of the assistant's track mark scared arms.

On a gurney next to Drake was a dead Python Lizard pirate. Half an autopsy had been performed on the body. It was cut down the middle with the rib cage sawn in half. The individual ribs stood straight up from the corpse like spines on a porcupine. The doctor was pulling organs out of the body and dumping them into a plastic bin marked "Phentari feed".

Drake was hungry and dehydrated. He croaked through broken lips. Pain from his cracked ribs shuddered up his frame. The healing injections had mended the wounds from the lasers, but couldn't make his broken bones knit faster. The doctor, alerted by Drake's moans, came over. His skin was taut, yellow, and unnaturally red around the rims of his eyes. His gums had receded so far up into his mouth that the teeth were hanging on by their barest roots.

"Still in pain, huh? I've got something that can help with that." The doctor licked his lips. "Course it'll have to cost you. Limited supplies ya know?"

Drake said nothing. The doctor touched his wounded side and he couldn't help but groan.

"Cause if you really needed something I might be able to dig up a pill or two, a shot, maybe a line of powder. All that comes from my personal stash, so I'd have to sell it as a private citizen, huh. Wouldn't be fair otherwise."

He gave no response, just slid off the table and began to awkwardly limp out the door. The assistant snorted as Drake passed him and woke briefly to wipe a gummy film of saliva from his chin before lapsing back into a sweet opiate haze.

"It's your choice, bojing. I'll be here when it all gets to be too much," the doctor called after him and went back to harvesting the dead pirate's body parts.

Drake dragged himself down the halls, past pirates laughing or crying, depending on their feelings towards the clan mates slain by the Mutzachans. Parg wasn't in his room, which gave Drake the brief hope that he had been killed. That was dashed when the Orion returned to grab some cash from his locker before running off to a gambling game in the ship's underbelly. Drake climbed into his bunk and passed out.

He held up for days in the locker room. Wallowing in grief, nursing the hurt. Dreaming of the touch and taste of his big, beautiful girl. He could feel her, almost smell her on his clothes. Food tasted like ash. The air was tainted by despair. Life had no meaning anymore.

To distract himself, he tapped into the newsfeeds, gathering snippets of information, reminding himself that there were worlds beyond his own. The war was moving on from Cassel to Jourheim. For a time, the Arachnids had been beaten back until their reinforcements arrived, which caused an even greater escalation of hostilities. The Merchants of Doom out of Harper's World was a lock for the Cyball championship this season. Spiff Blasthandy was renewed for season eight. The Galactic Stock index was up ten points. Jaquassarious Phentari had broken several of his colleagues out of a maximum security prison in a raid that left twenty dead. It was no good, he couldn't get her out of his mind.

There was a faint hope that he would be able to make it back to her one day. But then how would she react? From her perspective he must have just disappeared. Another lousy pirate with a line of talk and an empty soul. What did she think of him? That was the worst part, the idea that she might hate him, might look upon their time together with disgust. That she might curse his name. The thought was overwhelming.

"There you are, ya little fuck. I been wandering over this here whole ship looking for yer dumb ass."

Jack Mace stood over him, his black fur now lush and shiny. He had somehow managed to find a shower and give himself a shampoo.

"Yer still agonizing over this slop wife?" he said. "Christ kid, when are you gon' toughen up?"

"Go away."

"Next port we'll get you another one. Better yet, a hooker."

"Go away."

"You know what they say. You don't pay hookers to have sex with you. You pay 'em to get lost afterwards."

"Go away!"

Drake rolled over to stare at the wall. Jack Mace fumed for a moment, angry at Drake's refusal to consider his sage advice. He sucked on a ginseng cigarette until his temper cooled. After he crushed the butt, he tossed a data tube at the sullen Gen-Human.

"Here. It's full of that Spiff Spaceshit that you like. Cheer the fuck up, will you?"

Then he walked out. But not far, Drake could hear him jawing with another pirate just down the hall. The Fott had that wild wheedling tint in his voice that came on whenever he talked conspiracies.

"It's the Pascians, man. The Pascians. Them little bowlin' pin shaped things with eight legs."

"What's a bowling pin?"

"It's an Earth thing, you know?"

"No I don't know."

"Shut up. Listen…"

Drake popped the tube into his data pad and cycled through the episodes. They were all illegal copies, of course, and mostly from season four. It was a pretty good season. He'd seen them all, but it had been awhile. Perhaps this would help purge the loneliness in his life. Junk food for the soul.

He flipped on a random episode. The title flooded the screen, showing Spiff Blasthandy's vow to defeat the Arachnid menace and save the universe. Spiff strutted proudly into the top secret control room. His feline Cizerack companion, Cloe, beside him. The Chief, grim and grizzled, with a mysterious past, gave him his orders as he did every week.

"Them Pascians, they're a Mutzachan conspiracy!"

"What, the whole race?"

"Yeah. They were genetically developed by the

Mutzachans to destroy us."

"They're just little babbling weirdos."

"That's a defensive technique built inta them. So that we ignore them while they work their evil."

Spiff, Cloe, and group of no-name Galactic Control agents blasted off from the secret base in the heart of the Earth's sun. Destination, Thoh. A rebel group operating out of there had suddenly acquired a host of advanced weaponry. Why are they rebelling? Because they hate freedom! The Chief smelled Arachnids behind the scenes.

"Let me put it this way. Where do these Pascian's come from?"

"I don't..."

"You don' know. No one does. Not even them."

"So?"

"They don' know because they were built in a lab by the Mutzachans."

"Yeah, but..."

"The Gen-Human's were created. Us Fotts too. So why not the Pascians?"

"Just because you were, doesn't mean they were."

"Then where do they come from? Look it up. You won't fucking find anything."

The Mutzachan ring of power on Spiff's hand glowed brightly as the group approached the planet. That meant Arachnids. Spiff's jaw set in steely determination. His worst fears were confirmed. The great enemy was behind these rebel outbreaks. They must be stopped.

Drake was moved. Yes! Yes! This was true

action, true heroes, true adventure. How he wished he could be part of them. Then he could truly come into his own.

"After all that shit went down with them fat head fucks blowing holes in everyone, how can you doubt it?"

"But that had nothing to do with the Pascians."

"It's all part of the Mutzachan master plan."

"And those babbling retards, how do they fit?"

"They got powers."

Spiff and crew descended onto the planet. All seemed peaceful at first, but Cloe the Cizerack sniffed trouble at the Independent Veteran Aid Society. Entering and searching it under the authority of Galactic Control, the group discovered a secret elevator that jetted down into a dark and sinister lair. There, they found the members of the rebel factions encased in cone shaped glass and metal containers. The tops of their heads had been removed. Thin wires and tubes pumped Arachnid poison into their vulnerable brains. It was all an Arachnid plot. It must be stopped.

"They can like change things."

"Ah, diabolical."

"You don't believe me?"

"Well what are you talking about? Change things?"

"They can adjust uh…what's the word? Like uh uh uh probability! They kin change probable outcomes, so the Mutzachans always come out on top."

"I've never heard that before."

"That's why it's so insidious. There was a ton of us down on the planet, right?"

"Yeah."

"And they knocked the shit out of us. How do you think they did that?"

"Because they can channel their energy matrices and…"

"No, because these Pascians like manipulated the probabilities so their chances were a hundred percent. That's the only way that makes sense."

"But we drove them off."

"They retreated, not the same thing. Musta run out of energy pellets or something."

"One of them died. How'd that happen if their chances were a hundred percent?"

Further on in the bowels of this abominable place, Spiff and his crew came across the Arachnid forces controlling the planet. A lengthy battle ensued with both sides spitting bolts of hot death across a lava filled cavern. Most of the no-name agents went down gloriously, taking Arachnid warriors with them, their bodies exploding with fantastic goriness. While Cloe ripped the throat out of a Maelstrom General, Spiff bravely faced the Arachnid Lord. Ferociously, they battled. Despite the danger, Spiff would not take cover, would not back down. He stood straight, firing round after round into the monster. It seemed undefeatable, until the Mutzachan ring of power glowed as brightly as the sun. Spiff aimed the ring at the Lord. The power was released and the Arachnid crumbled beneath the blast. It fell, bleeding from a hundred wounds and leaked its life across a stone floor. Spiff left the planet triumphant in his righteousness. He radioed to the Chief. Mission accomplished. Arachnid threat neutralized. The End.

Wow. Just wow.

"That coulda been a ruse."

"Its skull was crushed, I saw it. You're out of your mind."

"I'll crush *your* fucking skull!"

Drake had had enough of this. He shook the creakiness out of his joints and stuck his face out of the doorway. Jack Mace had an Orion pirate pinned to the wall, a laser pointed at his head, its muzzle buried deep into the Orion's cheek. The Fott's ears were pulled back, nearly sticking out straight, indicating intense homicidal anger. The crew member must have been new, Drake didn't recognize him.

"You know," Drake said loudly, stepping into the hall, "probability isn't a force or energy that can be manipulated. It's a mathematical construct that attempts to determine the likelihood of an outcome. Math, numbers, equations, don't exist outside of the brain. If you fiddle the figures it doesn't change anything in the real world."

Jack Mace dropped the pirate who ran off.

"Look who's back from the dead to be an asshole."

He shoved the gun in Drake's face. When they first met, Drake would have cowered, but one of the things he'd learned was that none of these pirates were brave. Most were straight up cartoon bullies. If you stood up for yourself, they'd usually back down quick. Drake stared Jack straight in his pink eyes.

The Fott's whiskers twitched excitedly.

"Now what are you going to do with that Jack? Weld on a bigger cock? The one you've got is a peashooter."

Jack's eyes narrowed. His tongue darted in and out of his mouth, licking bits of debris from the front teeth. Everything was tense. Very tense. Then… relaxed. Mace burst out laughing.

"You're starting to come into yourself, punk. Good for you."

Drake sighed inwardly. Had Mace wanted to kill him, he would've fell like a house of cards. The Fott draped an arm over Drake's shoulders and led him away.

"Let's see if we can scare up a drink. You know you're lucky. I was about to burn off your face, but we get along all right."

It was the friendliest thing Drake had heard on the pirate ship.

***

After four weeks of straight hyperspace travel, the Arc of Blood reached its destination. It would have been much faster to use a stargate, there had been one in a nearby system. However, word had gotten around the clan that there was a priority alert out to Galactic Navy vessels ordering them to board any ship suspected of being affiliated with Black Flag. One ship, The Eon Raptor, had attempted to enter a gate and was destroyed in a firefight after several light cruisers descended on it. It was weird, considering the heightened conflict of the war. The navy should definitely have had higher priorities. Jack Mace blamed it on the Mutzachans as usual. This was the first time that Drake believed him.

During the month of travel, Drake stopped even pretending to work. He interacted little with the crew, usually trading insults or making promises to fix things that he immediately forgot about.

The crew was on edge. Despite the carnage at the end, they had enjoyed their time on Myntal 5. For most of them it had been broads and booze, gambling and gorging. Now the party was over and the daily drudgery felt even worse.

"Why can't it just be like that all the time?" many of them openly whined.

To add to the general malaise, by the time they had rendezvoused with the other pirate ships behind the moon of Stilt, the ship was dry. Every drop of alcohol had been soaked up, which upset Parg more than anyone. A still had been briefly erected, brewing a concoction made from fermented fungus, industrial lubricant, and some green fluid found leaking down a wall. But after several pirates went permanently blind and another died when the solution burned a hole in his stomach, the Captain clamped down. Craw threatened to space anyone even holding a bottle of the stuff. Those caught brewing it would be turned into sweet meat.

Drake shuddered when he heard that proclamation. He'd caught a whisper that the last of the captured sweet meat from the Orion freighter was "gone". He didn't want to know what that meant.

Occasionally he sensed greedy eyes feeling him up, but for now no one made a move.

Parg flipped out over the ban.

"I'm on strike," he declared, parking himself in his stolen lawn chair. "They can't treat people like this."

The Orion's hand trembled as he gripped the chair arms. All four of his thumbs twitched uncontrollably. He was true to his word. Parg did not get up for anything, spending hours watching incredibly violent movies, usually starring some monosyllabic hero who wiped out entire tribes of indigenous peoples. Other times, he lapsed into a deep sleep that lasted days, voiding himself where he sat. Drake did not clean him up.

Drake was idling the day away with Jack Mace when the call came for a full crew meeting.

"This is it boy," Jack slapped him on the chest. "We're 'bout to see some action."

The cafeteria was used for the meeting. Every bench was jammed, every inch of wall was being leaned on. Jack and Drake stood at the back. Most of the crew was present, except for those piloting, a few in engineering, and Parg. At the front of the assembly stood the Captain, Craw, Skel, Oxtiern, Ika Dhole, and a Gen-Human. The stranger was dressed in a Galactic Marine uniform with lieutenant's insignia. He had a bandage around his head and a glassy stare. The Gen-Human swayed back and forth uneasily.

"Pay attention," The Captain began. "The target is a military supply depot located on the planet below. They are currently storing a thousand brand new suits of ultra armor. We plan to take them all."

Low whistles came from the crew. This was going to be tricky. Those things weighed two tons each and were bulky as hell. Timing was going to have to be precise.

"The coordinates of the depot and the garrison strength have been supplied by our friend Oxtiern," the Captain gestured to the Zen. "We will be doing this raid jointly with our cousin ships, the Slioshotanizi and the Ergenstrasse. But even with their aid, we will need every hand to shift the cargo before the military can retaliate."

The captain pushed a button and a topographical map of Stilt appeared on the ceiling. He zoomed in on the image until the depot, highlighted in red, was in sharp focus.

"The actual garrison won't present much of a problem," the Captain continued. "As usual, we'll bombard the area with comwave jamming spikes. How many, Skel?"

"Around four hundred," the Zen first mate replied.

"Right. Then we will send in the heavy gunners to strafe the auto defenses, while the ground boys kill the remaining staff. No prisoners."

The Captain stepped back and motioned to Skel. The first mate cleared his throat.

"Everyone needs to be fully suited up," he said. "Even those just shifting cargo, because it seems that one of our cousins got greedy and sent down a raiding party to loot a few warehouses. None of them made it back."

The Arc of Blood crew groaned. Bastards. Greedy idiots.

"So the marines may be alerted to a larger raid. Be careful and kill anything that's not ours. Craw will give you the details of the operation and landing squad rosters."

Craw stomped out, butting Skel out of the way. The first officer retreated, but everyone saw a smirk plainly on his face. He must've gotten something over on the Cizerack recently. In his sing-song voice, Craw listed off name after name. As usual, Drake found himself lumped in with Jack Mace and Parg. They would be operating lifts to haul the ultra armor onto the shuttles. He was surprised to see that Oxtiern, Skel, and Craw would also be on-hand below, helping in the raid. The Captain truly meant everyone.

Drake was very happy. An idea of escape bloomed in his mind. *Maybe, with all of the activity I can slip away. Then I can hitchhike on another vessel and get back to Myntal 5.*

What could go wrong?

Chapter 15 – Stilt

Galactic Alliance: The Galactic Alliance is the most prominent ruling body in the Milky Way Galaxy. It was formed in 2108 as a mutual defense pact against the First Arachnid Invasion and has remained in operation ever since. There are 4 basic bodies to the Alliance infrastructure: executive, legislative, judicial, and administrative. The executive branch is run by the Council of Timar (each member race has two representatives) and headed by the Galactic President. It formulates polices and new laws. The legislative lower council, each with a representative from the 11, 917 member worlds, officially votes on said laws. The administrative branch deals with military and enforcement duties, and also handles various bureaucratic agencies necessary to run a government. And the judicial branch adjudicates trade disputes, handles civil complaints, and rules on criminal violations. After the first invasion, the Alliance expanded rapidly and now that the second invasion is underway, it is actively pushing for new races and worlds to join them.

***

The Mutzachans were dead tired and barely talking to each other. On the journey from Myntal 5 they kept their words to a bare minimum. Quandle's death hung between them like a toxic cloud. Even when they aided each other with the necessary blood cleansing to rid the fattened reed worms from their system, they communicated only in grunts.

Now they sat in a reception area waiting for an audience with the military governor of Stilt. The pair had been given irradiated water in lead cans, which they sipped at patiently, while the general's Gen-Human secretary sat behind a desk and spoke monotonously into a tablet, reciting figure after figure about water purity, concrete reclamation, and infrastructure integrity. Almon nearly dropped off listening to her. He cleared his throat.

"The General has been alerted to your presence and will be with you shortly. There is just so much to do," the secretary said brightly, then went back to her droning.

Molphus rubbed his throbbing temples. They had barely gotten off of Myntal 5 in one piece. After escaping the massacre, the pair had hidden out in D'puppup's charred rooms. Almon was near incoherent with rage, demanding that they charge back in and slaughter all of the pirates. No matter that they were wounded. No matter that they had expended all of their stored energy. No matter that it meant certain death for both of them.

He had given his mentor a flat refusal and injected him with healing serum, then dressed his injuries. The wounded Mutzachan would have to have an operation later to remove the bullets, but for now he was out of trouble. He left to keep an eye on the corridor, while Almon licked at an electrical socket. He wondered about D'puppup's fate, hoping that the Misha was still alive. Molphus had firmly planned on rescuing the dream merchant and nursing him back to health. It was his obligation.

But that proved to be a wild dream. While the pirates pulled a hasty withdrawal to their respected ships, Oxtiern had brought down a little surprise from the Arc of Blood. A legacy left behind by his criminal uncle, Vargeneit. A G-Series plague bomb of the sort used to wipe out an entire city on the planet Langoon.

Molphus realized what was coming when the municipal speaker, designed only to function during an atmospheric breech, crackled to life. Oxtiern's guttural voice filled the air.

"Hello. You may not know who I am, but that isn't going to stop me from killing you. I'm afraid the actions of several recently arrived Mutzachans have compelled me to cause the extinction of this entire city. Now I could say that if you yokels bring me the Mutzachan's massive heads I'd let you live, but it's just easier to kill you all."

He paused for a moment to yell instructions at several people in the background. There were a few gunshots, then Oxtiern returned to speaking.

"Look at it this way. An entire city's populace executed by one non-nuclear device is quite unusual, something for the history books. An event to be mulled over and studied by historians. Thus in a paradoxical way, I am making you immortal. Say, 'thank you'."

To say this caused a panic is an understatement. The city collectively roared as one. The pirates had taken over the underground monorail system leading to the hangar, making sure their own people left quickly. They fired wildly into the rapidly rising crowds, but no matter how many bullet casings and bodies hit the floor, the panic in the hearts of the residents overrode any danger instinct. They stormed the station, climbing over corpses, trampling any who tripped or fell behind, and engaged in hand-to-hand combat with the pirates. Each side brutally tearing the other to shreds.

"Tick tock. Tick tock," laughed Oxtiern over the speaker.

Almon stumbled over to Molphus and grabbed his shoulder.

"Come on, I know what he's planning. We have to get deeper into the tunnels."

Molphus began to protest but Almon walked past him, disappearing into the dank passageways that sank down into the barren crust of the planet. The halls were deserted except for those too old, ill, or drugged up to move.

"What does he have?" Molphus asked after he caught up. Imminent death had spurred the elder to move faster than anyone would have guessed.

"A plague bomb, probably G-series. We had always suspected that his family had a few secured somewhere."

"If that's true, then it won't make any difference where we are. All of the air is cycled through the central atmosphere reclamation processors and shunted out in a tube system." Molphus pointed to an open ended metal pipe sticking out from the ceiling. "Any airborne viruses will be pumped into every quarter of the city. And the processors can't be shut off or we'd all suffocate."

Almon leaned against the wall. The wounds in his leg were starting to reopen under the bandages. Molphus swooped in and supported him. The elder gestured that they had to move faster.

"You've forgotten that this used to be an Eridani mining settlement. There will be certain protocols in place in case of explosive emergencies."

"Are you sure?"

"Despite what you may think of them, you can always count on an Eridani to stick to their regulations."

"The city's mining days were a long time ago, will the disaster pod still be operational?"

"We better hope so or we're dead."

Even the King's Men emerged from their hidey-hole to storm the monorail station. They shot through their own people, savagely beating them aside, and sent a hail of bullets into the pirates, who took cover and returned fire. They fought each other to a standstill. Both sides began to run out of ammunition.

"Tick tock."

The Mutzachans raced down until the air grew cold and stale. At a cross section of shafts they found a circular steel cover entrenched in the ground with Eridani writing etched into it. Almon stooped and pushed his hand on the center of the cover. A handle popped out. It took both of them to twist it off, revealing a dark chamber beneath.

"Tick tock."

The pirates couldn't hold out any longer. The last

carload of them pulled out over the monorail track, jam packed with Black Flag members. Pirates clung to the outside, dangled on by the windows. A few crawled around on top, firing blindly into the thronging masses. Those still on the platform were torn apart by the mob's vengeance.

At the other end of the track, the pirates scrambled to their individual shuttles and embarked back to their ships in orbit. The monorail track was blown up, the car disabled, and the computer systems ripped out to prevent anyone from following them.

"Oh my, time is up."

The disaster pod had been completely gutted. All electronics, all power sources, any scrap of food or water was gone. Even the metal bench, normally embedded into the thick cement walls, had been pulled out, leaving behind large crumbling holes. Almon inspected the hatch.

"At least the seals are still intact. It will be completely airtight."

"How long are we going to have to be in here?"

Almon closed the hatch and the room became encased in darkness. Molphus channeled an energy matrix and light sprang from his fingertips. He didn't have enough power to sustain it for long. Almon was lying uncomfortably, transparent blood from his wound had stained what was left of his pants. The youngster knelt by him and gave him another healing injection.

"The G-series plague bomb was initially designed for use by the Alliance military," Almon said, as the injection worked its magic. "Its purpose was to depopulate an area with no structural collateral damage. While they have neutron bombs that can do that, even those devices caused some damage and fried electronics. The military wanted something to hit the Arachnids so that their equipment could be salvaged and examined with greater ease."

Molphus shivered. Atrocity upon atrocity.

"But it wouldn't be useful to have thousands of diseases lingering about, each manipulated to be as virulent as possible," Almon continued. "So a failsafe was encoded in every one. They will eventually burn themselves out after three days or so."

How much effort was put into this thing? Molphus thought. *How much evil cultivated? How much good could have been done with the resources wasted?*

"It was the work of a lifetime," Almon said, as if reading his former student's thoughts. "With the appropriate astronomical cost overruns. Then budget cuts went into effect and the capital was redirected elsewhere. Oxtiern's uncle had given it his all. No wonder he was so intent on using it. To prove his legacy. His only real child."

"You sympathize with him?" Molphus's tone quivered with… was that anger?

"No, but I understand why he dropped the bomb on that city."

Molphus settled back. This entire journey had clubbed his senses. He'd wanted some enlightenment and had found it. But the light was horrible and illuminated every scar and flaw in this war torn galaxy he lived in. The truth was terror.

In the distance they heard a faint "poof." The tiniest murmur of a sound that penetrated their deep hole. At ground zero their eardrums would've been bleeding.

"There it goes," Almon said.

"Have you been in situations like this before?"

"Once or twice. I was almost crushed to death during an attack on one of the Misha planets. On Sharron, when the planet detonated, I was nearly left behind. I've been wounded more than a few times." Almon looked over at Molphus. The light from his fingertips cast bar like shadows over his large head, "You'll get used to it."

"I don't want to get used to it."

"You probably won't have a choice."

That was all the comfort his mentor offered. It was odd how quickly he'd calmed down. Only an hour before he'd been spitting blood, braying for Oxtiern's heart. Molphus gauged the size of the room. It must have been designed to house about twenty people, but that's when there was still power and localized air scrubbers. Not that the Eridani equipment would've helped them, that race being methane breathers.

"We might not have enough air to last three days."

"I know."

"And we have no water, and…," He dug through his pockets, uncovering only a packet of large salt tablets with a sliver of uranium 235 in the center of each one. Mutzachan candy. "Barely anything to eat."

"Then we had better conserve our energy. Less movement. Less talk."

"Are you sure about how long it will take for the plagues to burn out."

"Very certain. Oxtiern doesn't have the technical skills to alter the device."

"Can you perform the kashonas matrix?"

Kashonas was a Mutzachan word that literally translated to "help me". It was a difficult and costly matrix, where the controller opened a hole to hyperspace, an electron width's wide, within their own brain and sent a distress pulse hurtling out to a receiver across ridiculous distances. It was developed to aid stranded Mutzachans in situations just like this. Molphus had never mastered it.

"I'm too drained," Almon replied sleepily.

He had given everything. That was contrary to all he had taught to Quandle and Molphus. Nearly from their first day of training, Almon had lectured them on the conservation of energy, on prudent expenditure, and the purpose of discipline.

He never intended to return. Molphus realized. *He was willing to die and take Quandle and I with him.* Then a further horrible realization. *He didn't care if I died as long as he got his kill.*

"Perhaps," he said, "we should concentrate on our meditation to conserve the air."

"As I've been saying."

The Mutzachan mediation trances were supposed to clear out the race's mental channels, allowing them to push the energy outward with greater efficiency.

One must focus on the infinity of space and purge all emotions from their minds. Molphus found it impossible to concentrate on anything but Almon's actions, of what he had done and what he had forced Molphus to do. Within those reflections, he found that any lingering love for his teacher had died.

After three days, they emerged into a dead and rotting city. The power still hummed, the air circulated, lights flared, water pumped through pipes, but there was nothing else. Except for corpse upon corpse, buried under even more corpses. The whole of the city of Myntal-Igas-Eridi had been converted into a mass grave.

They plunged through the tunnels, the wide markets, past the junk piled metal shacks, the slick stone old Eridani buildings, witnessing every cadaver about them. Some people had committed suicide. Others had tried to shoot everyone else. Many people clung to religious icons and holy texts up to the end. There were plenty who had died in mundane positions. Lying in bed, propped up in front of a flexi-screens – banality still blaring away on it- or squatting on a toilet. Others died with hallucinogenic serums on their lips or wonderfully numbing narcotics pumping through their veins, suppressing the absolutely certainty of death under a drug euphoria. Molphus had no tears left. They stopped for a moment and took turns sucking electricity from a downed and sparking power line.

Other sentients were spotted near the fusion power plant, the "King's Castle" as the locals called it, *used* to call it. Apparently the pair of them weren't the only ones who had the idea to hide away in a disaster pod. The King himself and about ten of his men had secluded themselves away, leaving the rest to die in the plague bomb.

"King rat crawling from his hole," Almon said.

How are we any different? Molphus thought.

The King and his men were moving metal canisters from the fusion plant and placing them onto a cargo hauler - a track driven vehicle powered by electrical energy from the fusion reactors. The King's Men spotted the Mutzachans and raised their weapons, calling their boss.

The King was a long nosed, red scaly plated Aeodronian. Short and squat for his kind, his triple forked tongue flicked in and out rapidly, a sign of indecision. Both of his hands had been replaced by cybernetic replicas that ended in needle like claws which sparkled with electricity. The rest of the King's Men were an odd collection. Four more Aeodronian, three Ram Pythons, an Orion, a scorpion-tailed insectoid Sarand, and a Gen-Human who must have broken his conditioning and stolen himself away from his corporate owners. All were ready to deal death. The King's red and green eyes flitted over the Mutzachans.

"So you're ta ones responsible for all dis," he said in a slivery voice that curled in weird spirals about the eardrums.

"No," Almon replied, "the ones who set off the bomb are responsible."

"And dey was ty'in to get at you."

Almon lifted a hand, which turned into a shrug. It

was true. He could not respond.

"I think maybe you owe me maybe," the King's mastery of the Standard Trade Dialect was shaky, Aeodronian syntax kept slipping in. "Fer death, property loss of, income loss of."

"Not one credit."

"Maybe kill you maybe."

"You might want to think on that. We attacked the most vicious pirate clan there is and walked away. We killed hundreds of them and walked away. They murdered an entire city to get us and we are walking away. What could you possibly do?"

The King's Men murmured. Most of them took a few steps back, except for the Rams. Their eyes sparkled and they grinned, showing their pointed carnivorous teeth, eager to see what they could do. The King's head cocked to the left, gauging his men, weighting the possibility of death, then he turned back to the Mutzachans. Apart from the flickering tongue, his facial expression was completely alien to them. He might do anything.

"The back… the past is dead," he said.

Literally.

"We're going now maybe. You stay away maybe from us. It's not worth it to kill you, but maybe it's not worth it for you to try us?" He stepped up to Almon. "Who knows? You might take a bullet in that head, big and fat, from us?"

They squared off for a few moments. Potent menace hung in the air between them. Who would strike first? Then, as if in telepathic agreement, they simultaneously turned and walked away. Almon grabbed Molphus by the arm and shoved him.

"Suppose they try to ambush us?" asked Molphus.

"I doubt it. He's going to be too busy scuttling back to Aeodronian space. He might even have enough to retire for life if his men don't kill him for his fortune."

"And once we leave this will be a true ghost city."

"Not for long. Places like this periodically get overrun, though not usually this thoroughly," Almon stepped over the bloated corpse of an Eridani, barely registering it. "Once word gets out, some group will come and take over. Or several of them and they'll battle it out to become lords of the corpse pile. Give it a few solar cycles and everything will be up and running again."

"I don't believe it. The Alliance should…"

"The Alliance is busy fulfilling its primary duty, repelling the Arachnids. One sunken city on an insignificant planet is not a priority."

What a place for Quandle to die. Molphus had known his classmate at least half his life, close to a hundred years. They had trained together, eaten together, helped, and argued with each other. He was a comforting constant from the past. He could be testy and bigoted and they had not been close in the last few decades, but Molphus had still considered Quandle as an old friend. The universe was dimmed without him.

They came upon a scene which drove the dead classmate from Molphus's head. Several thousand

Pascians, the race's entire population in the city, were piled together in a pyramid. Ten thousand wispy legs bristled over the pile like fallen whiskers off a grizzled giant. Was this some death ritual of the Pascians, to huddle together at death's door? Or was It a biological imperative which they hadn't outgrown? It was hideous and fascinating. Molphus's pondered whether someone shouldn't do a greater study of the species. Insane thoughts under the circumstances. Almon bumped him, forcing him to restart the trudge through tragedy.

After several hours, they reached the monorail station. It took them some time to work through the bodies and into the frozen rock of the tunnel. Channeling light through their hands to navigate by, they discovered that they weren't the only ones to make this trek. Here and there, the light uncovered some unfortunate who had tried to flee, only to collapse and shake out their last breath in total darkness.

It was a long journey. Molphus's legs grew numb. He had no idea how Almon managed to pull himself along. Eventually they spotted the literal light at the end of the tunnel. Bit by bit, it crept up on them until the Mutzachan's emerged into the shuttle hangar, still fully functional apart from the destroyed monorail system.

They pulled themselves up onto the hangar floor. It was devoid of life and death, just cold machinery waiting to be commanded. Almon found the shuttle of the Cizerack family that had brought them here.

Ion of Logic! Thought Molphus, coming as close

to blasphemy as one of his race could. *That family. I hadn't even thought of them. Not one flick of wonder at their fate. What's happening to me?* It had been a mother, father, two older siblings, and litter of three cubs. Dead and decaying away. *If we hadn't come...* He let that thought dangle, the end of it would only bring him more misery.

Almon placed his hands on the shuttle locking mechanism and power flowed forth. Molphus could sense it lightly tickling his nerve endings. Almon guided the energy inside, feeding it through the shuttle's circuitry, coaxing it here and there until the right linkage was established and the shuttle opened. It was an ancient Mutzachan matrix and another reason they were so feared. Put a Mutzachan in the right place and all of the enemy's technology would be theirs.

Inside, he saw all of the Cizerack's gear. The children's toys, snapshots of friends and family, clothes, the odd sustenance they cooked, the low oval couches they sat on (chairs were useless to the quadruped Cizerack). Their entire life strewn about. Molphus snapped.

"No we can't," he blurted. "We can't just leave them. We have to…"

He collapsed, exhausted in every conceivable way.

When he awoke, he was on a berth near the navigation deck. Almon was at the helm, working the controls. Well *working*, he sat by the controls, a faint glow before him. The Cizerack ship was designed for exclusive use by that race and, as they had no thumbs, the system controls had to be operated by the mouth and tongue using a set of faceplates, contoured to the Cizerack's physiology. They were nearly unusable by any other race, but were not beyond the Mutzachan's energy manipulations. Both of them sat on padded mats raised slightly above the floor.

"How long was I…?"

"Difficult to tell," Almon said in a strained voice. "A long time."

"Do you want me to take over?"

"…yes."

Molphus slipped into his spot, generating the energy matrix a second after Almon stopped. His senses seeped into the machinery. Control systems, thruster relays, life support circuitry… navigation computer? Navigation was locked off.

"It's practically on autopilot," Almon said lounging back. His voice dipped sleepily. "Next destination is set. Just maintain stability."

Molphus popped a jury-rigged electrical line, made from thick copper cable, into his mouth. Almon had wired it into the system to keep himself powered up as he preserved the vessel's course. A crude method and physically demanding, but it worked.

"Whe' a' we he'ded?" he asked, the cable gnarling his words.

"The planet Xensera in the Plains of Desolation."

"Wh' the'?"

"Perhaps you know it better as Stilt?"

"N'. Wh' the'?"

"Oh, why there? Because that's where the Rul is. That's where Oxtiern must be headed. How did

D'Puppup put it? 'A passage unto Passage.'"

D'Puppup. The dream merchant's name played havoc with Molphus's concentration. Surely he must be dead. If not from the diseases, then from his burns. Another one left behind with no rituals or remembrances said of them. A forgotten body turning into an anonymous pile of goo.

"Passage is a shade world. Its appearance in the Plains of Desolation sector is due to the quantum ripple effect generated by the Motaran Rift."

The Motaran Rift, the ultimate mystery. That chaotic cut of impossibility sliced right into the fabric of reality. It kept popping up in this business. Molphus knew little about it (no one knew much really), except that ninety nine of those who investigated it died or aged so much that they became senile. Scientifically speaking, nearly all of the effects associated with the Rift were absurd, the greatest demonstration of preposterousness. Yet there it was.

"So wh' go t' Xense'a?"

"Around the moon of Stilt is a wormhole channel to Passage," continued Almon. "We've long since known that there is a Rul developing inside of the planet."

"Wh' didn' we go the' fi'st?"

"Because going to Stilt means bringing in a lot of others. We have to co-opt the military for help, use fake credentials, answer questions, have our genetic profiles logged. All of that is evidence of our involvement. Myntal 5 was our best shot at keeping it all quiet."

What's the definition of situational irony?

"But I guess we have no choice."

Molphus pulled the copper cable from his mouth to better ask his next question, "What is a Rul exactly? And what would Oxtiern want with it?"

"What it is, is classified. As for his intentions… there are too many possibilities. And honestly his reasons don't interest me, only his actions."

Fatigue still clung to Molphus, "Why don't we just pass it off to the Alliance military then?"

"What?" Almon said, leaping from the floor, anger trumping weariness. "We have to handle this ourselves."

"Why?'

He grew silent for a moment. Molphus could hear the synaptic circuits connecting in his bilious brain.

"We have to do this for Quandle," he said flatly. "Don't you want revenge for his murder?"

Murder? A desperate attempt to play on Molphus's emotions. *Didn't he die in combat? Didn't we attack first?*

"I'd rather have peace."

"Oh, peace," Almon spat the words out in distaste.

He looked as if he were going to say something else but dropped off. He fell onto the oval couch, snoring lightly. Molphus replaced the cable and carried on.

And now on Stilt they were waiting, waiting, waiting. Their Galactic Control credentials passed inspection. The surly Eridani they had met from immigration control barely uttered more than a few grumbles before clearing them. Molphus wondered if his papers were that good of a forgery or if he had been unknowingly drafted by the intelligence agency.

After a few more hassles, Almon secured the access he wanted to the local military data-hub and while sitting in the crumbling hotel room provided to them, he made a few discoveries that disturbed him. Some cross-referencing later, he had kicked Molphus awake and insisted that they needed to see the General immediately.

"The General will see you now," chirped the secretary. "Bear in mind that his time is pressed. He can only spare you about ten minutes."

Almon rose to his full height. He was short, but from what Molphus had been told, Mutzachans had a natural mystique to them that intimidated other races.

"We will take as long as we need to," he said and stormed into the General's office.

Like all of the military facilities on the planet, the office was makeshift. Converted from an old schoolroom, reinforced steel had been welded over the windows and fluorescent lights buzzed above, their bare wires taped along the walls. A standard issue military field desk had been snapped together in a far corner with the General's personal effects installed in it. All of the chairs were uncomfortable fold-out metal things with no padding. The only indulgence was a lush blue rug bearing a gold Galactic Marine's insignia in the center. It did not fit the dimensions of the room, leaving bare patches around the edges.

General Lowe was a dumpy human, nearly bald with a wispy white fringe clinging on for dear life. His jowls sagged with age and had a bright knotted nose to complete the image. He was not pleased by the appearance of what he thought were a pair of Galactic Control agents.

"Now," he began after the Mutzachan's had seated themselves, "Almon and Molphus, no sur name of course." Mutzachan's did not indulge in the practice of family names. "We are always happy to help members of your agency, but I'm afraid the exact nature of your business is a mystery to me. You didn't fill out your forms properly."

Almon pushed a few buttons on his data pad, a three dimensional image of Oxtiern's head appeared.

"We are looking for this male. His name is Oxtiern Lomasi."

"I see. And is he a resident of this planet?"

"No, but he has been here very recently. Culling through your records, I discovered he attempted to enter Stilt…"

"Xensera," The General corrected. "That is the proper name."

"Quite. He came on what was determined to be false diplomatic credentials. Your immigration officer, a Captain Raskor-idan, denied him entry and apparently Oxtiern escaped before he could be arrested."

"Well, if he is no longer planetside..."

"He is with a group of pirates who plan to infiltrate the nearby wormhole and raid the planet Passage."

"What for? It's a rock."

"Unimportant. He had no reason to come to Sti… Xensera."

"Then I don't see how I can help you."

"You misunderstand. *Why* did he come here? What did he hope to gain?"

The General appeared stumped. He put up his hands in surrender. It was unlikely that he had even heard of the incident. These things were handled by subordinates. Almon pressed his advantage.

"Upon further inspection we discovered that this same Raskor-idan actually served as Oxtiern's commander for several years, while the latter was enlisted. Why did he not arrest him? He must have known that the name on the papers was false, if nothing else."

The General wiped some sweat from his brow and called out for his secretary to summon the Eridani immediately. Fifteen minutes later, a very annoyed Raskor-idan entered. Molphus had seen him when they first arrived, but now he fully took the officer in. The missing hand, the white disgrace, the penance scars. He had seen very few of the race in his life and had never talked to one before, but the stereotypical image that Molphus had picked up was not encouraging. Racist, brutal, a fascistic government, the concept of a war crime was foreign to them, but they were also sticklers for rules and regulations. He doubted this one would be much different. The captain's adherence to the white disgrace indicated that.

Under the stern gaze of the General, Almon

recited the information again. Raskor-idan took it with a bored indifference, tapping his foot with impatience.

"And it seems," Almon concluded, "that he was a field medic in your unit back when you were a lieutenant."

"Was he?"

"Yes captain. So the question is, why didn't you arrest him?"

"Arrest him for what?" The General cleared his throat and Raskor-idan threw in a belated, "Sir."

"Arrest him for having a fake passport."

"We didn't determine that they were fake until the next day. By then he had left. As for arresting him, I have yet to see any warrant issued for a Zen Rigeln by that name."

"You knew Oxtiern. You knew that wasn't his name on the file, despite the genetic checks."

"That was years ago. I've served with a hundred more troops since then," the captain replied. "Quite frankly, all of these Zen's look the same to me."

Possible. Molphus didn't like to admit it, but he had difficulty distinguishing between the Zen Rigeln's as well.

"The reason he left was because you denied him entry. That was before the forgery was discovered. Adding to that is the fact that he lists you by name on his entrance visa. This is all very suspicious."

Business considerations and to visit my old friend Raskor-idan. But what was the business?

Raskor-idan flinched. Not exactly a poker face. It was all too apparent he was hiding something, but the captain became mute.

"What did you and Oxtiern talk about?" Almon pressed.

"Nothing… unusual. He inquired about the mineral rights on the planet. He was looking, so he said, to secure a monopoly on behalf of his government. I thought it was strange."

"Indeed," harrumphed the General. "Such a thing is absolutely impossible."

"Plus his adjunct was a Ram Python. Extremely odd for a pacifist government and useless for diplomacy. He wasn't a very tough specimen, but still a Ram."

Molphus thought he could detect the remnants of bruising on the Eridani's face. Was there more to this?

Raskor-idan continued, "So I denied him entry. If he had another reason to see me, he didn't mention it. Perhaps he changed his mind after he realized I didn't recognize him."

The Eridani looked too smug when he gave that answer for Molphus's liking. Why was he being obstinate? His military records were standard, campaigns here and there, and until recently there was no disciplinary marks or records of personal confrontations. The word "adequate" appeared regularly in his performance reviews.

Almon turned to the General.

"I want this man interrogated by an empath," he demanded.

"Absolutely not."

"The facilities are available. You have a number

of them garrisoned…"

"I will not allow one of my men to have his mind dissected on flimsy evidence."

"I have the authority!"

"To investigate the whereabouts of this Oxtiern certainly, not to order Galactic Marine personnel about or to question one using extraordinary methods."

"Empaths are standard in questioning."

"For military prisoners," replied the General. "Captain Raskor-idan isn't under arrest nor is he likely to be. I don't see any criminal actions here, only sloppy paperwork and poor judgement."

"Fine," gave in Almon, "but according to the Interagency Cooperation Act, I am entitled to have a military liaison while operating in your jurisdiction. I request Captain Raskor-idan."

The General pondered. *Raskor-idan must be even more a problem than we thought*, Molphus gathered. Almon had filled him in on the innumerable pissing contests between every service branch of the galactic military machine. It had taken legislation rammed down their throats to even get them to talk to each other.

"I will agree to it," The General decided. "However he is not to be interrogated formally or informally without a proconsul provided by the Solicitor General's office. And under no conditions is an empath to be used."

"Agreed."

Raskor-idan was not happy. He stepped up to the General's desk, arrogance and hostility plainly chiseled on his face.

"If that's the case *sir,* then I request Sergeant Aebisher be assigned with me as my aide."

"Captain, we are short staffed as it is. If we did that, the whole of your section would have to be reabsorbed with the other immigration department."

"The work we do, or lack of work to be accurate, could be handled in half an hour a week."

"Still..."

"According to regulation 815.55d, a commissioned officer is required to have aide when assigned to field, liaison, or diplomatic duties. I will take the sergeant. Or is there anyone else you can spare?"

The captain had him and the General was clearly ready to be done with the matter.

"Take him. All of you go and finish whatever dirty business that you have cooked up."

The com, wired into the General's desk, lit up. Over it, the Gen-Human secretary squeaked, "Sir, we've just received a report of an attack currently underway on depot A6. They baffled our sensors and struck. It appears to be a pirate clan."

Chapter 16 – Stilt

Species: Cizerack

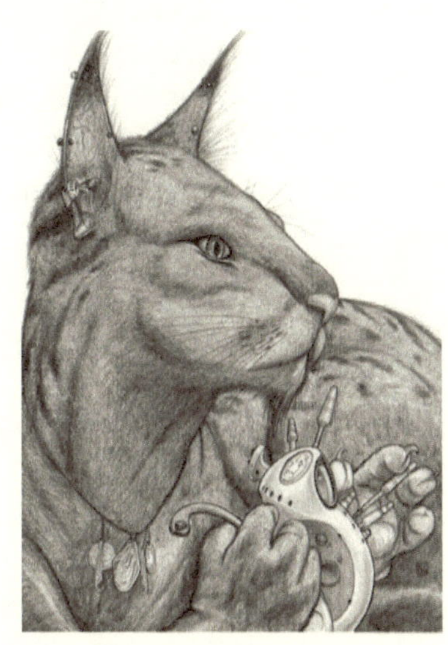

Planet of Origin:
Cashoulis in the 61-Verginis system

Description:
A large quadruped race sporting blue/black fur roughly similar in appearance to the Earth panther with some slight differences in the jaw and voice box, allowing them to speak in an intelligible manner. They are the only known species to develop space flight without the use of an opposable thumb. Due to religious doctrines, they are a matriarchal society with males placed into a lower caste and unable to hold positions of authority or political power. They have no central government and are primarily broken up into clan-states which war continuously amongst themselves over territorial sovereignty. Their representatives in the Alliance were chosen from the Fenib Maturt, the strongest clan, much to the anger of all the others. For this reason, Alliance directives are routinely ignored on Cizerack planets

Freaky Fact: The *nall*, or eunuch, are the only males

allowed to serve in any higher capacity in government or business. Castrated shortly after birth and sold to a patroness, they are a despised class but heavily used in business middle management and administrative roles. The practice has been condemned by several sentient rights organizations, but for now it is too engrained in Cizerack culture to be abandoned.

***

Supply Depot A6 was in an isolated area. Located two miles from Jericho City, it was on the only useable foundation large enough for the military's needs. The collapsed building that lay upon it had been bulldozed and a structure, using fortified portable wall units, was snapped together. These were designed to make movable field barracks and command huts. A plan was developed to build a permanent structure if the war remained in this sector, but the manpower, credits, and equipment had yet to be budgeted.

The pirate raid started well. A shuttle roared through the atmosphere and swooped over the depot, dropping comspikes - two meter long shafts of titanium steel with a scrambler fixed in the tail end. This jumbled all electronic signals, turning transmissions into static gibberish.

A container of spherical drones, each packed with explosives, was dropped and sent on a kamikaze run. Defensive emplacements, the makeshift warehouse doors, and any loose soldiers outside were targeted. The automated defenses retaliated. Only one drone got through for every five dropped, but it was enough. Fire twisted metal and shattered circuitry lay all about.

Pirate fighter ships descended, joyfully targeting anything that the drones were unable to destroy. Then the cargo shuttles came down like rain, packed with pirates eager to blow away some soldier boys. They stormed the warehouse, shattering the main doors.

The remaining marines, while shaken, were not down. They retreated behind the depot's walls and ventilated the first wave of pirates who charged the breech. For a brief time, it was a deadlock. The marines were better trained, better armed, and in a defensible position, but what the pirates lacked in discipline, they made up for in manpower. The lieutenant in charge of the depot had been blown up by a drone, so the first sergeant took command. The building was too large to defend in an extended firefight and as long as the coms were down there would be no reinforcements. The standoff wouldn't last. Every bullet the pirates landed cut the marine's odds just a bit.

The first sergeant made the decision not to waste his men's lives suicidally holding off a pack of thieves. He ordered one half of the troops to hold the line and the rest to make an exit. The wall plates were anchored together using thick iron bolts fused into place by specialized equipment. Luckily, the needed apparatus was stored in the warehouse.

They spent fifteen nerve wracking minutes unscrewing a plate, while the invaders screamed for their death. The first sergeant and two others raided the crates, grabbing weapons and a few other bits and pieces. They jury-rigged several automatic gun emplacements, programming them to fire at regular bursts every twenty seconds at the warehouse entry. Once the work was done, the first sergeant crept up and recalled his men one by one, replacing each with the jury rigged pulse rifle. As they retreated, they left behind a few proximity mines, just to kill a few more of the bastards.

The escape hole was opposite the landing platform, facing away from Jericho. Not ideal. Once gathered together, the eighteen marines sprinted for the perimeter. The first sergeant's rough-hewn plan was to get out of the jamming range, call in an alert, and hole up in a rocky alcove until the cavalry blared its bugle.

Up above, he saw the shuttles still descending. The pirate ships had come dangerously close into Stilt's gravity well. He could make them out. Three little dots far off in the sky. A series of explosions rocked the depot. Someone had tripped the mines. How long would it take them to sift the wreckage? How many precious minutes would it give them?

Not many. They were spotted by shuttles as they ran. The jamming spikes prevented the pirates from communicating, so it took several minutes to relay the information, giving the marines that much needed extra distance. Three shuttles were sent after the fleeing men. The pirates strafed the marines and dropped grenades from open hatches. Having no cover from an air attack, they could only feebly fire back, keep running, or die. Most opted to keep moving. Two stopped and fired skywards, but all that did was to provide a stationary target for the pirate's guns.

On an order from the first sergeant, the men split and ran in opposite directions, each shamefully hoping that the pirates would go after the others and allow them to escape. Several bullets hit the ground near him and blew apart a rock. Fragments of it shot up into his face, knocking him over. He stayed down, playing possum. Blood from another murdered marine, his body practically ground to hamburger by the pirate's guns, splattered all over him, adding to the illusion.

The ruse paid off. After gunning down the others, the shuttles didn't bother to land and make sure everyone was dead. Instead they returned to their comrades, boasting of their big victory. Once they were out of sight, the first sergeant picked himself up and ran out of jamming range. He called in the report to Command and hid himself as best he could.

That was the Black Flag pirate's first mistake. The second had to do with the cargo itself.

After they had secured the depot, loading of the ultra armor began in earnest. It was quickly discovered that the units weighed twice as much as was estimated. Meaning that it would take twice as long to get the damn things up to the pirate vessels, the shuttles not being able to handle the extra weight. They buckled down to the task. Craw was on the platform, pacing about on all fours, yelling at his men to get moving. But they hurried in vain.

The first sign of the counterattack came when a few pirates spotted drones flitting about in the cloud line, sending data back to the marines on the strength and disposition of the pirate forces. This was reported to the ground officers, but there was little that could be done. Most of the defense emplacements having just been blown up by the pirates themselves.

The marine assault was swift and brutal. Normally they would have bombed the place or fired a missile from near orbit, but Command was determined to get all of their equipment back, so in they went.

The initial wave came as a flight of atmospheric fighters. They dropped EMP cluster bombs, frying all unshielded electronics, including the comspikes. Close to half of the shuttles hadn't been properly fitted with EMP shielding. Two fell out of the air, reducing their occupants to a jellied substance mixed with powdered bone. Fighters strafed the pirates, scattering them before the ground assault began. Troop transports rumbled up, each mounted with pulse cannons that blasted indiscriminately into the invader's ranks.

Preferring to take on targets that couldn't really fight back, the pirates decided to cut their losses and run. Despite orders to the contrary, despite the howling of their officers, the main body of pirates scrambled to get away.

***

Almon had bullied his way into the counterattack by threatening to send unfavorable reports to this or that group, but he couldn't convince the General to let him be part of the main assault. He was forced to watch everything from the mobile command tank, a wide bodied reinforced tracked vehicle, to which the drone and body camera footage was relayed. He stomped from one monitor to another, peering in as closely as he could at the image, his head blocking the picture, annoying the communication officer to no end.

Molphus was uncomfortably crammed in on a narrow row of seats at the back of the tank. Next to him was a still angry Raskor-idan and a subdued Sergeant Aebisher. When he first saw the Mutzachans, the human grew wide eyed and hadn't uttered a word since.

As it should be, thought Almon.

He stared out at the scattering pirates. Vermin. Scum. All of them. Very fitting for Oxtiern. No doubt he had lured them in with fantasy tales of easy plunder. He flipped from one screen to another, trying to catch a glimpse of the Zen. He was out there somewhere, Almon knew it, could almost smell him.

He saw a Cizerack in full body armor, a rotating pulse rifle attached to its back- the trigger linked to its eye movements- valiantly struggling against the marines. The cat tried to lead a charge only to have all of his men abandon him. Several shots took him down, a vicious hole ripped in his side. He breathed several deep gasps and died.

The last of the operational shuttles were taking

off. With nowhere near enough room to fit them all, the pirates fought one another to get in. They tried clinging to the sides as it ascended, falling like flakes of dandruff. One pirate hung onto the door hatch and prevented it from closing. As they gained altitude, he slipped, his feet dangling on empty air. A black-furred Fott appeared at the hatch and kicked the pirate in the face, sending him plummeting to splatter below.

"Cruiser engaging pirate vessels," the coms officer relayed back to Command.

Almon turned to a different screen. The marine cruiser had barreled in, laying into the pirate ships with pulse cannons, fighters, and missiles. The three vessels reacted, turning around to encircle the marine ship from above and below. However, they underestimated the prowess of the military. The marine cruiser pushed forward at the ship blocking their immediate trajectory, absorbing hits from the other two.

"We've identified the three as known criminal vessels, the Slioshotanizi, the Ergenstrasse, and the Arc of Blood."

The cruiser laid on everything it had at the Ergenstrasse, using pulse cannons to crack the hull, then targeting missiles to widen the breech. Explosive decompression rippled through the midsection, cutting power to half the ship, including one of its main engines and the artificial gravity generators. The Ergenstrasse spun out of control. Marine fighters zipped in and destroyed the second engine. The spinning ship, unable to generate forward momentum, was essentially a dead hulk, vulnerable to any predator.

The Arc of Blood attempted to ram the cruiser, its Arachnid spike poised for a breaching blow. The marine vessel deftly outmaneuvered it in thrust after thrust while firing blasts at the Slioshotanizi. The marine fighters harried the Arc of Blood, plinking off armor plating, zipping in under its poor flux shield and destroying external sensors.

After taking multiple dead on blasts, the Slioshotanizi disengaged. It veered into the black and engaged its hyperspace drives. The Arc of Blood, realizing it was in a losing battle, spun about and shot off towards the moon at a reckless pace.

Towards the damn wormhole! Almon cursed.

The marine cruiser captain relayed that it was planning to intercept the Arc of Blood. Tension clutched Almon's guts. This was it! He would've preferred to be in there for the kill, but this would be a fair enough substitute.

Then an override signal came through from Command, directing the cruiser back to the Slioshotanizi. Its hyperspace drives had stalled, shorting out the whole system. The ship was running on a quarter power, barely able to maintain its main engine. The General, directing things from a cozy desk, ordered the Slioshotanizi destroyed. Almon angrily leaped on the com.

"General, the Arc of Blood is slipping away. It's heading straight for Passage. The other two are disabled, not a primary target."

"Incorrect. That one ship is a cornered animal. It

could easily swing around and rain hell down on our civilian and military centers. We have a million refugees down here. Our priority is to protect them. There is no choice."

"I have to insist…"

"Your recommendation has been noted by the system logs. Now clear the line, we have actual work to do."

Should I tell him? Tell the awful truth. That a million lives was an acceptable loss to end Oxtiern. Doing so violated every principle he had adhered to over the past hundred years. *I should do it.* But to admit to the existence of the Rul, here in front of these loose lipped grunts was unthinkable. No matter how many threats and regulations were thrown at them, they would spill the beans after their first swig of aviation fuel. Almon knew the type.

Someone laughed behind the Mutzachan. He turned to see Raskor-idan sneering at him. The smug Eridani had his arms crossed, his foot tapped impatiently. *I'm going to bury you*, Almon vowed. *Whatever sleazy deal you had with Oxtiern will be uncovered. And I will go to Eridine with it and embarrass your entire house!* He savored the idea of crushing this fallen soldier, the embodiment of everything wrong with his race.

"Sir, weren't we looking for a Zen?" a coms operative said. "I think I've spotted him."

Almon dove to the screen. If this were true, the Arc of Blood could go off to rape and loot as much as it wanted.

"Roll the image back," he ordered. The coms

operative complied after a nod from his officer.

The ground battle had essentially ended. The majority of the pirates had either died or surrendered, except a small group that had decided to fight on. The rolled back footage showed them entering the warehouse, weapons blazing.

"Stop there."

The image froze on a Zen in full battle armor, gun raised. Was that him? The picture was from a high angle and filtered through gun smoke, but… Same eyes. Possibly the same height. That was clear enough. Firing a pulse rifle. Oxtiern was combat trained. Was it…? Yes! Yes, it must be!

"Take him down," Almon ordered.

"Yes sir," the coms officer said condescendingly, "we were going to do that anyway."

The troops went in. It didn't take long for the pirates to be surrounded and put down. They ducked behind crates and were killed. Some tried to escape through the hole and were killed. A few tried to surrender, but the time was past for that. They were killed.

Then came the moment, the great money shot Almon was hoping for. The Zen staggered into view, firing his weapon. A shaft of superheated plasma spat onto his head. Instinctively the Zen clutched as his melting face, burning his hands deeply in the process. He tottered, then fell. Most of his head dissolving away into a mucusy liquid.

That's it. He was dead! Dead, dead, dead, dead, dead!

Chapter 17 – Stilt

Species: Chatilian Empath

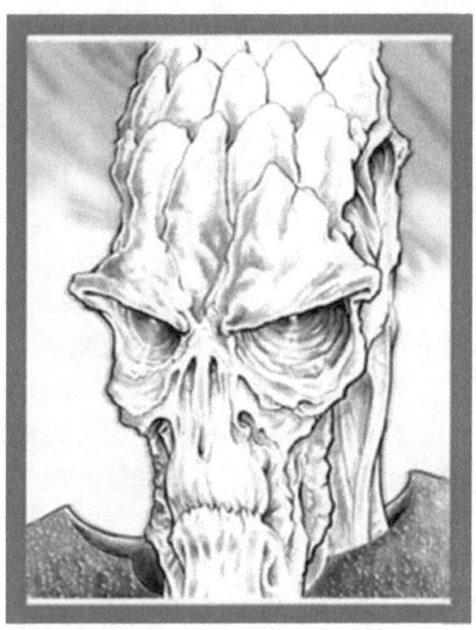

Planet of Origin: Chatil in the Fomalhaut system

Description: The shortest of the Alliance races and the only sentient herbivore race ever discovered. The Chatilian transitions from an endo-skeleton in the body to a greenish hued exo-skeleton surrounding the neck and head. They are able to harvest their brains overabundance of energy and expel it on psychic wavelengths through resonating nodes in their plated skull. While technologically less advanced than most Alliance races, their prized empathic interrogation techniques, lie detection abilities, and therapeutic systems have allowed them to be granted full membership into the Alliance.

Freaky Fact: Chatilians are chronic sleepwalkers and their architecture is entirely designed around this trait. Often their bedrooms are padded time locked chambers with mundane household tasks laid out to occupy the wandering sleeper. Some date back ten thousand years and use a water clock wheel system that unlocked the room when a certain number of hollowed out gourds were full.

***

"It wasn't fucking him?"

Molphus had never heard his mentor use profanity before. The genetic scans from mutilated body of the Zen killed in the warehouse confirmed its identity as Rabin Atol, a multiple felon and known Black Flag pirate, who went by the moniker, Skel. Sensor sweeps determined that the Arc of Blood had definitely escaped down the wormhole and by now must be orbiting Passage.

The mop up operation had turned into a bit of a bonanza for the Alliance law and order statistics this quarter. There were an estimated three hundred pirates killed (they were still sifting the wreckage) and forty captured, with a combined total of fifteen hundred criminals warrants cleared. The General was taking full credit, sending communications out to all military and civilian branches, crowing about his achievement. Part of the announcement was damage control. The General was trying to blur the fact that the remaining pirates had escaped with close to two hundred suits of ultra armor, rebranding the theft as a victory.

Almon didn't care, let him hog the praise as long

as no one paid attention to the Mutzachan's presence. In this vicious war, a fight over a depot was a minor debacle at best. Easily overlooked.

The General was so happy with the results that he allowed the Mutzachans to interrogate the captured pirates as much as they wanted, granting them the use of a marine empath as well.

"What's the point?" Molphus asked darkly. "We know where we're headed."

Almon was getting tired to Molphus's worsening attitude. He would have dismissed the boy, sent him back to Trishmag, if he could spare the manpower.

"This is intelligence work," he replied sharply. "We gather as much information as possible. It looks like half of the Arc of Blood's officers were killed. So who will take command after that? What are their strengths and weaknesses? Who is Oxtiern close to? Who would he take down to Passage with him? What is his ultimate goal? Where is their next destination if they succeed on Passage? How many able bodied crew might be left on the ship? How many pirates are actually trained in the use of ultra armor? It's not just something that can be slipped on. How does the crew feel about Oxtiern? Could they be persuaded to turn on him for a price? All this is extremely valuable."

"I'm glad that we're not *just* assassins. Some of that would have been good to know before."

"We weren't in the same position as before. We have to press our advantage."

"Advantage?"

"We've got him on the run. Cut down part of his power base. Oxtiern's allies must be rethinking their arraignments with him now."

"They still carried away a lot of valuable equipment."

"But at what price?"

Almon didn't mention it to Molphus, but he needed something to enlarge the threat that the Arc of Blood posed to the military presence on Stilt. The General had refused to aid them in mounting an expedition through the wormhole. Instead he had planted sensor satellites around it, in case the ship emerged. Almon still couldn't bring himself to tell the General that if something did come out, it would mean the death of them all.

Raskor-idan entered, followed by a Chatilian Empath. It stood level with the Eridani's thigh, features immobile, unreadable. A piece of burning celery stuck out of his mouth, dried out and lit at one end. The race found inhaling the exhaust intoxicating. The empath was decked out in Galactic Marine Corp field fatigues, a corporal's insignia glowing from its breast.

As races went, the Chaitlians were held with fear and wariness, ranking just below the Mutzachans. No one could deny, however, just how useful the race was. Like lawyers, everyone hated the Chatilians until they needed one.

Almon spoke over the empath's head to Raskor-idan.

"Where is Sergeant Aebisher?"

"He's arraigning to have the prisoners brought in. The first one is set up in the room." Raskor-idan had dropped saying "sir" the minute they had left the

General's office.

"We are primarily looking for..."

"I'm just the liaison here. Your business will reveal itself, I'm sure."

Aren't we just so happy that Oxtiern got away, thought Almon. *Hasn't it just been a load off of your mind.*

They entered the interrogation chamber. It was made from the same portable wall units as the warehouse, with one important exception. Each piece - ceiling, walls, and floor - had a large crystal inserted into it. The crystal, when stimulated by a small battery, sent out a sonic pulse that resonated in the empath's exo-nodules, amplifying its powers immeasurably.

Standard issue now, Almon remembered when the proposal to build the special plates was first placed before the Marine budgeting committee a century ago. It had cost over a quarter of a billion credits to develop and come up against some serious resistance.

A metal chair and table had been bolted to the floor. Handcuffed to the table was a blonde Orion with a prodigious paunch. His hands shook due to a chemical dependency on fermented vegetables. According to the medical scan administered to all the prisoners, he also suffered from several ulcers in his intestines and stomachs, rotting gums, degenerative nerve damage, and the Orion equivalent of scurvy. The end results of a toxic waste lifestyle. Camera footage showed that he had dropped his weapon and surrendered the minute the bulk of the Marine forces showed up.

A few privates entered and screwed chairs into the floor for the interrogators, then disappeared. Molphus, Almon, Raskor-idan and the Chatilian seated themselves. The empath closed his eyes, attuning his senses to the crystals with a series of squawks above the range of most sentient's hearing. Almon flipped on the profile of the career criminal before him. Raskor-idan snorted, his racism against the species apparent and stereotypical.

"Parg Mildue," the elder said. "Theft, smuggling, arson, rape, vehicular manslaughter, armed robbery, along with some minor vandalism and drunk-and-disorderly charges. And those are just the open warrants."

"The manslaughter thing was an accident."

"Not to mention the crimes you are suspected to have been involved with. Plus the list of your convictions, which is still incomplete. The full record has yet to come in from Taos…"

"Is it my fault if kids are too stupid to look up? No, it is not!"

"And now add to that pile, treason. A capital charge."

"Whoa whoa. Treason? Where'ja get that, cholly wuzzle?" Parg raised a shaking hand. "Let's not get carried away."

"You and your organization attacked a vital military installation during wartime. What else but treason?"

"Organization? We're just a bunch of guys fucking around in a ship."

Raskor-idan pointed at the Black Flag insignia on Parg's flak jacket, "What do you call that, you vermin?"

"It's just a club."

That one didn't pass the laugh test. "He's lying," the Chatilian said between chuckles.

"Hey wait a minute," Parg yelled, gesturing at the empath with his cuffed hand. "Is he reading my thoughts."

"What else would he be doing?"

"I didn't agree to this. Where's my fucking advocate, you assholes? I'm demanding it, so you need to stop now. You can't read me either."

Arrogance and ignorance personified. "You're a military prisoner," Almon informed him slowly. "This planet is under marine jurisdiction. Their penal code is the only one that applies. No advocate, no speedy trial, no right to mental privacy, no jury, no civilian judge. All you get is a military tribunal- some of which probably knew the Marines your *club* killed personally."

"And with a freighter load of you criminals to go through, I'm sure your case will be given the two minutes it deserves," added Raskor-idan.

"Then I want to talk to a person from the Orion diplomatic core."

"On this planet? There isn't one."

"Then I guess we'll just have to wait."

Almon smirked. A pathetic delaying tactic. "We'll put the request through the normal channels, but no law states that we have to wait for them to show up. You are an *Alliance* citizen. Diplomatic consul is a courtesy, not a right."

The Orion's shaking went past the DTs and was overtaken by fear. Fat bullets of sweat slid down his fleshy face, dripping off his nose and clustered around his armpits. He let out low whooshing moans, spreading the rotting meat stench of his receding gums around the table and up the interrogator's noses.

"It's a pity," Almon said, sticking a piece of cloth over his face, "that you can't offer us anything."

"Sure I can!" Parg leapt at the bait with snarling ferocity. "I'll tell you anything you want to know. I've got dope on all of the officers. Like Craw."

"He's dead."

"Skel then."

"Dead."

"The Captain?"

"He doesn't know anything," inserted the empath.

"What about Oxtiern?"

"Oh he's bad, the fucking worst. Really bad news. There's tons of evil about him."

"Yes....?"

"He like likes to torture people."

Almon sighed. "What are his plans?"

"Um."

"All right, what are Black Flag's plans for the ultra-armor?"

"What?"

"The items you people were stealing."

"Is that what it was? I missed the briefing."

"How about where your group plans to strike?"

"Uhhhh..."

"After Passage."

"Passage?"

"You are completely useless," bellowed Almon. He buzzed for the marine guards, who appeared immediately. "Get him out of here."

The guards shackled Parg's arms behind his back and frog marched him out.

"Hey no, wait," protested the Orion. "There's the Fott, Jack Mace. I can give you all kinds of dirt on him."

The door closed.

"He was telling the truth," offered the empath, sparking laughter from the others.

Next up was a young Gen-Human with scars curving out from the corners of his mouth. He was the exception in the group of prisoners. No criminal record, no warrants, but he had escaped from the Brethia Stargate Project. That was crime enough in itself.

Almon could read the boy like a big pink book. He was sweating, shifting his eyes nervously from alien to alien, silently pleading in despair as he was handcuffed to the table.

"Drake-DKE-k0018," Almon said.

All of the Gen-Human's life scrolled up in front of him, snagged wirelessly from the chip implanted in his skull. *Odd that it hadn't been removed*, Almon thought. Usually when a Gen-Human went rogue, the first thing they did was pull it out of their head.

"Ye…yes," the Gen-Human stammered.

"The charge you will be facing is treason. There

may be a number of other ones: murder, theft and destruction of military property. These are all covered under the main blanket charge. The death penalty will be in effect."

"I didn't want to. I didn't want to."

"But you did."

"I didn't have a choice. They kidnapped me at Brethia and forced me to work for them. I wanted to escape every day I was among them."

"Truth," said the empath.

Almon could have belted the empath right then. He wanted leverage, even if the boy was innocent.

"You see," Drake jumped on the information. "I didn't commit any crimes that I wasn't forced to."

"Your very presence here is a crime. You've only completed three months of your twenty year lease to the Stargate Comglomerate."

Gen-Humans were indentured for twenty years to their manufacturing company, then leased out to other corporations. Once the two decades were over, they had the option to sign up again or become free agents. Originally they were considered property and owned by their businesses for life, then all of the wealthy do-gooders and activists decided to step away from their vacant lives to rally around sentient rights for the organic product.

Damn liberal whiners, thought Almon. Eventually it was settled and the twenty year limit was legislated. Still it was also around that age when the schizophrenic trait, common in Gen-Humans, was likely to manifest, so it spared the corporations from having to deal with that headache. Prefect democratic compromise in action.

There was also the fear that when the Gen-Human's were first developed they would be used as "disposables", objects to be worn down and cast off by their leaseholders, Almon remembered with mirth. However, when the final bill was tallied, each Gen-Human cost so much that the corporations treated them not as trash, but valuable pieces of equipment, preferring and pampering them over their regular human workers.

Many of the same activists who had been fighting for their rights did a 180 and began protesting against the Gen-Humans. Now they claimed that the corporations had created an unfair genetic caste system. But as usual, monetary value and usefulness won out over emotional hand-wringing. The Gen-Human became a staple of industry and the disposable workers continued to be trawled from their traditional pools, from amongst the poor, the unskilled, and the uneducated.

"I'm not responsible for that. I didn't do it on purpose. I'll go back to work."

The boy was near tears, just how Almon wanted him. He noted a frown on Molphus's face. It had been there for a while, now it deepened tenfold. How could he ever have seriously considered his student for employment by the agency? Brilliant energy manipulator that he was, Molphus was too soft. Although he had shown a glimmer of steel on Myntal 5, that must have been just the survival instinct kicking in when death threatened.

"If you're lucky, you'll go back to work. I may

be able to help you with the treason charges." *They probably wouldn't stand up in a tribunal case anyway*. "But you must help me with my inquiries."

"Am I going to say no? Sure!"

"What was your forced occupation on the Arc of Blood?"

"They made me the shit surgeon."

"The what?" blurted Molphus, caught off guard.

"Septic maintenance," answered Almon. To Drake he said, "So nothing to do with weapon systems, navigation, engineering functionality, things like that."

"Well…I…"

"Tell the truth," Almon pointed to the empath.

"No." Drake was defeated.

"Did you have any contact with a Zen Rigeln named Oxtiern?"

The Gen-Human's face darkened. He rubbed his scars reflexively. Almon noted that Raskor-idan leaned in to better hear the answer.

"He's a pig fucker. He did this to me," Drake roared, pointing at the mutilations on his face, onc up one down. "Just for a laugh. If I could get my hands around his neck I'd strange him until his eyes popped out of his face, then I'd cut them off and piss in the sockets."

"He's telling the truth."

"That's perfectly obvious," replied Raskor-idan. "Don't need a green head to tell us that."

Almon liked the boy's enthusiasm. Though his diction indicated that he had been corrupted by the pirates away from his initial fetal programming. Such things were natural. As a Gen-Human gathered individual experiences additional to their pre-programing, their behavior was bound to change and mold itself to its surroundings. That's why Brethia was so controlled and seeped in corporate culture. The pirates were the exact opposite. He might not be of any more use back at the Stargate Project.

"What can you tell us about him? Besides your dislike."

"You mean like that golden needle he uses to control people's minds?"

That tidbit caught everyone's attention. Drake clammed up at that reaction.

"Elaborate on your last statement," ordered Almon.

"I…I…"

"Answer!"

"Please," interjected Molphus. He placed his hand on Almon shoulder. "You won't be in any trouble. We need to know. We're trying to stop Oxtiern."

Drake calmed a bit. "I saw it jammed into the brain of Oxtiern's Ram Python bodyguard. Before that, the Ram used to attack the pirates whenever he could. Afterwards, the pair were inseparable."

Almon pondered this. So Oxtiern had mastered the use of the bionucleotide restructurer. Not good. Almon flicked an eye at the Eridani seated to his left. Did Oxtien co-opt him with the golden needle? Was he a pawn put into play to relay information back to the Zen? After a few seconds of clicking it over, he ruled it unlikely. The pirates had been caught unaware at the depot. He would have surely tried to warn them if his brain's had been rewired… unless he had been given a different purpose. Like to murder the Mutachans! Had Oxtiern's visa application been a ploy to get his agent close enough to them to strike?

His thoughts raced further on, twisting inside on themselves, until all they had encountered, from D'puppup down to the General, was in league with Oxtiern, conspiring to destroy them. Too many years in espionage, too many foul deeds and backstabs, too much of…everything. He shook his head. It never ended, causing you to suspect everyone and everything.

"I know where Oxtiern's headed," Drake said, snapping Almon back to reality.

"How?"

"Well I guess the Arc of Blood got away. They're probably heading for Passage, right?"

Almon didn't answer.

"It's still an entire planet. But I came across a map when I was trashing Oxtiern's quarters. He is going to the Rul Excavation."

The boy knows too much. Where on Passage Oxtiern was going was not news. Almon's organization had built the excavation site and there was nothing else of interest on the planet. But simply knowing the name Rul was enough to condemn him in Almon's mind, not to mention his knowledge of the golden needle.

"Have you been discussing this with the others?"

"I don't talk to them if I don't have to.

"Truth," said the empath.

We'll have to take him with us. Can't have him mixing with the others and spilling his guts. Will have to decide later on his fate, one way or the other.

Almon hit the buzzer and the guards appeared. He gestured to Drake.

"Isolate this one. He is to have no contact with any other prisoner, nor are any personnel to talk to him. Understood?"

The guards saluted and dragged Drake off.

***

Ten hours and a hundred interrogations of vile people later, Almon was done. Except for Drake, each were multiple felons, having committed every crime conceivable and a few Almon had never heard of before. He felt he needed another blood cleansing to wipe the filth out of his system.

They had uncovered nothing of any use, the Black Flag commanders kept their grunts in the dark, giving them just enough to know where to shoot, shit, and eat. No information was gained that would persuade the General to cough up a ship to go down the wormhole. He had requested another meeting, but the General's office refused, stating that all information be relayed through the liaison officer.

"After all," the secretary had chirped, "that's why one was assigned to you."

He didn't trust the unhelpful Rakor-idan to do anything. Almon wasn't entirely without means however. There was one way left for him to get to Passage. It was a card he had held back for an emergency and, once played, all of his dark secrets would be revealed to his companions. Which might mean that their deaths would be ordered by his own agency. The Eridani, the Human, and the Gen-Human…well, these were the losses one had to expect when dealing with the most dangerous business in the galaxy. Molphus's death would be the one that he truly regretted…just as he did with Quandle's. He never should have brought him along.

He squatted on floor of his dirty hotel room and began the kashonas matrix. Opening the hole to hyperspace within his brain and spitting out the distress pulse into the space between spaces.

Chapter 18 – Leaving Stilt aboard a Strange Vessel

Species: Phentari

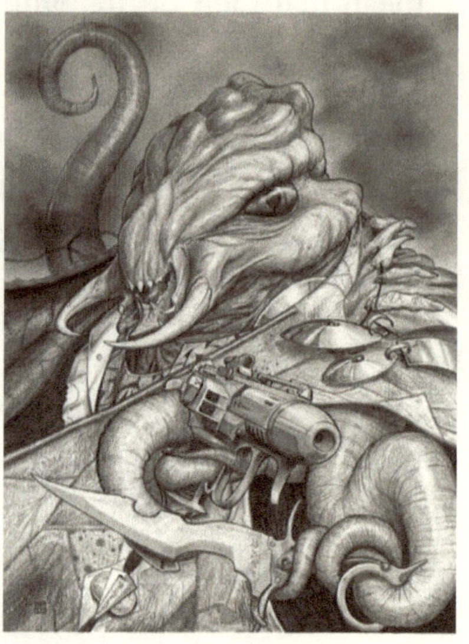

Planet of Origin: Phena in the Tau Ceti system

Description: With four tentacles serving as its primary manipulation appendages, the methane breathing Phentari are an exclusively carnivorous race with an ability to eat meat in an advanced state of decay. The primary governmental system on the planet is a matriarchal militocracy, due to the female being twice the size of her male counterparts.

Freaky Fact: Phentari have a very bad reputation for "interspecies cannibalism" or the hunting of another sentient races for food. While exaggerated, the stereotype is not without some basis in fact. The Alliance has made such activities illegal and the Phentari's various Shulesso (High Commandresses; as the term is translated) agreed to officially outlaw the practice after joining the organization. It seems not all of their subjects received the memo however.

***

It was the dead of night as Almon, Molphus, Raskor-idan, Drake, and Aebisher waited on the edge of a landing platform. Flood lights illuminated all about them, casting long shadows across the cement surface.

Something was coming, only Almon knew what. After he had recovered from sending the mayday beacon, he had Raskor-idan clear a flight path for an unidentified vessel. Using his Galactic Control credentials, he had somehow managed to erase its arrival and future departure from the system logs. Molphus was astonished. Usually such records were inviolate, even with espionage work. He heaped that surprise onto the pile of unpleasant ones he'd already discovered on this carnage filled journey.

He didn't understand what he was still doing here. This wasn't Myntal 5. Stilt was an Alliance planet. He could arrange transport back to Trishmag, leave all of this behind, reunite with his love, marry, and never leave her side.

But could he? The blood was on his hands. The corpses he had created, no matter if they were good or evil, stained his mind. Would he ever be capable of living on his homeworld again? He wanted to. But could he? It was that fear which kept him here, not loyalty to Almon.

In Molphus's mind, Almon had caused all this trouble. He had dug his own grave and Molphus felt no responsibility to keep him out of it. Oxtiern, the pirates, the dead city on Myntal 5. Had Almon been open about everything so many lives could have been saved.

Drake stood next to him, shivering a bit in the night air. Molphus had spent a few hours talking to the young Gen-Human. The manufacturing of the race was primarily done by Mutzachan corporations, so Drake had felt at ease with him.

The conversation hadn't been encouraging. Molphus brought some food to his minuscule isolation cell, knowing that the captive probably had not been fed. He was unsure what was planned for the boy, but he assumed it wasn't anything good.

"Thanks," Drake had said, accepting the candy bars the Mutzachan offered.

"Well, you need to keep up your vitamin levels," he replied. Alien physiology was not Molphus's strong suit. He just knew a lot of humans ate candy and assumed it must be nutritious.

"Are you really going to lock me up? I never wanted to do any of that stuff."

"I doubt it. You'll probably just be returned to the stargate project so you can finish out your lease. The time you've been missing won't count against the time owed, but…"

Drake's face sank. His eyes darted about the small cell, molars absent mindedly gnashing on the tail end of a chewy chocolate bar.

"What's wrong with that?"

"Well," the Gen-Human said, "isn't there some way I can get out of my lease?"

"Not legally, no."

"So no way to get back to Myntal 5? I suppose the Brethia Stargate Cooperative doesn't have any dealings with the place."

Especially not now. "Why would you want to go back there?"

Drake burst into a long description of his beloved Annette. What she looked like, how she smiled, her scent, all her vagaries and nuances and quirks. Proclaiming his eternal love for her, he wanted to show Molphus a holo-picture of the woman, but his data pad had been confiscated by the military police.

Molphus paused. That sounded familiar. Where had he met this man before? He couldn't place him. Again a lot of the alien races looked very similar to each other. The differences in facial construction were too subtle for Molphus to pick up on. That aside, he was confused why Drake was going on about this dead woman? Did he want to bury her?

"So I was hoping to get out of my decanting contract somehow and marry her. I know it's a long shot..."

He doesn't know! That tossed the Mutzachan into a quandary. What should he do? His moral duty, Molphus supposed, was to inform Drake of recent history on Myntal 5. But after looking into Drake's smiling face, the flood of love accompanying every word he spoke of her, he couldn't bring himself to speak the truth. It would have been the cruelest act he had ever done.

"I'm sure we can organize something," he said hoarsely.

Besides, Molphus justified to himself, *I don't know for sure that she perished in the plague bomb.* It was just extremely likely. The King had survived, so maybe her.

He then recognized Drake, or thought he did. The Gen-Human had been with Parg and the black furred Fott when they accosted him in the underground city. He didn't have the curving burn scars at the corners of his mouth then. Was it him?

"Have we met before now? On another planet?"

"Wh…maybe?"

"You don't remember?"

Odd. Molphus remembered the incident. Mostly Parg stuck out in his memory, but Mutzachans scored below the Gen-Humans on the Oskowitz scale, at 0.851.

"I remember a Mutzachan but…"

"But we all look alike."

"No, I've spent a lot of time around you people, I can tell the difference. I just didn't really look."

The term "a lot" being extremely relative. Molphus remembered Drake's record, a very brief file. *Six months away from us. A bucket drop to me, but two thirds of his life.* At two hundred and sixty five years Molphus was still considered young for his race, yet Drake at nine months might've just been shunted out of the birth canal. Molphus knew that whatever problems had fallen on him, the terror must have been ten-fold for Drake. He made a pledge to protect the boy from Almon. He had failed to protect anyone else, but this one wouldn't die.

A shimmering oblong pearl, ten meters wide, dropped from the sky and nestled silently onto the platform. Molphus had never seen a ship of its make. It conformed to no technology he had ever heard of.

It seemed to be formed from one continuous frame. No rivets, seams, plates, or bolts showed on its surface. A hatch rippled from the ship's side, flowing out like water and then solidifying. Almon gestured for everyone to enter.

Inside were six cushioned chairs the same pearl color as the rest of the vessel. Their bottoms flowed into the floor as if it were cast from the same mold. There was no one inside. No controls, mechanisms, or engines either. It was incredible. A perfectly fluid ship, something that made Mutzachan technology look like prehistoric scrap. For decades, Molphus had worked developing and refining the ion drives which powered the Mutzachan fleet and their most advanced designs did not come close to this. Pure magic. Beautiful and terrible.

The hatch shut or, more accurately, it melted back into the frame. A few minutes later it reopened, having docked with a ship, to everyone but Almon's surprise. There hadn't been any bump from lift off, no sense of motion, no stress from the trust needed to break gravity. Nothing at all. The pod had been a dead space.

They entered a pristine world. Everything about them was sleek, white, sterile, glowing and shining softly. Molphus felt unclean, his very presence dirtying up this antiseptic world. He was out of place in the perfection.

The ship was one long room with the occasional table, chair, or bunk flowing up from the floor. It was devoid of any windows, instrumentation, flexi-screens, or control stations. Except for at the far end.

A large chair, more akin to a throne, loomed. Tubes ran up from the floor to a white helmet. An arm swung around the right side of the chair holding up a single blank panel, which the figure seated in it traced a tentacle across. Even at this distance Molphus could tell the creature was a Phentari. The throne, tubes, and panel all glided across the floor towards them, leaving no trace of having moved on the floor behind. The Phentari removed its helmet and …no!

***

Shock, dismay, roars of anger. Raskor-idan pulled a weapon. Aebisher followed his lead. He even heard the young Mutzachan power up a blast. Drake cowered behind them all. Almon stepped in front of the Phentari, his arm raised, a flux shield humming about him to ward off any weapon discharges.

"Wait. Wait."

"Wait?" yelled Raskor-idan. "You protect this…this…."

Words failed him. And well they should, for behind Almon was the most vicious mass murderer the Alliance had ever seen. Jaquassarious Phentari. Number one on the Alliance most wanted lists. He had committed over three billion murders when he destroyed the entire planet of Sharron. A killer that put Oxtiern to shame.

There was no mistaking him. His evil countenance had been plastered over every news feed for months after Sharron. They had to even create a new word for the crime he had committed. Biocide - the complete destruction of a planetary biosphere. His further audacious crimes had kept him in the headlines ever since.

He had distinctive red vine tattoos curling down his four tentacles and his feeding tusks had been replaced by gilded steel biters. Of all the sentients the Eridani might've guessed would be on board, this was the last one.

"He is," Almon carefully measured his words. "My associate."

Silence, shocked silence. The assembled group held their breath, waiting for the bubble to pop, the dream to end, the hallucinogens to wear off. Anything that would prove this not to be reality.

But it was.

"How is this cannibalistic butcher your associate?" challenged Molphus. "What kind of business are you in?"

Almon placed a gentle hand on the younger Mutzachan, but he jerked angrily away. *Trouble in the brotherhood of fat heads*, thought Raskor-idan. Not that he was any less angry. It was just good to know that if it came to a fight, he might not have to take on two of the energy spitting race. Aebisher was on edge, waiting to be told to pull the trigger. Even Drake had his fists clenched. *Not that he'd be any use.*

"Follow me and I will explain everything."

With a nod to the criminal, Almon led them towards the center of the room and laid his hand on the floor. The substance of the floor liquefied and flowed upwards, spitting in the face of the artificial gravity. Five chairs and a table solidified. The table edges curved upwards creating a basin. A bump with a hole on its top popped up in the table's center. Crystal water dribbled out, filling up the basin.

Where is this ship from? There was no possible way the Phentari had developed this technology. No one could. Was it Arachnid? It didn't conform to anything Raskor-idan had picked through on the battlefields. Perhaps this was some sort of pleasure cruise liner. That seemed a stretch.

"Please be seated."

Before he could move, Jaquassarious Phentari bumped into Raskor-idan, lightly touching his chest with a scaly tentacle.

"I will let you keep your weapon, little solider pup," the criminal whispered to him in the Eridani tongue. "Because it will do you no good. I'm hoping you will try to prove me wrong."

The Phentari walked away laughing and plugged himself back into the chair, the headpiece flowing about his features. The throne glided away.

Hate! Hate! All of his childhood indoctrination took hold. The hundreds of years of history of racial hatred, all ground into his brain since it first learned speech, spread a flame of rage. This creature wanted to fight? He would show this shit what a true Eridani was all about.

Aebisher restrained his commander, grabbing the weapon from his hand. "He's the most wanted criminal in the galaxy for a reason," the sergeant said calmly. "And he's got the home field advantage. Let's be careful."

Raskor-idan didn't understand the idiom, but recognized the meaning underneath. He wrestled his emotions, forcing them back down deep into his writhing soul, and sat with the others.

"We're waiting," he said briskly to Almon.

"The Phentari," Almon began with a deep sigh, "is a member of my agency. One of our best operatives."

Another round of shocked silences. Then Molphus blurted, "He's an agent for Galactic Control?"

"There is no way that's true," Raskor-idan retorted.

"That's correct, he is not… and neither am I."

"Then who…"

"We. Our pilot, Oxtiern, and myself are members of Galactic X."

Galactic X, the ultra-secret espionage agency. Its membership and missions were among the most classified information in the Alliance. They dealt with matters far above and beyond the scope of Galactic Control. Shrouded in absolute secrecy, the organization was the go-to spook society for every crackpot conspiracy theory. It had taken forever for the Alliance high assembly to even admit its existence. Any other attempts to discover what they were up to had been shot down. They had one mandate…

"To protect Alliance integrity at all costs," spat Raskor-idan. "How does employing the worst criminals in the galaxy achieve that?"

"Because they get the job done."

Raskor-idan pointed at the Phentari on the other side of the room. "That creature detonated an entire planet. Killing how many? An Alliance planet at that. How… how…"

"He had to destroy the planet in order to save lives."

What? Raskor-idan knew little about Sharron, except about its destruction and who lit the fuse, but he remembered enough about its location to understand…

"That planet was nowhere near the front line of the war. It had no strategic value to the Arachnids at the time. So assuming that's who you are fighting…"

"That is a large assumption."

"Is it?"

"Yes, because the Arachnids are not the real enemy."

Not the real enemy. Blood soaked memories stabbed Raskor-idan's mind. The mountains of corpses, lakes of blood, the ruined societies. *Not the real enemy*. He saw the crushed bodies of his men, slaughtered by Arachnids forces. He recalled the lists and lists and lists of causalities after each engagement. How many dead? How many crippled? How many broken minds? *Not the real enemy*. The Alliance only existed to repel the Arachnid advance. What could be worse?

"Then who the hell is?"

"The Rul?" said Molphus.

"Oh yes."

"What is a Rul?" demanded Raskor-idan.

"The most ancient of races," said Almon. "From a planet long since destroyed by the Proto 1 Scattering, billions of years ago. But they survive. Listen to me Raskor-idan. Have you never wondered why the Arachnids are invading? What they want?"

This was a no-brainer. "To gain more territory, wealth, and slaves."

"If they were Eridani I'd agree that would be the motivation," said Almon. "But they are beaten back by the Alliance every time. At a great cost to us true, but they are still being defeated. So why do they continue?"

"I'm sure you'll inform me."

"The Arachnids have to relocate because all of their planets are being destroyed by the Rul. They literally have no choice but to move the whole of their civilization elsewhere. They have chosen our area of space to colonize."

"What does this have to do with blowing up planets?"

"The Rul survived by completely restructuring their genetic make-up. They reproduce asexually, implanting their embryos in planets. The gestation period takes millions of years. They are completely self-contained creatures. All accumulated knowledge, race memories, and education is gestated as their technology is grown within. You might consider them to be cyborgs, but their technology is much more advanced than that. They have seeded themselves everywhere."

"Including our space?" asked Raskor-idan.

"Correct. We have detected several of them. A fully grown Rul is the size of a large moon. Once gestated, they explode out of a planet, rendering it useless for any habitation, sometimes reducing it to rubble and creating a new asteroid belt. They then sterilize any planet in that system containing life. Not just sentient life either, if a bacteria grows someplace it is vaporized."

"And Oxtiern is planning to wake one up?"

"Precisely."

***

There is no war. Drake recalled Jack Mace's conspiratorial words. *They'll need servants to mow their lawns and clip their toenails once they cause the apocalypse.* He noticed that Mutzachans didn't have finger or toenails. A fact that had never registered before.

All of this was too much. He had dreamed of action, adventure, intrigue, secret agencies, but the reality stunk. Soulless men doing foul deeds. It made him long for the boredom of his old job, where the danger all took place in virtual reality.

"We know almost nothing about them," Almon continued. "Their culture, language, thought patterns, and barely anything but the basics of their physiology. We don't even know their given race name. Rul is the Arachnid word for them. It means Dark Overlord."

"So you have been unable to create a dialogue?" asked Molphus.

"We don't know how they communicate. As their natural habitat is space, it can't be verbally, and no empath has been able to lock onto a brainwave. They may not even recognize us as sentient beings. Some speculative theories, to misuse the word, think that they have a meta-intelligence that might overlook us, which views cosmological events as we would a rainstorm. To them, a trip around the solar system is a walk downtown."

What else had Jack said?

Something…something…planets blowing up by a virus. Ridiculous. But the planets *were* destroyed. Drake cut in.

"Where these Rul in Ering Crasb and Ampyria and Efrafa?"

Almon looked at the Gen-Human, surprised that he dare speak, even more surprised by his insight. All eyes, each hostile, turned to Drake, who tried to shrink into the seat. The Mutzachan nodded.

"Yes. Those were operations of ours. Each with a Rul buried in its heart."

"Did you even try to evacuate the planet?" said Molphus.

"We couldn't. The decision was made at the highest level to keep people in the dark. The Arachnid Invasion is worrisome enough, but the revelation of the Rul would cause panic beyond panic. Confidence would falter, the Alliance would shatter, and then we are all doomed."

Molphus was enraged. "Don't hide your own guilt. 'The decision was made at the highest levels'. It's a decision that you *agree* with. All those people sacrificed. You couldn't come up with a cover story to justify an evacuation? Just something to get them moving?"

"Any scientific explanation we cooked up would've been debunked within hours. There was no way. The knowledge had to be protected."

"I kept wondering why Oxtiern was so obvious about everything he was doing. It's because he knew your agency would spend just as much time covering up as tracking him down. This silence has allowed him to run riot. Quandle dead, the workers caught in the middle of the Brethia Stargate heist, all the marines murdered by his pirate allies, the whole city on Myntal 5 killed! All of it!"

What? What was that? Everyone in the city…dead? Not Annette? No, no, it couldn't be. A ball of ice solidified in his stomach. His fingers and toes grew numb. He slouched in his chair and stared at nothing, contemplating over and over the nightmare thought that his love was gone.

***

Molphus was defiant. This had been building for quite a while. Now that all the pieces fit, he could see the entire evil image for what it was.

"I was hoping that you would understand," Almon said.

"You commit mass murder and destruction on a scale that is almost inconceivable. How am I supposed to understand that?"

"Because had the Rul been born, those people

would have died anyway. And not just them, whole worlds would have been sterilized and who knows if we could have stopped it or what it would have taken to do so."

Almon leaned closer, staring Molphus in his large eyes, "Planet after planet. What if it had gone after our world, Trishmag?"

He flipped to Raskor-idan. "Or Eridine?"

To Aebisher. "Or Earth? What would you do to prevent that? Or a better question, what wouldn't you do to protect your planet?"

They rolled that question around their heads. None had an answer.

"That's why we kept it quiet. That's why Oxtiern must be stopped at all costs on Passage."

"Why didn't you detonate that planet as well?" asked Raskor-idan.

"Passage doesn't physically exist in Alliance space. Its image is reflected here because of a quantum ribbon from the Motaran Rift. When the creature matures and cracks the planet to be born, its travel to our space is unlikely. Administration deemed it important to gather as much information as possible. Maybe some weakness could be found, something to give us an edge."

"Have you found one?"

"No."

What did D'puppup say? What were his words? '*If his hand is not taken from the thread it will rip a hole in the tapestry of your civilization and the Alliance will fragment then fall'*. Did Almon have a point? He personally had withheld the truth from

Drake earlier to spare him pain. To help him maintain an illusion so he could be happier in his life. Was this that much different?

He shook his head. What the hell was he thinking? One little omission did not equate to a conspiracy that resulted in holocaust upon holocaust and threatened to do more.

"Why are we fighting the Arachnids if we both face the same threat?" said Molphus. "Why haven't we negotiated a truce or defense pact?"

"Nothing you say is a new idea. You're a thousand steps behind. We've tried multiple times and failed. They will not accept a treaty. Their societal structure is dominated by religious zealotry. Their holy scripts state that the Arachnids are destined, by the grace of their invisible deities, to conquer the universe. All acceptable races were created by these same Gods to serve them. The rest were conjured up by some personification of evil to thwart them and must be destroyed. I'm afraid everyone here falls into the latter category. It is their religious obligation to subdue and destroy, thus proving their worth to their deities. Occasionally we've run across a few commanders and lords who agree with us, but they're afraid to do anything. If they proposed a truce, they would be cast down and their genetic lines purged for having a blasphemous trait. We're on our own here."

"This is a nightmare."

"The nightmare of our lives. You can condemn me for the people I have to associate with, but I chose them because they will not hesitate to pull the trigger.

They will not crack under the moral weight of what they've done. And they will continue with their mission."

"But they are..."

"The worst specimens of every race. But they can handle the knife's edge we are all living on. Can you? Can you really blame me for protecting people from this awful knowledge?"

"Yes."

***

The argument sped on and circled around in loop after loop with nothing new added. The two Mutzachan's reached a deadlock, neither willing to philosophically concede anything more to the other. Eventually it spread out into such metaphysical concepts as the nature of truth and the need for honesty, stepping further and further away from the practical. By this time, Aebisher was lost and Drake had sunk into some kind of stupor, so Raskor-idan stepped up to bring the Mutzachans back to reality. He slapped Almon on the side of the head.

"This one's got a point," he stepped between Almon and Molphus, staring down the elder Mutzachan. "But not just about keeping us in the dark about these monsters." He waved a hand about him. "You've got tech that's above and beyond. If the military had this stuff we could've wiped out the Arachnids long ago. Why have you kept it secret?"

Almon raised a hand. A translucent ball appeared in it briefly, then blasted into Raskor-idan's chest.

The Eridani flew back, knocking over Molphus, and crashed hard into the seat beyond. He rolled out, unholstering his weapon, angry heat blazing across his face.

Energy crackled between Almon's fingers.

"Don't try it," he said. "You will not survive."

Raskor-idan glanced towards Aebisher, but the human just sat there, staring fearfully at the scene, hands far away from his weapon. Raskor-idan swore. He'd be damned if every human wasn't brainwashed by the alien's propaganda machine. The scar-faced Gen-Human was probably doubly so. They'd be no help at all. Reluctantly, he put the weapon away and took his place on the chair, rubbing his aching back.

"You raise a good point," Almon conceded, glowering at the captain. "This is ship is … well not unique, but it's the only one we have. There is no way to make more."

"You can reverse-engineer…"

"That would take fifty years. We need it *now*."

"Then where the hell does it come from?"

"We fished it out of the Montarian Rift. It took us years just to restart the primary systems. Since then we've been exploring more and more uses for it. It is very effective in dealing with the Rul."

"So who created it?" Molphus asked. He had pulled himself up by this time and slapped some water on his face from the table basin.

"There are speculations… but that's all they are. With the Rift, time and space, cause and effect, become blended into a variable order. Could be some civilization from the past, or the future, or some other part of the universe. It doesn't matter."

"So," said Raskor-idan, "you took a super evolved piece of tech and gave it to the worst criminal in the Alliance."

"He's only the worst criminal *because* we gave it to him. This is the vessel he used to destroy Sharron."

"Well, that makes it so much better."

"Your opinion is not important. Focus on the objective," said Almon. "Are you going to help us stop Oxtiern? Or do we return you back to the planet?"

More like eject me into space. The words didn't fool Raskor-idan one bit. He had a suspicion that the elder Mutzachan was planning to kill him or do something to his brain the moment this was all over. By rights he should attack Almon now. That would be acceptable in the Buddon warrior code. But he had a grudge against Oxtiern too. Plus, there was something about the Zen's plan….

***

They were still babbling away. Drake had tuned everyone out long ago. Nothing mattered. Worlds destroyed, colonies exterminated, dark forces from the beginning of time. Who cares? Then only person he would ever love ever was dead.

He never had the chance to say goodbye. To hold her one last time. To kiss her. Anything. He just dropped out of her life and then she died. Nothing would be good again. There was no beauty. Death could claim him now.

"Well Drake?" someone said.

Everyone was looking at him. He had slouched in his seat and was planning to starve to death in that spot. Nothing would rouse him.

"What?"

"Are you ready to go after Oxtiern?"

Except that. He stood bolt upright.

"Let's go!"

Chapter 19 – Passage

Body Rehabilitation Injection: Considered by most to be *the* breakthrough discovery for military field medics, the body rehabilitation injection (BRI) stimulates a body's white blood cells, rapidly increasing tissue regeneration. Created from the refined nectar of the ganoir plant located on the Orion's sister planet of Taos 3, the serum is not without risks and can be habit forming if injected too many times. But when a person is gut shot on a battlefield in hostile territory, most are willing to take the risk.

***

When all was agreed upon, they acted at once. Jaquassarious Phentari's strange vessel entered the wormhole conduit. In theory, entering a wormhole was simple. In reality, it took some careful piloting. One had to approach it at an exact angle to trigger the time/space dilation effect. Through this pinpoint anomaly, they shifted incalculable distances, skipping past stars, planets, galaxies, and all manner of undiscovered life. The only effect the shift had on the passengers was a slight pulling sensation. Each felt dragged down, as if the artificial gravity had doubled.

Passage, a ghost world no longer, floated in front of them. Not much to look at, it was filled with dismal, nearly vegetation-free, continents and placid seas brimming with primeval life. A young planet, relatively speaking, on the verge of blossoming into a unique ecosystem. Or it would be if the ancient time bomb planted in it was defused.

The vessel took a position above the planet's gravitational pull. They reckoned that the pirates would take a geo-stationary position above the Galactic X observation rig to give support if needed and to allow the landing party to have a quick escape path. So they waited patiently, donning their armor and checking weapons, until the Arc of Blood revolved towards them.

***

Oxtiern stood at the railing of the Galactic X observation rig and peered deep down into the volcanic fissure. At the bottom lay the nascent Rul, suckling itself on heat like a newborn spider. He was so close he could taste it through the acrid tang of the planetary atmosphere.

There wasn't much to the outpost. Not meant for long term visitors, only three pre-fab steel bungalows had been erected. One held the instrumentation used in analyzing and storing data on the Rul. The second was set up with a few bunks and sealed packets of flavorless food for the semi-annual visits from Galactic X technicians. The last was fitted to be an airtight storage unit for genetic samples cultivated from the creature below. These all connected to a central steel platform that supported a large lift that lowered a carriage down into the fissure with metal cables thick as a man's arm.

He backed away and looked at his crew. Six pirates, not very healthy looking. Undesirables and loafers, no doubt. Definitely unfit. The ones that would not be missed if things went wrong. Such faith the Captain had in him…Ah well, no matter. He still had the brainwashed Ika Dhole to protect him.

After their trouncing on Stilt, the pirates had cold feet. All of their enthusiasm was sucked away as it suddenly dawned on them that the attack on the Zen Rigeln's home planet might actually take some effort.

Oxtiern had gotten into a long argument with the Arc of Blood's captain, who tried to pull the plug on the entire gambit. Much to Oxtiern's amusement, he used the excuse that the job would be impossible because they hadn't stolen the full complement of ultra armor. He reminded the Captain that he would have to answer to the Admiral and all his cousin captains if he ran away now. Granted only a fifth of the units had been taken, but they were meant for support, not as their big guns. As long as they controlled the Rul, the plan would work.

Currently the men were busy jury rigging a bypass around the lift controls. The ones in the central bungalow couldn't be hacked in the time frame they were on. Galactic X kept their secrets well hidden. He kicked the Orion techie wiring up the new box.

"How much longer?" he hissed.

"It's gonna take as long as it needs to. You keep buggin' me ain't gonna move it faster, cholly wuzzle."

The Zen turned away, hands twitching, feet sweating, brain cells sizzling with anticipation. So close. Oh, so close!

He took out the golden needle and tossed it from hand to hand. Such a beautiful little device, so elegant, so potent. Its mechanics were well beyond his comprehension. Luckily Galactic X basic training included a data chip brain implant with a comprehensive vocabulary of the Mutzachan language, otherwise none of this would be possible. Hell, the agency had almost handed him the keys to global annihilation. On reflection, his plan wasn't much different from some of their missions. Oxtiern had simply taken their own methods and repurposed them, adding a few creative flairs.

Or he would if the damn pirates would do their job. The anticipation was choking him. How much longer? Hurry, hurry, hurry! He wanted to yell.

He stood still. *Peace brother skin, peace.* It was all good. It would all be done in time, he reassured himself. He had skulked for too many years, played violent errand boy for the agency for too long, to lose everything now.

Near him, Ika Dhole was spending his time picking up a rock and dropping it back onto the ground. He stared at it intently every time the stone landed, as if he thought something interesting was going to happen, then picked it up again. The creature had been acting odd lately. His senses seemed dulled. Reactions weakened. Possibly a long term effect of the golden needle. Well, it was still an experimental device, bound to be some teething troubles. He had gotten the lizard a new thwack-'em'-stick to pull him out of his funk, but it didn't seem to help. Or did it? Difficult to tell.

Oxtiern considered his life. How far he had come! Before he had been scooped up by the agency, he was just another military castaway. His ideas before Galactic X had been so petty. Almon had showed him a different life. Had bequeathed upon him the scope of the great struggle the Alliance was secretly engaged in. What was the torture of a single person or the destruction of a solitary city, when he could inflict pain over an entire planet? And now he was about to paint the final brushstroke on his masterpiece.

He had Almon to thank for that. For inspiring him. For showing him his true destiny. He was grateful. He would still kill the old melon head if he got his fingers around the Mutzachan's throat, but he would impart a silent 'thank you' over the lifeless corpse.

"I think we're done here," the techie yelled.

Finally! He strode over to the lift. Then his wrist pad crackled. Someone was screaming in an alien tongue over the Arc of Blood's com channel. There was noise behind him. What was going on?

***

The landing party took a shuttle to the surface when the Arc of Blood appeared on the Phentari's instruments. The larger ship waited to attack the pirate vessel until the landing party was in position.

To avoid detection, they entered the atmosphere out of range of the pirate ship's sensors and flew nape-of-the-earth to an area five miles away from the observation rig. After deposting them, the pearl shuttle took off on its own, leaving them all stranded.

"Still don't like that part of the plan," Aebisher whispered to Raskor-idan.

"There was no way for us to pilot it anyway. I'm sure your Mutzachan masters will be kind and offer you a way home."

"Ah knock it off with that…sir. They've done a lot for my planet. It's easy to get star struck."

Maybe for you.

Raskor-idan and Aebisher had their standard marine issued plasma rifles. Almon and Molphus were fully powered up. Drake had been supplied with Molphus's back-up laser that he had been allotted at the beginning of this journey. There had been some objections by Raskor-idan about bringing the Gen-Human with them at all. Drake had no military training, the Eridani argued, and would be more of a liability than help. Almon had put his foot down and that ended the argument.

If he gets killed that will solve one problem for me, Almon thought. The group took position behind a small hill and monitored the pirates around the rig through military binoculars that could be switched to pick out heat traces and energy emissions. Almon counted them off. One, two, three… eight of them. Two by their shuttle, four by the rig, the others idling by a bungalow. Where was Oxtiern? There! By the lift. He was tossing the golden needle about like it was a toy and grinning insanely. The smug bastard.

The pirates were smart enough to place a pair of sensor drones fifty feet from the rig to the southeast and southwest, no doubt positioned with overlapping zones of detection. Any movement sensed would send them into attack mode, while emitting an eardrum shattering shriek.

The party consulted and, after some heated words and unnecessary profanity, grudgingly decided on a plan. The Mutzachans could use their abilities to generate a static field around them, baffling the drone's sensors and allowing them to get close enough to shut the hardware down. Then they would take cover behind one of the bungalows, while Rakor-idan, Aebisher, and Drake attacked. Their main goal was to take down all of the peon pirates and Ika Dhole, while Almon and Molphus slipped around back to kill Oxtiern. Almon was certain that the Zen would not jump into the fray, but hang behind.

That settled, the Mutzachans left the cover of the hill. Almon concentrated, felt the buzz of power flow around him then focused, keying it up, flipping the electrons this way and that, harmonizing it to the pitch he needed. There it was. He walked slowly around the hill, stepping lightly on the grey slate rocks that made up the terrain.

He spotted Molphus on the other side, walking slowly as well, nearly mirroring his own steps. This energy matrix was effective as long as one moved carefully. A sudden shift in the field would alert the sensors.

What was he to do with the boy? His stubbornness and refusal to see reality would almost certainly mean his termination. Couldn't he see that? But could he, Almon, personally bring himself to give the order. He had to admit, probably not. Dying for the cause was one thing, even if the person didn't realize what they had been killed for, but a cold-blooded execution of someone he cared about was not something he could do. The decision would be taken out of his hands at any rate. Someone higher up would look at the paperwork and choose. It was so much easier when it was a disembodied name on a screen.

Focus. Focus on the task. He chided himself. *The rest doesn't matter.* He had reached the drone and touched it lightly with a finger. He did a mental balancing act. One side of his brain maintaining the static buzz, the other channeling energy up into the machine, probing for the shutdown mechanisms.

Molphus got his first, catching the drone as it fell from the air. Almon struggled. Come on, where was it? Finally he made the linkage and the drone fell. He tried to grab it, but it slipped through his fingers and clanked to the ground.

Damn it. He looked about, collecting energy in his fist to lash out at any enemy eyeing his way. It was all good. The pirates were too engrossed in getting the machinery ready or chowing down on stolen food packets to notice.

Molphus crept over to him.

"Are you all right?"

"Of course I am," he snapped.

What was he getting at? Old didn't mean enfeebled. Molphus grabbed his arm and pulled him along. They snuck around the perimeter, keeping careful watch on the pirates, who still noticed nothing. The pair hid behind one of the bungalows and waited for the others to strike. Almon tapped on his data pad signaling to the Phentari's ship to begin its attack on the Arc of Blood.

Plasma fire, shotgun blasts, the searing hiss of lasers. Almon poked his head out. The battle was in full swing. It looked like Drake was down, shot either in the chest or the shoulder. He was lying on the ground kicking his legs about and screaming. And Oxtiern…

Was over by the rig lift. His hands and eyes glowing blue, looking in the opposite direction from their position. He tapped Molphus and pointed to a further building, one that would give them an unhindered view of the villain. They slipped over to the next bungalow and took aim, their fingers humming with power.

"Now," said Almon. "NOW!"

***

After the Mutzachans left, the others took sniper positions. Raskor-idan had to drag Drake up the hill as the Gen-Human had been preoccupied during the strategy argument and thought they were going to charge in like idiots. Then the Eridani had to pull him down, because he had propped himself up too high, making a good bullseye.

"Pick your mark," Raskor-idan said. "I have the Ram Python leaning on the railing."

"I got two zeroed in by the second shelter," replied Aebisher. "Might be able to take both."

"Umm...I think I can hit the green one too," Drake said.

"That's my shot, stupid," snarled Raskor-idan. "Go for a different one."

"Wouldn't more shots on one be better?"

"Don't argue with me," Raskor-idan punched Drake hard in the face. A bruised swelled up almost instantly. Drake had no way of knowing that Raskor-idan had marked the Ram as his personal kill for the battle, a time honored custom of his people, and the Eridani wasn't in the mood to explain. To his credit, Drake didn't cry.

"All right," he said. "That one in the back."

"Fire."

They did. Raskor-idan hit Ika Dhole center mass. The great Ram Python roared in rage. Aebisher, true to his word, shot the two pirates eating food. Hitting one in the leg, sending him down, and nailing the second with a headshot. Both slumped on top of each other, the wounded one trying to drag himself into the bungalow. Drake missed.

The rest of the pirates took cover, except for Ika Dhole who charged at the hill. His thick reptilian hide absorbing fire from Aebisher and Raskor-idan's weapons. Seemingly impervious to pain, the Ram Python ran on, waving his metal tipped quarterstaff about his head like a baton.

Two pirates darted up from behind some

machinery with cylinders in their hands. Pop. Pop. Grenades arced out of both.

"Take cover!"

BOOM. Reality shattered around Raskor-idan. Everything became a bright light with a low hum beneath. Things lost all meaning. Was this really the world? How long had it been like this? Was there ever any other life? Or was it all just a dream and he was lord of infinite space? Perhaps, but then what was that darkness?

A smack from Ika Dhole knocked the world back into place. He was sprawled out, the Ram Python's weapon had cracked his chest piece in half. His methane converter barely hanging onto his face. The lizard swung at him and somehow he managed, dragging up energy from the depths of his reserve, to get out of the way. He raised his weapon to fire, then realized he was only holding onto the grip. The rest of it had been smashed on the ground.

He scrambled back. His feet slipped against loose shale and slate. Aebisher was at the bottom of the hill in several pieces. His head and upper torso pulped. The left arm detached from the body at the elbow. Drake was nowhere to be seen.

Ika Dhole leered up at him. Several of his pointed carnivorous teeth had been knocked out and he was bleeding openly, but that didn't diminish his ferocious presence. He waggled the thwack-'em-stick with two hands tauntingly in front of him like a massive phallus. Raskor-idan drew the only weapon he had left, his Buddon blade. The edged weapon that all Eridani carried into battle, symbolically demonstrating their link to their ancestral warrior kin.

How fitting it was. If he were to die here, let him go down in the old way. Let that be his last testament. He may have failed in the way of his Buddon code, but he never abandoned it. He raised the sword and lunged.

Tempered steel met hardened wood. Hack and slash. Ram and repel. The two warriors met. Straining every muscle. Prepared to sacrifice every corpuscle of blood to end the other's life. The universe beyond collapsed and compacted, reducing all infinity down to simply the two of them dancing on this pin prick of time.

They hammered and railed and wounded each other until both their weapons broke. Then they bit, clawed, and pounded until their bodies were one continuous bruise. No words were uttered, just bestial snarls in-between gasps of pain and gurgles of blood. They kept on until finally, finally, with his cybernetic hand jammed down Ika Dhole's throat, trying to choke him from within, and the other digging into an open wound, the Ram Python croaked his last and the dim light of life left his eyes forever.

Broken and bruised, Raskor-idan crawled on top of the corpse and raised an arm of victory. One eye was blinded, probably permanently, a tooth from the lizard was lodged deep in it. He had multiple fractures all across his skeletal structure. And the blood loss was prodigious. But he had prevailed.

He pulled a body rejuvenating injection from his kit and stabbed it into his leg. That should stop the bleeding at least. As he waited for the serum to run through him, he spotted the laser that Drake had been issued lying under a rock by his feet. He laughed. What a joke. Had he spotted it before, the battle could've ended with much quicker. On reflection however, he was glad it didn't. He was cleansed now, purified in the old traditions of Eridine. It made his next decision that much easier.

Aebisher's body still lay there, less than intact. He made a short Eridani sign of farewell to a dead soldier that he was sure Aebisher wouldn't have understood. He could muster up no emotions for his splattered comrade. He had lost too many to be able to grieve and it would not be the last of his companions to die.

There were no sounds of battle from the other side of the hill. Raskor-idan emerged cautiously around it to discover that they had won. The pirates were all dead, shot or burnt to death. Oxtiern lay sprawled out, head exploded. Drake sat in the dirt next to him cradling Aebisher's backup revolver close to his chest. Molphus was inside one of the pre-fab huts doing whatever. Almon was standing by the rig, examining the golden needle. So it had survived. Good. He stepped up behind the elder.

"Everything check out?"

"Hmmm? Oh, yes. We got here just in time. They managed to bypass the lift controls and were about to descend."

"What about the Arc of Blood?"

"Jaquassarious checked in. He drove the ship back out of the wormhole and is in pursuit. It may be a bit of time before he returns."

Jaquassarious now, was it? Very comfortable being on a first name basis with a mass murderer. But then you're no different.

"And the device?"

"It seems to be completely functional."

"Good."

Raskor-idan raised the laser.

***

After the grenade attack, Drake's senses shattered. There was the boom, he was cut by blasted shards of rock, the sonic reverberation deafened him, and the resulting dust cloud blinded him. Some foul smelling glop, part of Aebisher's midsection, splashed on his face. A metallic item hit his legs and knocked him over.

He felt around, grabbed the item and ran madly in a random direction. He had no idea where he was going. He just wanted away. From here, from blood, from fear, from death. Why did this stuff seem like so much fun in the Tri-V shows? It was god awful.

Drake fumbled with the object he had grabbed and found it to be Aebisher's backup piece, probably blown off of his body. *Well, now I can defend myself*, he thought, just as he ran headlong into a metal wall and fell over, nose broken.

Shouts and gunshots and screams filled his ears. Deciding to lay there for a bit, he rubbed his eyes, trying to force out the crap swimming around in there. His own blood, mixed with Aebisher's, dripped into his mouth. Ugh. Someone tripped over him and thudded to the ground. Who was it?

"Wat dat?"

Pirate slang. Orion accent. He heard the figure stand. Drake hefted the gun and pulled the trigger, aiming where he thought the pirate might be. The loud retort deafened him again and when his senses finally cleared, a dead Orion lay next to him.

Drake stared at the body for a moment. That was… easy. Should he feel bad about this? The pirate certainly would've killed him given the chance. He felt that he should feel *something*, but he didn't.

He rose to find all the other enemies dead, except…was that Oxtiern? It was.

The Zen Rigeln lay on the ground, scarred and seared, still moving slightly. He ran over. The Mutzachans were occupied elsewhere. Drake guessed they had left him to die in peace.

He looked down at the monster. Most of his face was melted, making it even more skull-like. The fingers on his left hand had fused together, like a clay model of a hand sculpted by a child. He kept moving his arms about, little lights of blue appearing on them then dying off instantly. The Zen was trying to heal himself, but didn't have the strength.

Yet his eyes were intact. Those electric blue orbs that burned with such joy when he tortured Drake, when he had carved the scars into Drake's face, that were probably laughing when he killed Drake's beloved Annette. He leveled the revolver at Oxtiern's face.

"You…you fucking…," he fumbled for the right curse, but none were vicious enough to voice his hate. “You’ve taken everything from me. My life, the only world I had known, where I was happy.” He had been happy back at the Stargate Project, he realized. Bored, but contently so. “And… and… and the only woman I ever loved. The only ray of joy I have ever known. You killed her like she was garbage!”

Oxtiern’s lips curled back. In pain? No. He was smiling. A hoarse excruciating laugh came out between crisped lips.

“S…say ‘thank you’.”

He pulled the trigger and stared at the ruined face. *Now* he felt something. Pain and grief. He cried for Annette, and his dead friend, Jake-DKE-r0865, but mostly for himself and an uncertain future. He sat crossed legged next to the body and pulled the gun close to him like a comfort animal.

Someone gripped his shoulder. It was Molphus, alerted by the shot. Kindness softened his alien eyes.

“It was an act of mercy.”

“What?”

“Almon said it was fitting to let him suffer, that‘s why we left him in that state. You did the right thing in ending his pain.”

The right thing. He had to laugh and then cry again. And keep on crying until he ran dry. Had he ever done the right thing? Was he capable of it? Could he even recognize it? Fuck it. Fuck it all.

“Do you want some food?” Molphus asked.

“Sure,” he mumbled.

The Mutzachan went to dig up something, Drake stayed where he was, holding the gun close to his bosom. He continued to do so, right up until Raskor-idan shot Almon in the head.

***

Molphus reemerged from the hut just in time to catch the flash of the laser and witness Almon's body crumple to the floor. The Eridani whirled and shot Drake in the arm, causing him to drop the half held revolver. After scooping up the golden needle, he pointed the weapon at Molphus.

"I can put a burn through your eye before you can power up a charge," he threatened.

Molphus wasn't sure that was true. The captain looked to be on his last legs, half blinded and bloodied, but equally he wasn't willing to risk his and Drake's life on it. The Eridani was a life-long soldier. He'd probably been killing sentients since he was old enough to heft a weapon. Why wasn't he attacking? Did he plan to make slaves of them as his race had of many other species? Not a good plan, by Alliance decree neither his nor Drake's race could be enslaved by the Eridani. But now, he reckoned, was not the time to debate points of law.

"I don't have a quarrel with either of you," Raskor-idan said, as if reading Molphus's mind. "But I need to redeem my family's honor. And this," he held up the golden needle. "*This* is how I'll do it."

"How is that device going to help your family?"

"Oxtiern was going to use this to force the Rul to attack a planet or something as massive, correct? Well, one planet is as good a target as another. Phena looks ready for an apocalypse."

"The Phentari homeworld? Why?"

The Eridani face became puzzled, as if the knowledge should be obvious.

"They razed our planet, looted our temples, killed indiscriminately. My family was crushed and never recovered. My life was hijacked generations before I was born. And it lead to this," he grabbed at his pale mohawk with his metal hand, at his white disgrace. "This is not who I was supposed to be!"

"That was over five hundred years ago. No one alive on Phena had anything to do with that war or who you are."

"They destroyed everything!"

"And it's all been rebuilt."

"My house…"

"You have to make your own destiny. Decide who you are going to be."

Raskor-idan shot a blast over Molphus's head.

"You are not Eridani. You will never understand. History is always with us. It defines us whether we want it to or not," he said imperiously. "This *will* happen. And if this is the last act of my house, and myself, let it count for something. You can either stay back or die." He paused, then added. "I know you two were pawns in this, so I will give you a chance to live. It's…it's the honorable way. Take the pirate shuttle and leave. You might make it."

With that, he hopped onto the lift and began the descent down the fissure into darkness.

Chapter 20 – Passage

Alliance Calendar: Due to the vast differences between the planetary rotations of Alliance worlds and the length of their solar orbits, the Alliance lower council created a standard calendar set for bureaucratic and military business. The fact that it was based on the Mutzachan's own units of measurement and the rotation period of their homeworld, Trishmag, did not go un-noted. After a lengthy debate, it was finally adopted. This, along with Galactic Basic, has been used by various separatist and rebel factions as proof of the Mutzachan dominance over their lives. The breakdown of time units is:

Standard Minute: 100 seconds
Standard Hour: 100 minutes
Standard Day: A 30 hour period of time.
Standard Week: 7 standard days.
Standard Month: 5 standard weeks.
Standard Year: 350 standard days, or ten standard months.

***

There they were. The last men standing, so to speak. The last that could conceivably be called heroes at any rate. Mutzachan and Gen-Human. Master and servant from a racial hierarchy standpoint. But right now the one was feeling anything but masterly and the other was in no mood to be servile.

Drake slapped an adhesive bandage over his laser wound and jabbed himself with a healing injection. The rig mechanism buzzed along, quietly unraveling cable, each meter bringing Raskor-idan closer to his destiny. Drake broke the deafening silence.

"Do you know how to pilot the shuttle?"

"We can't leave."

"Why not? He said…"

"What he said isn't important. Time to be strong."

"I'm plenty strong," Drake retorted, not very convincingly. "I'm just tired of being beaten up and shot. I just want to get out of here."

"We have a moral duty to stop him."

"Moral duty? In the last six months, I've been across this entire galaxy and from what I've seen morality is an illusion. Something for comfortable snobs and academics to debate over. No one in the real world listens to them."

Considering how many of his preconceived notions had been blasted to atoms in the past few months, this wasn't a point Molphus felt up to arguing. But an entire planet of sentients killed? There was no justification for that. Deep down his soul revolted at the idea. Others could make their excuses. Raskor-idan could claim revenge. Almon could intellectualize it away. Oxtiern and Jaquassarious Phentari… who knew how they rationalized it. Both seemed to be gleeful villains. Perhaps they just lacked a soul. Perhaps they truly enjoyed it.

Whatever the case, the Eridani had to be stopped. Even if it meant that he personally must die. Drake seemed to take issue with this.

"Why does it have to be me that has to stop him? Why is the moral obligation pressed on me? No one else lives by it."

"Because you're the only other one here!"

"Everyone else gets to do as they please. Like Parg…"

"That Orion drunk? The one who's going to spend the rest of his life in a penitentiary? That's your baseline for morality."

"No, but…but can't we just go?"

The childish outburst angered Molphus. No! They couldn't just go. He had to remind himself of Drake's relative age, which was deceptive due to his older appearance. Of all the marvelous things scientists had been able to introduce to the developing Gen-Human, maturity was not one they ever conquered.

"I won't force you. I'm not sure that pirate shuttle has the range to reach Stilt, but maybe you can get out of orbit and send a distress beacon, assuming you can pilot it successfully back through the wormhole."

Drake jumped into the pirate shuttle and reemerged five minutes later.

"I don't know what any of those controls do. I was never checked out on any of that stuff. We always had others to handle the flying."

He sat down outside the shuttle and buried his head in his hands, refusing to budge. *Fine, let him sulk.* Molphus would handle Raskor-idan himself. First, he had to make sure he was powerful enough. He went into the pirate shuttle and opened a maintenance hatch. Generating a laser from a finger, he sliced open a power line and popped it into his mouth like a licorice stick.

The power pulsed through him, snapping in his synapsis, darting between cells. He focused, concentrating on storage, sneaking it away until the power core was drained, rendering the ship a dead husk.

Drake was still sitting outside, but his head was up.

"Well I guess I'll help you," said Drake, resigning himself to the fact that he had no way to leave. "Killing him will be best thing to do."

"Yes it is, unfortunately."

Killing a person being the best thing? How he had changed. If he could meet himself from the beginning of this journey they would not agree on anything. The old him, while agreeing that Raskor-idan needed to be stopped, would argue unceasingly about the need to put the Eridani down. He could come up with emotional reason after emotional reason about reaching his enemy's heart and showing him the error of his ways. About the universal bond of all sentient creatures. And that the villain just needed to be shown a better way. Naïve intellectual bullshit.

He had seen the fanatic's eyes. All of Raskor-idan's training and culture told him this *was* the better way. Even if they managed to destroy the golden needle and foil the genocidal plans, the Eridani would do everything he could to kill them. Molphus wasn't ready to die yet.

"Let's go," Molphus said. "I can get us down there. Hopefully catch him by surprise."

***

Down, down he went. The cold and black enveloping him. Light headed, Raskor-idan had kept his weapon ready in case those above had fired down at him or tried to pull the rig back up. After half an hour, he relaxed his vigilance.

His eye bothered him something fierce. It itched and stung, giving him a throbbing pain in his head. The eye matched what was happening in the other parts of his body. It all ached and cracked. He jammed another healing injection into his thigh and chomped on a fistful of pain meds. That should keep him going for a few more hours.

The lift chugged on.

Had he been right to spare the two up top? The Buddon code allowed for mercy if the foe unconditionally surrendered. Whether the warrior accepted it was a personal choice. Usually surrender meant enslavement. But he hadn't done that. He had told them to leave. That was more than mercy, that was... his language didn't have a word to describe the concept.

Had Drake and Molphus had really been enemies though? Almon was, or had been. No doubt about that. The others were just bystanders. Both seemed to have been roped into this escapade. Neither had lifted a hand against him. Yes. Letting them live was the honorable thing. He was in the right. He had to cling to that.

Details, details. It was done. Time to focus on the task at hand. He began fiddling with the golden needle. How did the damn thing work? The large lift had flood lights built into it, he flipped them on and examined the object closer. The human symbols didn't activate anything. He turned the knob at the end and an interactive hologram keyboard projected from it. Seventy two alien characters stared at him. These were Mutzachan symbols. Uh oh. Raskor-idan knew nothing about the language, not even basic phrases. Plus his mind, clouded by drugs and pain, wasn't in the best position to figure out the intricacies of a foreign language. He keyed through his data pad looking for the translation program standard in all units. Unfortunately, these were notoriously inaccurate, especially when dealing with idioms, syntax, and diction. He was going to be here for a long time.

The lift shuddered to a halt. Raskor-idan noticed that the air had grown considerably warmer, the opposite of what it should have been. He was nowhere near the core, he would probably be dead if he had been, but the air was thick. He looked over the side of the lift and saw the Rul.

There it was, the great nightmare creature, radiating heat at immense volumes. The mere act of leaning over the railing sent a blast of hot air into his face. He wheeled a floodlight around and looked closer, ignoring the discomfort. It was embedded deep in the fissure, plugging it up like a black tarp that had been draped over the area.

All he could make out was a mass of pitch black flesh that shifted constantly. Rippling and bulging, little pockets of its malleable dermis folded into bubbles and popped. Arcs of purple light ran across its surface in irregular patterns. Occasionally the energy, whatever it was, leapt off the surface and crackled in the air. There were no organs or limbs that Raskor-idan could see. It was just a blob, a super evolved mollusk. Not the harbinger of destruction that had been presented to him.

Had he been lied to?

***

It took them a while to descend into the shaft. They tied themselves to one of the cables and jumped. Molphus was able to slow down their pace with successive blasts of counter force. Occasionally they stopped and rested on a ledge or a minor alcove they happened upon. They talked little, just stared down the shaft at the lift's flood lights which grew steadily larger.

The actual death was anticlimactic. There were no speeches or a grand standoff. The pair used Raskor-idan's own surprise tactic. They simply took a position above him and rained laser and gunfire down on him. The Eridani did not fall immediately. Most of the volley was absorbed by his battle armor's ablative lining, but he had neglected to put on his helmet and gained a vicious burn across his head. He stumbled forward, his wounds reopening, dropping the golden needle.

Barely working through the pain, Raskor-idan drew his weapon but never had a chance to get a blast off. Drake had landed on the lift and fired three shots into the warrior's chest. The first two knocked holes in the already damaged plating, but the last got through, hitting the Eridani square on, exploding his heart and killing him instantly.

Molphus landed. He picked up the golden needle and ran his fingers over it. It was cold. Despite the heat, it was somehow cold. Such an innocuous looking object, hardly the sort of thing that would be the cause of so much evil. He smashed it against the railing and threw its broken pieces over the side into the Rul.

Chapter 21 – Trishmag

Galactic X: The dark open secret of the Alliance government. Officially the agency has no operatives, no hierarchy, and no budget. The only acknowledged location linked to the group is a single data-hub on the Mutzachan's home planet of Trishmag. The Alliance only admitted to the existence of Galactic X two decades ago, but it was known to be in operation for at least a hundred and fifty years prior. The agency's mandate is to "maintain the integrity of the Alliance at all costs". At first their operations were mainly deep range infiltration missions against the Arachnids, but the discovery of the Rul changed their focus towards defeating this overarching threat.

***

Six months later, an exploratory vessel of unusual configuration entered the wormhole and sent several shuttles down to the Galactic X observation rig. Apart from the equipment, they found a number of hastily dug graves and two survivors living rough. Both were malnourished and exhausted.

The pair had managed to sustain themselves by rationing out the rig's food parcels on a starvation diet and when those ran out, by licking fungi and slimes from the bottom of rocks on river beds. They had cannibalized some equipment to make a purifier that boiled water and collected the condensation into a barely potable brew. The survivors were quickly evacuated back to the Mutzachan homeworld.

Upon returning home, Molphus had been isolated. He hadn't seen Drake since the landing. The Gen-Human probably having been sequestered in a specially shielded building, as the planet's background radiation was way above the tolerance levels of most other races. At first, he had been placed in an empty room and forced to give his report to a blank wall. It was all recorded, no doubt, but the instrumentation was expertly hidden. He was then moved to more comfortable quarters. Apart from service and medical drones, Molphus hadn't seen anyone. He had not been allowed to contact his family or fiancée. But he was fed well and after a few weeks he felt normal again. At least physically.

Then came the summons, the official debrief, and he was whisked away to the other side of the planet, only to find himself back in Malon's office where this adventure had begun. Malon sat behind the same desk, still sucking on his irradiated gold ring. Molphus was not nostalgic about the reunion.

Off to the side sat a human, possibly a Gen-Human, with an odd greenish hue to her skin. She had on no protective clothing, but somehow was able to fend off the rads. Molphus was completely uncurious about how she managed it.

"Are you sufficiently recuperated?" asked Malon.

"You have access to the medical drone's readings of my bio-scans, so you tell me."

"Indeed."

Malon tapped a few buttons on his desk. The

entire surface glowed, streams of information poured across it at breakneck speed. He absorbed it all.

"Well, your account was thorough, almost a waste to have the empath poke your brain while you were asleep. I'm glad you didn't obfuscate any details. Very sensible."

"What's going to happen to Drake?"

Malon smirked.

"The Gen-Human's been corrupted well away from his original designations. He's practically feral, useless for admin work anymore. He'll be repurposed."

"To what?"

"That's beyond your clearance."

"So death."

The woman stirred.

"No," she said, waving a hand at Malon's half voiced objection. The Mutzachan clammed up immediately. "It won't hurt you to know he'll be given a chance. We'll retrain him. If it works, he'll be brought on board as an operative."

"Of Galactic X."

Silence.

"Can't you people even admit it in a sealed room?" Molphus exclaimed. "You're going to turn him into a killer."

"He's already killed once under your direction."

"That was different. That was necessary."

"As is our work. In fact, what you did *was* our work."

Molphus rubbed his head and sighed. He couldn't argue moral absolutes anymore. Black and white had blurred into a thousand tones of grey. Today, and for the rest of his life, he longed to bury himself in willful ignorance, live a quiet life, and have a quiet death.

"But that's not what this meeting is for," continued Malon. "Almon's death by this renegade marine captain is a bit of a blow. He was a valuable individual to us."

"I know that… now."

"Is there anything you'd like to add to the official statement? Any facts or errors that you'd like to correct?"

"None."

"The device was broken during the fight with Raskor-idan."

"Yes."

"And Almon was shot from behind by this same person."

"Your crew exhumed his body. I'm sure you've done an autopsy."

"Quite."

"Why did you do that? You only took DNA swabs from the others, even Oxtiern."

"We felt he deserved a hero's burial, properly credited. He was a secret champion of the Alliance. For over 100 years he had kept it safe, sacrificing even his own life for his ideals. A rare and wondrous thing in this hedonistic time, don't you agree?"

Molphus did agree, but wasn't convinced by the explanation. These people lied too easily, the truth always had to be shaken out of them. Almon's memory was a tainted one. For all of the good he had done Molphus in his youth, the ruthlessness his mentor had displayed at the end clouded every other pleasant memory.

At this point it didn't matter. Almon was dead. His motives buried with him. Let his spirit lie in peace. He was a person of conviction. That was epithet enough.

"Where's he buried? I'd like to pay my respects."

"That's classified."

He had to laugh. Of course it was. Why the hell not? He refused to engage after that. Malon went through a speech that, judging from his wearied tone, he'd squawked off many many times before. About the need for integrity and secrecy. About how Molphus was now bound under law and oath to Galactic X. About the penalties to himself and his family where he to relate any portion his activities on this endeavor, or identities of Galactic X personnel, or any other information gleaned about the agency's operations. By the end, he happily signed volumes of documents just so he could get out of that room and back to life.

Molphus had had doubts before about his ability to return, but now that was the only thing on his mind. He wanted away from these people and their filthy secrets. Let them keep them. Maybe their job was necessary, but he didn't have to do it. He was free.

***

The gleaming white door slid silently shut behind Molphus. Malon leaned back, licking his ring, and typed a few random thoughts into the desk panel. The green-hued woman did not move.

"Well…," he began.

"Keep him under surveillance," the woman barked. "Ground him. Deny him access to anything off planet. Monitor all of his communications. Get him employment somewhere near. He can go back to designing ion engines, but he is not to step foot on a ship."

"Just as I was going to suggest. Let him live his life. I believe he plans to marry."

"Good. If he has a family of his own that gives us more leverage."

"And if he tries to talk?"

"Follow the standard termination protocol. But let's see if we can keep him alive, on the back burner for emergencies. He exceeded the expectations Almon wrote about him in the mission profile. He may still be useful."

"Right." Malon tapped a few final phrases into the desk and it went blank. File closed. "Pity about the device," he added.

The woman rose and brushed away a thin film of radioactive dust that had collected on her.

"We still have the schematics. It can be rebuilt. The cost is prohibitive, but if nothing else Oxtiern's little extracurricular outing demonstrated that it works well in the field. And we're going to need it."

"Is it becoming that bad?" asked Malon, miserably.

"Oh yes. There's a dangerous future ahead."

THE END

OTHER BOOKS BY REX HURST

In the same universe as *Wounded Galaxy*

SPIFF BLASTHANDY: BEHIND THE SCREEN

On an Earth rebuilding from an apocalypse, the star of the Spiff Blasthandy show, the most popular drama of the day, must recover from a public scandal while simultaneously dealing with personal loss and tragedy. Even his popularity won't save him from a beating. As the virtual world gathers to spit on everything in his life, the demons of his past rise and threaten to destroy his life. He must question everything in order to survive.

TWIN VILLAINS

Two stories of alien villains in a galaxy at war. The first deals with a space pirate serving a life sentence in a military prison on a bleak planet. Rather than rot away for the rest of his life, he makes one last desperate attempt to escape. The second deals with a hidden cult on a planet dedicated to pacifism. The leader of this ancient religion must do anything he can to prevent its exposure or else his family will lose everything.

Stand Alone Books

THE FOOT DOCTOR LETTERS

A serial killer speaks out. Collected here are the ramblings of the notorious Andrew "the Foot Doctor" Masters - the rapist and murderer who terrorized a city in the early nineties. Read in his own words how this madman recounts his life, from his violent upbringing, to his life on the streets, to his eventual rise into criminal infamy.

ABOUT THE AUTHOR

Rex Hurst is a writer from the prestigious Hurst family of Hurstberg, Germany. He first emigrated to the United States knowing only a slight smattering of English and taught himself up to a proficient level working as a taxi driver in the urban blight of New York City. He has eventually obtained Master's Degrees in Forensic Psychology and Linguistic Taxonomy. He is a writer and a university instructor after relocating to South Carolina. He also is attempting to discover if one can grow wheat in a pot sitting by the window.

Answer: You can, but it’s not that great.

www.ingramcontent.com/pod-product-compliance
Lightning Source LLC
Chambersburg PA
CBHW051327250626
47155CB00007B/2481

* 9 7 8 0 9 9 9 3 8 0 3 0 7 *